THE
CANE

THE
CANE

MARYROSE
CUSKELLY

ALLEN&UNWIN
SYDNEY · MELBOURNE · AUCKLAND · LONDON

This is a work of fiction. Names, characters, places and incidents are products of the author's imagination or are used fictitiously. Any resemblance to actual events, locales, or persons, living or dead, is entirely coincidental.

First published in 2022

Copyright © Maryrose Cuskelly 2022

All rights reserved. No part of this book may be reproduced or transmitted in any form or by any means, electronic or mechanical, including photocopying, recording or by any information storage and retrieval system, without prior permission in writing from the publisher. The Australian *Copyright Act 1968* (the Act) allows a maximum of one chapter or 10 per cent of this book, whichever is the greater, to be photocopied by any educational institution for its educational purposes provided that the educational institution (or body that administers it) has given a remuneration notice to the Copyright Agency (Australia) under the Act.

Allen & Unwin
83 Alexander Street
Crows Nest NSW 2065
Australia
Phone: (61 2) 8425 0100
Email: info@allenandunwin.com
Web: www.allenandunwin.com

 A catalogue record for this book is available from the National Library of Australia

ISBN 978 1 76087 985 3

Set in 13/18 pt Granjon LT Std by Bookhouse, Sydney
Printed and bound in Australia by Griffin Press, part of Ovato

10 9 8 7 6 5 4 3 2 1

The paper in this book is FSC® certified. FSC® promotes environmentally responsible, socially beneficial and economically viable management of the world's forests.

For my father, Terry Cuskelly,
and in memory of my mother, Irene Cuskelly.
In your house, I have always felt safe.

ONE

THEY'RE LIGHTING THE cane and Janet McClymont has not been found.

A week after she disappeared, her mother Barbara walked into Jensens' shop and bought every box of matches and all the Bic cigarette lighters on the shelves. She then stood outside striking the head of each and every match against the phosphorus strip, watching it flare before shaking out the flame and dropping the spent stick on the road. Then she drove down to the inlet and threw the lighters into the water.

No one knew what the hell she was playing at. Then it dawned on me. With the crush about to start, and all of us believing that her daughter's body must be lying in the cane, some harebrained notion had got hold of her. She thought she could stave off the lighting of the cane fires until Janet's body was found. You see, in Barbara's mind, on top of everything else that probably happened to her daughter, burning her body would be yet another desecration. But nothing is going to stop the sugar crush. It's already been delayed. We're almost at the end of June, what with all the searching and the upset.

I mean, I understand Barbara's need to hope that after all this time someone will find Janet's body lying unblemished in the cane fields near where she found her daughter's bag. Or maybe even that the girl herself is alive. You have to remember, apart from the fact that she's been missing for so long, there's no evidence that Janet's dead. But hundreds of people combed through those drills from Quala to Kaliope and back again for weeks looking for her and found nothing. That hasn't stopped Barbara, though. She still goes out every morning by herself, walking through the cane fields belonging to the Creadies and the Tranters, looking for her daughter's remains. She comes back hours later, covered in dust and dirt.

I've got all the sympathy under the sun for her and Ted and what they're going through, but if their girl is in the cane, she's dead, and burning isn't going to change that. And I tell you what, I'd rather find her bones after they've been scorched clean by fire than see what she'd look like after a month of lying in this heat. Fire's cleansing, I reckon. When it goes through the cane, it burns off the dreck and drives out the rats, the snakes and those filthy toads. Sure, everything is scorched and black and there's ash everywhere, but the real muck, the stuff you can't bear to look at, it's all been burnt away.

Not that Barbara sees it like that, and I'm not saying I blame her. It put me in mind of that time Dot dropped her pearl earring that had belonged to her mother on the kitchen floor. We heard it bounce and there were only a few square feet of floorboards where it could've possibly landed, but it was as if it'd disappeared into thin air. Just like poor little Janet McClymont disappeared into the cane as if something unseen had swallowed her up. But those fields have been searched thoroughly—dozens of times—and the cane must be harvested, and for that to happen it has to be burnt. Even the Tranters, with Connie Tranter being so close to Barbara, aren't going to be able to hold off much longer.

Connie was very taken with Barbara right from the start. Barbara's an artist, you see, and Connie knows a bit about that sort of thing. Culture and whatnot. Before she married Cam she had a public service job with Queensland Arts Council or some such. Gave it all up when she got married.

Barbara being an artist was why the McClymonts lived at Quala, rather than in town, in Kaliope, despite how much bigger it is. She'd only agreed to come north for Ted's job on condition that they bought a house with a view of the sea. As soon as they moved in she set up a studio with canvasses and brushes and paints in their big sleep-out on the eastern side of the house. All you could see from up there was ocean. That, and the cane, of course. There's nowhere you can't see the cane around here.

There's a few people around Quala who do arts and crafts, the kind of stuff you see sold in Kaliope for the tourists. Macramé owls, clocks with numbers made from shells, woven bags, that sort of thing. But Barbara, she's the genuine article, a real artist. She paints landscapes mainly. Big bloody canvasses. I had a bit of a gander at some of them hanging up at that housewarming they had not long after they arrived. They invited everyone in

Quala, even old blokes like me. I'd just got myself a beer when Barbara walked up behind me while I was having a look at one of her paintings she had up in the hall. Straight up, she asked, 'Well, what do you think, Arthur?' I told her it was very impressive. A close-up view of the rainforest up on Mount Tamborine, that's what Barbara said it was. A bit strange, but in a good way. Moody, I suppose you'd call it. Dense. Splashes of bright colour among the darkness of the trees. Not that I know anything about it—art, that is.

Anyway, Connie thought an awful lot of Barbara. They had a bit in common, I suppose. Neither of them being locals. Now, I know how that sounds. Connie's been living in Quala for what, almost thirteen years? But you know what I mean. It takes a while to be seen as part of the furniture in little places like this one.

Janet was walking up to the Tranters' place when she went missing. It was a Saturday evening, just on dusk. Connie had asked her to babysit her girls, Essie and the little one, Helen, overnight. Cam Tranter's brother had just got engaged and there was a bit of a shindig planned. Cam and Connie were going to be away till Sunday morning.

The McClymonts' house is right on the edge of Quala township and up against the boundary of the Creadies' place, and the Tranters are the next one over. Janet would have taken the track that runs through the Creadies' two biggest fields to get there. Lots of the local kids use that track—or used to—to walk to the main road to catch the bus to the high school in Kaliope of a weekday morning, or the one that goes late on a Saturday arvo if they're going to the pictures in town.

About twenty past six, Connie rang Barbara to see why Janet hadn't turned up. She was a reliable girl, you see. Barbara was in a tizz right away. Janet had left the house at least an hour earlier, maybe more, she said, which surprised Connie, because it would have only taken Janet twenty minutes to walk over to their place. Later on, the fact that Janet set out so early was enough to make people twig to the possibility that she'd arranged to meet someone—a boyfriend maybe—before she went to the Tranters'. It made things hot for Joe Cassar for a bit, because it had got about that he and Janet were keen on each other.

Anyway, Barbara was so worried that Cam left Connie with the girls to go and help Barbara look. And when he wasn't back within half an hour, Connie called John Creadie to see if he could help. He and his father Vince took off in the ute to look for Janet as well. After an hour or so Connie herself, still with all her makeup on and her hair curled, dropped her girls over to Jean Creadie to mind and she joined the men and Barbara in the search. Connie and Cam ended up missing his brother's engagement party altogether. Not that that's a tragedy, not compared to a young girl going missing.

For Cam and Connie, it immediately brought up memories of when Jean and Vince Creadie's daughter, Cathy, went missing. Of course, it must've hit the Creadies even worse. It must be nine, almost ten years ago that Cathy disappeared swimming off the rocks up at Danger Point. It was several days before they found her body. Cathy was about the same age as the McClymont girl when she died. Sixteen, I reckon, and John about four years older, I suppose. A terrible thing.

Terrible in all sorts of ways and for all sorts of reasons. Mind you, the McClymonts have had weeks to endure the uncertainty of what's happened to their daughter, and it's not over yet.

It took them a while to track down Ted McClymont that night. He'd gone out fishing with Les Comerford in the afternoon. Ted works for the Department of Primary Industries and he'd helped Les with a compensation claim against the state electricity commission. His cane crop had been damaged when they were replacing power poles or something. I can't remember exactly. Anyway, Ted knows a bit about these things and Les offered to take Ted out on his boat because he'd done such a good job for him. They'd stopped off for a few beers with Les's mates after they tied up the boat at the jetty.

Ted'd been drinking for a few hours by the time they found him, but he sobered up pretty quick smart once they told him Janet was missing, and he got stuck into searching for his daughter as well. Cam and the Creadies had searched alongside the track Janet would have taken, so Ted drove up and down the highway mostly. Cam went into Kaliope on a hunch and went round the pubs, but she wasn't there. Then he drove out to George and Nola Cassar's place because Barbara mentioned that Janet had dropped a few hints that she and Joe were going around together. No one was home. They were at one of Nola's people's place, apparently. A bit of a family get-together. Nola's the eldest of eight, so there's always birthdays and whatnot to celebrate.

The police weren't called until about ten o'clock that night. Some young bloke just out of the academy was the only copper at Kaliope station. There'd been a brawl earlier in the day at the footy game in Candleford, between their blokes and the Kaliope team. It's still early in the season but there's a bit of bad blood left over from last year's grand final. All hell had broken loose again later at the Commercial Hotel in town when the Candleford boys turned up for another go. So there was no one around with any brains to take a report of a missing teenage girl seriously. The young constable didn't even let Bill Wren—he's the local sergeant—know about Janet until early the next day.

Barbara and Ted were out all night looking for their daughter, of course. As were Cam Tranter and John Creadie. Connie tried to persuade Barbara to get an hour's sleep, but she wouldn't hear a word of it. At sparrow's fart the next morning, before the local cops even turned up and got a proper search going, Barbara found Janet's shoulder bag a couple of drills into one of the Creadies' fields. Jean Creadie said she heard Barbara screaming her daughter's name all the way from their place up on the hill. I suppose it was then that Barbara knew her worst fears had probably been realised, because no woman I know, young or old, willingly goes anywhere without a bag of some sort. It was the only clue as to what had befallen her daughter, and a pretty strong indication she hadn't gone of her own accord.

The bag was open, all of Janet's things spilled out onto the grass. Her purse, I suppose, perhaps some homework to catch up on and whatever else it is that young girls carry round with them. Maybe a handkerchief. I think she would have had a handkerchief. She was a neat, clean little thing. I'd seen her round and about. She always had some little bit of feminine frippery like the butterfly hair slide she was wearing in that photo they published in the paper. She had a knack for looking smart, well put-together—even I could see that—like her mother. Well, like her mother used to.

By the time the Kaliope coppers arrived, most of the McClymonts' neighbours had joined in the search for the girl. Even Dot and me were helping as best we could. There were blokes on horses, blokes driving tractors, others on motorbikes tearing through the bush, and four-wheel drives roaring up hills and along the beach down at the inlet. We'd just about thrashed our way through the entire field where Barbara had found her daughter's things, as well as the one opposite and all along the riverbank. And a few men had already fanned out into the field beyond the creek further up. We'd found no other trace of her.

When the police managed to get a few of the searchers together, someone said they'd seen footprints in the sand by the river, but by the time the coppers went to look for them all the ground there had turned to mud, churned up by those who'd come running when word had got out.

None of us locals were saying it, but we were all thinking it—the same way we were when Vince and Jean's daughter Cathy first went missing—just how bloody easy it would be to hide something or somebody in this type of country. The cane fields are just the start of it; then there's the creeks, the gullies, the swamps, and the bloody mangroves, of course. The guinea grass was that tall, not to mention the cane. Most of us were soaking wet, our boots caked in mud from pushing through the waist-high grass and the gullies filled with muck. There'd been so much rain in the months before that water was lying everywhere, and the growth was that thick. Plenty of snakes too.

I was half afraid of blundering across a wild sow and her piglets, but not much chance of that given the noise we were making. I gave myself a hell of a fright when I caught a glimpse of something white in an overgrown gully. They'd told us Janet had been wearing cropped white pants, you see, pedal pushers they called them, and a blue sleeveless top. Thought I was going to shit myself. I called over one of the Froome boys. Too bloody scared to find her by myself. Turned out to be a dead horse. Most of it was hidden in the long grass. It was one of its legs I'd seen poking out of the end of the gully. It had a white fetlock. We laughed, if you can believe it.

The search was all a bit bloody ad hoc, if you want the truth. At least on the first day. It wasn't until that afternoon when some of the women—Dot and Connie and Meg and Jean Creadie and a few others—brought sandwiches and tea and set up a canteen that the coppers got all the searchers together in one spot. The Jensens even donated soft drinks and chips, which was a bit of a turn-up for the books. Anyway, one of the coppers, I think it was Bill Wren, finally got around to marking off sections of a map of the surrounding area. It was only then that they got us to break into groups of two or three to systematically search within a four-mile radius of where Janet's bag had been found. Before that, we'd just been tearing off in whatever direction we got into our heads.

We searched all day. People came from everywhere to help. Even the tourists from the caravan park and hippies from that commune up near Danger Point, blokes from the dive shop.

There must have been hundreds of us charging around the place. And not just men. There were plenty of women too. At about five-thirty the coppers called it off for the day. It was too bloody dark to see anything. Ted McClymont made a point of shaking the hand of every man that was there. He was kind of hearty, trying to smile, slapping our backs and that. It was bloody cruel. I couldn't look him in the face.

On Monday, the principal of Kaliope West High, Ern Shaw, told all the students they could have the day off to join the search, and before long every man and his dog from Kaliope was traipsing round the place. Over the next five days, thousands of people turned out to look for her. We searched every creek, every waterhole. There were people tramping along the beaches north and south, a couple of army helicopters buzzing over-head, vehicles driving up and down the highway looking in ditches by the side of the road. Ted McClymont even hired a pilot with a private plane to fly him over the area. Apart from Barbara finding her daughter's bag that first morning, we found nothing. Absolutely nothing.

That's when the fear really set in. The fact that a young girl had just disappeared without a trace and no one knew what had happened to her, like something had just swallowed her up. Everyone was watching their kids like a hawk; they still are. No child within a two-hundred-mile radius of the place is allowed to walk to school. People on the farms have organised rosters to pick up their kids and drive them into town every morning. No more riding their bikes. Even kids who only live a couple of doors away from the school have to walk there in a group or with a parent. I'm glad my grandkids are just about grown up. The fear must be something awful if you've got young ones. And the poor kids. What's being a kid if you don't have a bit of freedom to muck about?

~

Four weeks have passed since Janet's disappearance and Ted McClymont still hasn't gone back to work. Lucky for him he works for a government department, because anywhere else and who knows what they'd be living on.

Ted hasn't accepted that Janet's dead; at least that's what he says. 'I've not given up hope, not by a long shot,' he shoots back at anyone who tells him how sorry they are about what's happened to Janet. He has this awful grin smeared across his face like a scrape of dough. His lips all twisted and baring his teeth. Mind you, when he thinks no one is watching, his mask drops away and something horrific happens to his eyes. It's as if he's watching his daughter being tormented with the worst things he can imagine.

Barbara, though, she knows her daughter's gone for good. She staggers about as if she's carrying Janet's corpse in her arms. She was a striking-looking woman, was Barbara, even though she dressed in a pretty peculiar way. Bohemian, I guess you'd call it. That's what Dot says. Hair all piled on top of her head, some bloody great pin or scarf securing the lot of it. I don't think I ever saw her in what I would call normal get-up. She was always going about in caftans and harem pants like that woman out of *I Dream of Jeannie*, her hands stained with paint.

Now of course, well, it's a different story. Poor woman. She looks terrible. I'm not saying that to be unkind, but hell's bells she's thin. From what I can see, she barely changes her clothes, just wanders around in what looks like a pair of Ted's old trousers and a T-shirt.

The women tried to keep Barbara and Ted fed at first. Dot and Jean Creadie and Connie Tranter and a few others would drop off casseroles at the house for them. Barbara was hardly ever there. Always trudging about in the cane, looking for Janet's body. Even when she was at home, more often than not she wouldn't answer the door. People left the food on the doorstep—spaghetti Bolognese, salmon loaf, sweet and sour pork. There were buckets of the stuff going off in the sun. All that trouble people went to going to waste. Ted eventually hosed out the dishes and left the empty pots and Tupperware containers at the gate to be picked up by whoever owned them. Not that anyone holds it against them. People can't be held to account for such things when they're grieving.

Some people say it'd be easier for Barbara and Ted if they knew exactly what happened to their girl; that what they imagine has to be worse than the reality. I don't reckon that's right. If it was my daughter, I wouldn't want to know. Not the details. There are men who are capable of anything; blokes whose instincts when they have something or someone in their power go beyond what decent people can imagine. If the McClymonts asked my advice, I'd tell them to accept that their daughter's gone, rage and howl for a while, and then settle quietly into their grief. It's what I would do.

But if those detectives from down south ever do catch that bastard who killed Janet—if they're lucky enough to trip over him and he holds up his hands and says, 'Yep, it was me' (because they're that bloody useless it would be the only way they'd find him)—then they should tie that black-hearted bastard to a tree, give Ted McClymont a cane cutter, and walk away. A few swings of that hooked blade and he'd be crying like a baby; crying like Janet would have been.

TWO

ESSIE DREAMS.

A shadow, vast, towers above her. The sun is blocked out by a figure looming on the track between the cane fields. As the shadow moves closer, her ears fill with a terrible rustling, and a huge male hand grasps the strap of her school port where it lies across her shoulder, pulling her upwards so that her feet dangle, air between the soles of her shoes and the ground. He is massive and enormously strong. Her weight is nothing to him. For a moment she hangs there until, with a shredding sound that frightens her more than anything else so far, the strap tears from its mounting on the bag and she drops, her legs collapsing beneath her so that she sprawls in the dirt. Her bag, unzipped, spills its contents on the ground—her school reader, her maths book, her pencil case—all her things scattered and smeared with mud.

Before she has time to scramble to her feet the hand descends again, grasps her wrist, and once more she is held aloft. Dangling, the weight of her body drags on the joint where her arm meets her shoulder. She fears her arm might shear off altogether. She turns her head to look up into the man's face, but he is so tall and holding her so close that she can't get a good look at him as she swings and bumps against him. In snatches, in bits, she sees that he is made entirely of cane. The hand clasping her so tightly is forged from leaves twisted into fingers. Their fine edges slice into the skin of her wrist and the thin cuts sting, sharp and hot. Blood trickles down her arm.

Within a few strides he has taken her deep into the field, the cane thwacking her in the face as he pulls her effortlessly through it. She tries to call for her mother, but it is as if stalks and leaves have been stuffed down her throat, lodging in her chest. She summons all her strength, opens her mouth wide, but she can't make a sound.

The strain of trying to scream shatters the dream and Essie wakes. She sits bolt upright, panting. In the bed on the other side of the room, her little sister Helen breathes easy.

~

The children of Quala slip through the humid air like eels in mud. They don't notice the close, damp heat. It is their natural habitat. They are mystified by the way their mothers constantly talk about it, plucking at their clothes and fanning themselves with their hands.

It is the other things, the under things, of which their mothers seem unaware that are more remarkable. These things usually appear at night. Rearing up out of nightmares, they have no name, being too big, too uncontainable to fit inside one word. The children struggle to describe the terrors that wake them to their hovering parents. 'A monster', they might say, or 'a bad man'—shrinking the thing that generates their fear into a form that has edges, confined to one shape or another. But it is not one thing, or in one place. It is not like that.

It has to do with the stories the children have heard all their lives: the strange lights seen hovering either side of the highway; the boy discovered wandering, his power of speech gone forever; the unexplained single-car accidents on a straight road; the girl mysteriously found dead in the mangroves when she'd been swimming off the rocks miles away. The stories span the generations. Some happened in their parents' time, while others are remembered by their grandparents. A few go back even further than that, way back to the olden days.

The children's games often revolve around these tales. They revisit and amplify them, giving themselves the willies. Favourites come and go, themes wax and wane, but unsurprisingly, right now they are absorbed by an event so recent that they themselves are part of the story. A girl wearing white pedal pushers was walking through the cane to babysit the Tranter kids. Then she vanished. Just. Like. That.

Their mothers make soothing noises, clucking nonsensical promises. *Mummy and Daddy would never let anything bad happen to you.* Everyone, parents and children alike, knows such assurances to be hollow. Janet McClymont's disappearance is proof enough of that.

Since Janet McClymont went missing, the adults' unease and constant attention to their children's activities have become stifling. Used to roaming the township, the inlet and the beaches, the countryside and all its hidden trails at will, schoolkids now find themselves constrained. They must continually account for themselves in the face of their parents' relentless questioning. *Where are you going and with whom? What will you be doing and when will you return?* More often than not, edicts are issued that they must stay close, in sight at all times.

At home, their mothers are shrill and brittle with anxiety, their fathers prone to explosions of anger and swipes of work-worn hands across the backs of legs or to the sides of heads. Often these outbursts are followed by stricken looks and hoarse, half-whispered apologies.

'Sorry, little mate, but just do what I say, alright?'

So the children are wary both of the nameless horror that has swallowed Janet McClymont, and of their parents' fickle-ness, their faces going from fury to quivering fondness with bewildering speed.

In the schoolyard, the talk is lurid and thick with real and imagined details of Janet McClymont's fate. Some of the children live in households with imprudent parents who allow them to take in the nightly television news along with their tea. They come to school brimming with importance, eager to report what they have learnt. Some have older siblings who attend Kaliope West High School, where Janet McClymont had gone for the six months she and her parents had lived in Quala, so there are plenty of rumours to repeat. Essie listens to their stories with the rest of them. Most of it is nonsense:

a finger was found in the ditch beside the cane field where she disappeared; the police read her diary and she was pregnant to an Islander boy; a huge crocodile was seen in the mangroves with a strip of white material that matched Janet's pedal pushers hanging from a tooth.

Fascinated and titillated, the children speculate and elaborate on the rumours and stories. They trade theories and snippets of information while kicking the footy on the oval or turning the skipping rope on the asphalt. They act out scenarios of Janet McClymont's abduction and possible murder in intricate games of pretend. In huddled knots of two or three, the littlies, the Grade 1s and 2s, and even some of the Grade 3s, entertain fantastical possibilities. They terrify each other with tales of monsters lurking in the cane and in the shaded gullies where stagnant water gathers.

All the children take a certain pride in their little town being so much in the news. Everyone in Australia is talking about them. It is only later, when their mothers turn out the lights and close the doors to their darkened bedrooms, that they are driven to dreaming grim nightmares.

～

A week after Janet went missing, Essie saw the new girl sitting on the steps of the pub as her father was driving her and Helen home from school. Her father must have seen the girl too, because when he followed Essie and her sister into the kitchen for afternoon tea he told their mother that it looked like the new owner had taken over the pub.

The girl, whose name is Raelene, started in Grade 7 at Quala Primary the following Monday. Susan and Sharon—the only other Grade 7 girls—made a point of telling Raelene that the two of them were best friends. Susan and Sharon usually exclude Essie too. So even though Essie is in Grade 6, because there are only twenty-nine kids in the whole school, Raelene ended up sitting at the desk next to her.

Raelene has a yeasty smell like the beer Essie's father drinks with his Sunday roast. And she wears a bra. Essie saw the impressions of the straps beneath the material of Raelene's blue school shift when she leant over her desk. She was wearing the uniform from her previous school rather than the green check of Quala Primary.

'I'm almost fourteen, but don't tell anyone,' Raelene told Essie as they got their snacks out of their school ports to eat at little lunch.

If Raelene had asked, Essie would have swapped her apple for Raelene's bag of barbecue-flavoured potato chips in a second. But Raelene didn't ask. She didn't offer Essie a single chip from her bag. Even so, Essie was pleased to be trusted with a confidence, and she promised to keep Raelene's secret.

Raelene explained that because she'd lived in heaps of different places with her dad, some that didn't even have a school, she'd been kept back a couple of times.

As Raelene spoke she shook back her coarse, straight, almost spiky dark hair. Her fringe lay heavy on her forehead and fell to her thick black eyebrows. At the back, her hair ended at the base of her neck in a blunt uneven line, as if someone had inexpertly cut across the entire width with one pass of the scissors.

When Danny Pine and Tim Froome brought around the crate with the bottles of milk, Essie offered Raelene half the Milo her mother had packed in a twist of wax paper.

'Where's your mum?' Essie asked as she tapped crunchy brown granules of Milo into Raelene's bottle of milk. Unlike Essie, who had steadily pressed down on the milk bottle's cap so that the edges gradually loosened and the foil lifted off in one piece, Raelene had simply pushed her thumb straight through it. The torn lid clung, jagged and untidy, to the rim of the bottle neck.

'She died.' Raelene licked cream off her fingernail and from the sides of the bottle where it had slopped out. Droplets of milk stained the bodice of her uniform. 'In a car crash. She went through the windscreen. Her head was cut almost completely off.'

Essie looked into Raelene's face. Could it be true?

Raelene, when she saw Essie staring, goggled back at her, her eyelids stretched wide so that her eyeballs were prominent like those of a horse. 'People die all the time.' She took a gulp of the Milo-flavoured milk. Gritty particles stuck to her teeth. 'Get used to it.'

Raelene said she already knew about the missing girl when Essie, with great ceremony, took her down to the mango tree at the far end of the schoolyard and got her to sit on the wooden bench at its foot. Here, beside the sports oval that was little more than a paddock, and in the deep shadow beneath the low branches, was Essie's favoured place for the exchange of confidences. Before she could tell Raelene that Janet had disappeared into 'thin air', that the search was still continuing and that Essie and her sister were no longer allowed to ride their bikes to school, Raelene cut her off.

'Duh, Fred.' Raelene goggled her eyes again and waggled her head, as if Essie had said something incredibly stupid. 'I've heard all about Janet McClymont. It's been in the news on the television and in the newspapers everywhere.'

Janet's disappearance was one of the reasons Raelene's father had bought the pub in Quala. He had been able to buy the building and the licence cheap.

'The owner was afraid he wouldn't be able to sell it with all the perverts that live around here.' Raelene looked at Essie from under her fierce eyebrows. 'Did you know her?'

'A bit. She babysat me and Helen a few times. She was nice,' said Essie, unsure about how much she wanted to tell Raelene, who spoke of death with such offhand familiarity.

Shortly after the McClymonts had moved to Quala from Brisbane, they held a party and invited almost everybody in town as well as the families from the farms nearby. They were hoping to make friends, Essie supposed, and her mum hit it off straight away with Mrs McClymont. At the party, when Mrs Zammit said that Barbara McClymont, in her harem pants and headband, was a bit too much for most people, Essie's mum said, 'I think she looks rather glamorous.'

Mrs Zammit pulled a face and took another curry puff from the tray of food on the coffee table.

Later, when Mrs McClymont offered a bowl of olives to old Mr Creadie, he had to ask what they were.

Janet had been kind to Essie that night. She gave her a Fanta after Essie told her she didn't like the Creaming Soda she'd been given, and she let Essie lie on her bed and read one of her books when Essie was tired and wanted to go home. Helen was already fast asleep in a beanbag by then.

When they drove home after the party, Essie's mum said to her dad that she was glad that the McClymonts had moved to Quala. 'They'll bring a bit of fresh air to the place. And I love those paintings of hers hanging in their lounge room. You know the Queensland Art Gallery acquired one of her landscapes last year?'

Essie's dad had raised an eyebrow. 'Is that so? Very fancy.'

Her mum had laughed and smacked him on the shoulder. 'Bumpkin.'

Perhaps Janet is dead like Raelene's mother, but no one knows for sure. But whether she is alive or not, Essie's protective of her memories of the girl who sometimes babysat her and her sister. She didn't tell Raelene about how Janet smelt faintly of strawberries, the flavour of the lip gloss she always wore, or that after Helen fell asleep on the couch Janet would show Essie how to apply eyeshadow and mascara. Or how Janet had told Essie that she had a boyfriend; his name was Joe, and he had the longest eyelashes Janet had ever seen on a boy.

~

Three weeks after moving to the town, it is Raelene who's become Quala Primary's authority on Janet McClymont. She hears things while sitting at the counter in the public bar where she has her tea every night. Not nice things. Some of the men toss their heads in her direction and tell the others to watch what they say. But after a few beers or a couple of rum and Cokes, their voices get loud again, and Raelene knows how to look as if she isn't listening, that she is just reading a book or doing her homework. And when her father, from behind the bar where he is pouring beer, tells her it's time to go upstairs to bed, she sometimes sits in the hall, just around the corner of the doorway and out of sight. He never checks whether she's gone up to her room. And if one of the drinkers catches sight of her, she puts a finger to her lips and they give her a wink and a nod and say nothing.

Her father turns a blind eye when some of the men bring their sons who are under eighteen, boys not much older than Raelene, into the pub. He will serve them a glass or two. When, as sometimes happens, a police car turns into the street, he will send the boys into the pub's private residence to wait until the coast is clear. Raelene will ask them for a sip of their rum and Coke and then gulp down as much as she can before they grab back their glass.

'Have you ever been drunk?' she asks Essie.

Of course Essie has never been drunk. Sometimes her dad lets her sip the froth from the top of his glass of beer. She doesn't think much of the taste, but the froth prickles pleasantly cold against her top lip.

'You'd like rum and Coke,' Raelene says. 'It tastes like caramel.'

Raelene heard one of the men in the bar saying Janet McClymont was a little slut and what did she think was going to happen walking around by herself in tight pants. There was almost a fight when John Creadie told the man to shut his mouth or he'd shut it for him.

Essie laps up this information greedily, and all the other things Raelene tells her, in the same way as she swallows down the lemonade she and Helen are only allowed on special occasions like birthdays and Christmas. Her parents don't let her read the newspaper and they no longer listen to the news on the radio at breakfast. But still, glimpses of and references to Janet McClymont are unavoidable: at the beginning of the television news before her mother changes the channel, on the stands outside the newsagent and on the covers of magazines. The effect is like a haunting. It's a terrible paradox. Janet McClymont is everywhere but nowhere. And try as they might, Essie's parents can't stop her and Helen from hearing the whispers and rumours that percolate through Quala Primary School.

~

'What's a pervert?' Helen asks from the back seat of the station wagon on their way home from school.

Essie swivels in the front passenger seat and glares at her little sister. If she was sitting beside Helen, she would give her a Chinese burn on her stupid arm. There is no point in asking the question: their mother will not tell them the real answer. She will bat the word 'pervert' away and all that will remain is the shame of having asked what it means. The source of the mortification is difficult to pinpoint, but it has to do with sex, forbidden and cloaked in mystery, and the exposure of wanting to know about it. From what Raelene has told her, Essie is sure Janet found out what a pervert is.

Despite her mother's prim refusal to discuss what happened to Janet beyond vague explanations of bad men, sometimes a crumb of information will drop. Some of her mother's friends are more cavalier, less careful of the ears of children. At the school gate, the women chat while they wait for their children to find lunch boxes and forgotten homework. If Essie makes herself inconspicuous, or the women forget themselves, the conversation will turn to Janet McClymont and what they imagine has happened to her. Essie is alert to these moments and stores up the morsels of information to share with Raelene later.

One afternoon at pick-up, Essie is sitting in the car outside school while her mother leans against the door waiting for Helen to find her hat. Essie has a book from the school library open in her lap. It is one that she has read before, but it is a story so alien and replete with other-worldly glamour that she borrows it again and again. It's about a girl whose mother, like Raelene's, has died in a car accident, and whose father is a pilot in the American air force. They have a housekeeper and during the holidays the girl goes to a country club where there are tennis courts and women lounge around the swimming pool wearing sharkskin bathing suits.

'I suppose you heard that a carload of darkies was seen in Kaliope the day before Janet McClymont disappeared?' Mrs Zammit asks Essie's mother. 'They weren't any of the local Islanders either. Some Abo mob from out of town, apparently.'

Essie stays silent, so quiet that perhaps her mother won't glance over her shoulder to see that the car's passenger-side window is wound down. But her mother does look. Then she turns back to Mrs Zammit, who Essie's dad calls 'the Quala

Bugle' because she's such a busybody. Essie can't see her mother's face, but she knows by the quick, sharp shake of her head that her lips are pressed together and pushed forward in a disapproving pout like a chook's bum.

From overheard conversations and skimming the front page of the *Kaliope Mail* as she waits for Mrs Jensen to ring up whatever small purchases her mother sends her in to buy, Essie learns of the anonymous phone calls made to police suggesting they search this house, beneath that bridge or along a dead-end track where teenagers drink and do other things their parents might not approve of.

THREE

AS I SAID, Janet McClymont's disappearance has brought back memories—not just for the Creadies, but for all of us locals. Except for the younger kids and a few of the blow-ins, all we could think about was the day Cathy Creadie went missing while swimming off Danger Point. It was dreadful for Vince and Jean, for John too, those few days before Cathy's body was recovered. And afterwards. No doubt about that.

Cathy was badly knocked about. Her body was. Deep gashes and bruising and that. To be expected given all the rocks beneath the point and the swell that day, I suppose. It was never clear why her body was found in the mangroves, though, rather than down on the rocks where you might have thought it would have washed up. I guess the tides could have taken it out and then brought it back in further up the coast. But, like I said, surprising.

She'd been at the point with a few of her friends, girls and boys. They'd been told, all of them at one time or another, that it was dangerous to jump into the water off the rocks there. But when have kids that age ever listened to adults when they try and tell them something? They think they're bloody indestructible.

I brought up Cathy's death with the Froome boys at the pub the other afternoon. It's a bit hazy now, but I recalled they were there at Danger Point at some stage that day. They were older than Cathy and her mates, but they used to knock around a bit with Chester Connolly, even after they were all married, like bloody overgrown kids. Still do a bit. Jimmy said that yeah, they were there, they'd turned up planning to go fishing. But they'd left, along with almost everybody else, shortly before Cathy jumped off the rocks for the last time. Just her and that young bloke who was her boyfriend were left. I vaguely remembered Vince saying something to that effect, but I don't really know anything about that part of it. Eric Shields. That was his name. He and his family left town not long afterwards. Moved further north. Cairns or somewhere.

It almost killed Vince, losing Cathy. He adored that girl, as cheeky and as wild as she was. She had him wrapped around her little finger. They were a real pair. Of course Jean loved Cathy too, but for Vince? Well, she was the apple of his eye.

You see, Vince and Jean, because of one thing and another, they ended up marrying relatively late in life. Jean sometimes says that they only got married because they were the last single people left in the district. She's joking, of course. At least, I think she is. Anyway, Vince was forty or thereabouts and Jean not much younger and it was several years before she fell pregnant. They'd just about given up hope they'd have a child after a couple of miscarriages. They were over the moon when John was born, and when Cathy came along four years later Vince couldn't take the smile off his face. He loved that little girl, by cripes, he did.

~

In broad daylight, when Essie is riding her bicycle around the farm—since Janet disappeared, she's no longer allowed to ride along the road—the cane usually seems neutral, unremarkable, even benign. But every now and then, if Essie finds herself alone because Helen has refused to come with her to check the mailbox or her father has asked her to run back to the shed and get the pliers, Essie might hear a whisper, something muttering and mithering too quietly for her to make out words. The papery raspings of cane leaves scraping against each other in the humid air crawl up the nape of her neck and into her hairline, sending a shiver down her back and fanning out to her shoulder blades, even in the day's warmth.

~

'Where?' Essie says.

'You know.' Raelene points at the place where Essie's legs meet her body.

'Where your *wee* comes out?'

Raelene rolls her eyes. 'No, retard. There's another place between there and your bum hole. Where do you think babies come from?'

'Yuck.' Essie squirms and splinters in the cracked bench beneath the mango tree hook through the thin cotton of her underpants, stabbing her skin. In the weeks since Raelene arrived in Quala, Essie has learnt more about sex than she accumulated in her previous eleven years. After Raelene's divulgences, Essie often feels queasy, like she did last Easter when she ate all her chocolate eggs before breakfast.

Raelene is still talking about disgusting things, though Essie is trying not to hear them. But when Raelene says the Kable boys' names, she can't not hear them. Brice and Darren are older. They live next door to Raelene's dad's pub and catch the bus into Kaliope to go to the same high school that Janet went to.

'Their dad was there too,' Raelene says. She pauses. She's been looking straight ahead, but now she turns towards Essie and her eyes harden to glass, cold and brittle. 'And your dad.'

Essie springs to her feet and stands over Raelene. '*Shut up!*'

It is a shout, but Raelene hears the sob beneath it, and she smiles. 'Don't be such a baby. I'm kidding. It was just Brice and Darren. God, as if. Your dad's ancient.'

Essie is still standing, she is rigid, her hands curled into fists. She sucks in huge gulps of air that rasp against her tonsils like stones.

Raelene, who hasn't shifted from the bench, punches Essie lightly on the hip. 'It was a joke. Your dad wasn't there.' And when Essie remains standing, 'I'm sorry, alright?'

'Don't say anything like that ever again.' Essie thinks she might cry. She hates Raelene in this moment. Can imagine scratching at her eyes and raking her face with her fingernails until there is blood.

'Jeez, Louise.' Raelene pulls her down beside her. 'Alright, I won't.'

Essie doesn't want to know any more, but Raelene tells her anyway and as much as Essie doesn't want to hear, fragments, like worms, work their way into her ears.

'It's big and pink,' Raelene says. 'And kind of stiff and springy.'

Essie remembers the German sausages, mottled and red, at the Kaliope agricultural show. Her dad bought two in buns with sauce for her and Helen. Wurst, he called them. 'These are what your grandma ate when she was a girl.'

Grandma's dad, his grandad, he told them, was from a country called Prussia that didn't exist anymore, and he used to make the wurst himself. Minced up the meat with spices and pushed it all through a sausage-making machine into casings made from pigs' guts.

Essie had always liked the stories about her grandma and eating the wurst, but now she doesn't think she could eat another one ever again.

The bell rings and Essie springs up from the bench. She runs ahead, wanting to be first in line, but Raelene catches her, grabs her elbow, pulls her up short and swings her around so they are facing each other.

Raelene glares into Essie's face. Essie stares back. Being Raelene's friend means always being tested.

'Don't tell anyone about the Kable boys,' Raelene says.

'I won't.'

Raelene takes a step towards her, hooks one leg behind Essie's knees and then shoves her in the chest with one quick, hard movement. Essie falls onto her back, sprawling in the dirt.

'Are you going to cry?' Raelene asks, glancing around, but their teacher Mr Day isn't looking. He has Tim Froome by the ear and is making him pick up the banana peel he just chucked on the ground.

'No.'

Raelene extends a hand and Essie lets her pull her up and into a run. At the foot of the stairs, they jostle with the other students, forming two straight lines. Raelene squeezes in front of Essie so that she is directly behind Gavan Connolly.

Essie leans into Raelene's back, her mouth at her shoulder. 'Did you touch it? Brice's thing?'

'Yes.' The word slides out of the corner of Raelene's mouth like a snake.

~

Raelene lies. Essie knows this. Raelene also embellishes, changes names and inserts herself and others into stories and situations in which, in reality, they took no part. She gleans things from newspapers and magazines, and from television programs, like *Matlock Police* and *Number 96*, that Essie's parents would never let her watch. She listens in on the tales and gossip exchanged between the farmers and the itinerant workers who drink in the front bar of her father's pub. She picks up strands and elements from all these sources and weaves them into her stories, adopting them as her own.

But Raelene doesn't lie all the time. There are things she tells Essie that ring true and speak to some knowledge deep and dark that eludes her. Things about bodies and what they are capable of; what one body might do to, and with, another. Essie has a sense of these baffling adult activities but in a vague, disconnected way. She lives on a farm. She sees the rooster subduing the scattering hens, how it burdens them with its weight, its taloned feet pressing into their feathered backs, and how it cruelly seizes their plumed necks in its beak. How it struts and beats its wings after the act is complete. She has seen the wet, pink tube of flesh that slips from the furry sheath beneath Tambo's belly as he lies panting in the dirt. And the blood on Sheba's bottom and the way she licks the place where it is red and swollen.

Raelene's stories are set in a shadowy landscape that lurks beneath the bright and shallow world where Essie's mother tries to keep her tethered. Raelene, on the other hand, is in it up to her neck. She is like the women who inhabit the big houses and hospital corridors of the television programs that Essie's mother occasionally lets her watch when she is home sick from school.

Raelene moans with exaggerated pleasure as she licks the Paddle Pops or Icy Poles they buy from Jensens' shop. She flings her limbs about in languid abandon when they sit on the benches near the drinking trough to eat lunch and giggles when Tim Froome says he can see her underpants. When they line up after the bell rings at the end of lunch, she makes sure that she is standing in front of Tim and Danny and Gavan. She puts her hands on her hips and swings her bum back and forth as she climbs the stairs to the classroom. Her dark brown eyes and barely there smile invite Essie to learn what it is she knows.

Essie is torn between knowing and not-knowing. She drinks in Raelene's dark and bitter stories. They fill her up like warm liquid until she feels at sea in her own body, jittery and languid at once. The feeling builds until, nauseous and off balance, she can bear it no longer. Propelled to her feet, Essie runs the perimeter of the school's big, wide yard, her arms outstretched, shrieking wordless expression of her tumult and breathing in great gulps of fresh air, the way she does when she is carsick.

~

'Do you think she's dead?' asks Essie, breaking the slice of her mother's homemade butter cake into two and giving a piece to Raelene.

''Course she is.' As a swap, Raelene tips beer nuts into Essie's waiting hand out of the torn-off corner of the packet she draws from her pocket. Every morning for her little lunch her dad lets her choose either a bag of chips or a packet of nuts from the stands he keeps behind the bar. Raelene bites into the cake, crumbs falling from her mouth as she speaks. 'She was probably cut into a million pieces and chucked into the mangroves. The mud crabs are eating her now.'

The yells and grunts of the boys kicking a footy on the oval below the schoolhouse drift across to the girls as they walk the circuit of the school fence.

'He would have done it to her first, though. Or maybe afterwards.' Raelene pulls viciously on a clump of foxtail grass.

'Aww, don't these look like baby mice?' She shows Essie the fluffy decapitated seed heads and then throws them in her face. 'She was a slut anyway, probably happy to meet a sex maniac.'

Essie isn't entirely sure what a sex maniac is, although she imagines someone male, naked and towering, with a long red protuberance swinging between his legs. Sluts, she knows, are always female. But the way the word fills Raelene's mouth, her tongue relishing the consonants packed tightly together in one abrupt parcel of sound, conveys a lewdness that is completely alien to the Janet who Essie knew. She doesn't challenge Raelene when she speaks about Janet like this. She knows enough not to reveal all her tender, sacred places to Raelene. Anything precious or delicate, whether a feeling or a favourite book, Raelene will find a way to besmirch it.

'I bet she's not happy now.' Essie runs her hands along the top wire of the fence. Her understanding lags behind all the meanings hidden in Raelene's words, but she feels their pull like an underground stream beneath her feet. The *it* that Raelene declares would have been done to Janet implies violence and something breached, the flow of unfamiliar fluids. It has to do with what she saw when she accidentally let Tambo into the barn with Sheba and with the strange coupling of their furry bodies.

She had only meant to go and pat Sheba, who would be lonely locked up in the barn away from Tambo. Essie just wanted to rub the rough fur between her ears and scratch her pink belly.

'Sheba's too young to have babies,' her father told Essie and Helen. 'It's just for a few days.'

But Tambo was sly. He followed Essie up the barn steps and slipped past her legs towards Sheba when Essie pulled the door open just a crack. Essie rushed in to haul Tambo out, but it was too late. The dogs were already locked together—Tambo dancing behind Sheba on his hind legs as she tried to pull away. Then it turned nightmarish when Tambo slipped off Sheba's back and was somehow facing in the other direction but, horrifically, still fused to her, end-to-end. Sheba was docile now, resigned to this strange bonding with her brother.

Essie stood frozen to the spot, until Tambo glanced at her, his tongue lolling from his mouth in a wide grin. She stumbled from the barn, calling for her mother.

Connie came running from the house, flour still on her hands. 'Is it a snake? Have you been bitten? Quick, quickly, show me.'

Essie pointed to the barn.

Her mother ran up the steps and through the barn door. 'Oh, Essie, they'll be alright,' she said as she emerged, brushing her floury hands on her apron.

'But what's happened to Sheba?'

'She'll be fine. You'll understand when you're older.'

~

'It's like your dad's the car and your mum's the garage,' Tim says at school the next day.

Essie had told Raelene what happened in the barn and she told Tim and Gavan and Danny. Now they're all standing there, grinning at her like idiots.

Essie turns on her heel and runs up the schoolhouse steps, away from their leering faces. 'I know all about that stuff,' she yells over her shoulder.

That only makes them laugh at her more. Like the hyenas she saw in that nature program on TV. Raelene is laughing too, laughing at Essie. Raelene's supposed to be her best friend, but sometimes with the boys, with Tim and Gavan and Danny, it's as if Raelene likes them better, or at least she wants them to like her and is happy to toss Essie into their grinning mouths with their sharp teeth if it makes them laugh. She knows Essie will come crawling back, even if she has her guts ripped out.

But Essie knows that Tim is wrong. A car is metal and plastic, a garage an empty, echoing space. The garage isn't changed by the car that drives into it, doesn't feel it, doesn't care if the car is there or not. The boundaries between each thing remain unaltered. That's not what sex is like.

What happens between bodies is dangerous, the contortions grotesque and strange. What she had caught a glimpse of in the barn was the least of it. When people speak about what might have happened to Janet, it leaves Essie with the same sick feeling.

⁓

Raelene is coming for a sleepover.

Even though it still hurt that she and the boys made fun of Essie about what she had seen in the barn, Essie asked Raelene if she would like to come over on Saturday afternoon and stay the night. Raelene shrugged as if she couldn't care less, but she said yes. Essie tried to act cool, as if it was no big deal, but later, in the dunnies alone, she hugged herself with pleasure.

'I'll tell my dad,' Raelene said. 'It'll be fine.'

But even so, Essie's mum rang the pub and spoke to Mr Mason to make sure that he was happy for Raelene to stay the night.

~

Essie's father is surprised when Raelene turns up on her bicycle alone on Saturday. 'I would have come in the car to pick you up if I'd known you were riding here by yourself,' he says to her.

Raelene looks equally surprised at the suggestion that she might need adult supervision for anything. She stands up straight, her hands on her hips. 'I'm not a little kid, Mr Tranter.'

They have afternoon tea in the kitchen. Essie's mum has baked a rainbow cake and Essie makes malted milkshakes flavoured with caramel sauce. Helen gets the food colouring out of the pantry and pours a whole capful over the ice cream in the blender's glass jug so that after drinking their milkshakes the girls all have blue lips and teeth.

Afterwards, Essie shows Raelene around the farm and Raelene asks to see the barn where Tambo mated with Sheba. Essie shows her where it is but refuses to go in.

'You can if you want,' she says, pretending she doesn't care one way or the other.

Raelene runs up the steps and looks inside. She turns to face Essie and makes a disgusting thrusting movement with her hips. Essie turns and runs back towards the house, and Raelene follows.

They play Twister until teatime, with Helen spinning the arrow to tell Essie and Raelene on which coloured dots to put their hands and feet. When Helen begins to whinge that she wants to have a go on the mat too, Essie's dad joins in. The four of them crawl over the plastic sheet while her mum takes over flicking the arrow. At first Essie is embarrassed, fearing Raelene's scorn at this childish game. But there is no trace of mockery in Raelene's laughter when they get so tangled they all fall in a heap.

Essie's dad sends them into the bathroom to wash their hands before they sit down at the table. Essie sees a small frown of dismay on her mother's face when she places a plate of tuna mornay on the table in front of Raelene and notices the line of grime around Raelene's neck.

'Would you like to have a bath after Essie and Helen have theirs, Raelene?' her mum asks.

Raelene breezily refuses. 'No, thanks, Mrs Tranter. I had a wash before I came.'

Later, when their mother tells them it's time for bed, Helen and Essie put on their seersucker shortie pyjamas. Essie's are pink with tiny red roses. Helen's are lemon yellow with white daisies. Raelene pulls off her shorts and tosses them under Essie's bed.

Their mother looks at Raelene in her grey cottontails and the grubby T-shirt she was wearing when she arrived on her bicycle. 'Didn't you bring pyjamas?'

'My dad says it's stupid to buy special clothes just to sleep in.'

Their mother doesn't argue, just kisses Essie and Helen goodnight and turns out the light before closing their bedroom door.

The three girls lie in silence for about twenty seconds before dragging the mattresses off the two single beds and onto the floor, piling them high with pillows, sheets, cotton blankets and the sleeping bag their mother had taken down from the top shelf of the wardrobe for Raelene. Raelene is supposed to be sleeping on the thin pallet from the bamboo recliner on the verandah, but the foam pad lies spurned on the floor between the denuded beds.

'Listen.' Raelene sits on top of the piled bedding, facing Essie and Helen. Her command is issued in a hoarse whisper.

The only light in the bedroom now comes from the small torch that Raelene has brought with her and retrieved from her shorts. Helen's pale brown hair is in the pigtails that her mother scraped it into that morning. Her eyes are round, the pupils huge in the dim light. Her thumb is in her mouth, and Essie, whose hands are trapped between her own tightly pressed thighs, doesn't slap it out.

'Can you hear it?' Raelene shines the torch into Essie's face.

'Hear what?' Essie stares into the bright light. Forces her eyelids to stay open, refusing to blink.

Helen has snuggled herself into Essie's side. She links one arm through hers and burrows her small paw along Essie's wrist to find her hand. Holds it. Essie doesn't push her away.

'That swishing sound,' Raelene says, her voice low, eyes darting towards the window. 'It's coming from the cane.'

Helen lets out a strangled sound, something between a giggle and a sob.

'Stop it,' Essie says. 'You're scaring her.'

'Or is it you who's scared?' Raelene flips the torch so that she is holding it vertically beneath her chin, illuminating the underside of her facial features. Her eyes are black pits. 'Listen. The swishing's getting louder. It's coming closer.'

'Please don't, Raelene.' There is no mistaking the quaver in Helen's voice. 'I don't like it.'

Raelene swivels her head towards Helen, widening her eyes, and says, her voice flat like a robot's, 'It doesn't care if you don't like it. But don't worry, when it comes for you, you won't even see it. Not until it's too late. You'll just think it's the sound of the wind blowing through the cane and then . . .'

Raelene pounces, snatches Helen from Essie's side, digs sharp fingers into her ribs.

Helen shrieks. She bounds up towards the bedroom door, driving her sharp little elbow into Essie's eye and smacking Raelene in the nose with her foot as she charges past them. Essie, one eye clenched shut and water streaming down her cheek, springs to her feet to stop Helen before she can open the door and spoil everything.

But it's too late. She hears her mother's footsteps thudding down the hall. The door flings open and Helen leaps into her mother's arms. Essie sees her father behind her.

~

Later, when Helen is asleep in her parents' bed, Essie and Raelene lie face upwards in the single beds. Essie's mum has taken Raelene's bloodstained T-shirt to soak in the laundry tub. She has persuaded Raelene to don one of her nighties.

'Do you think he's still out there?' Essie says.

'Who?'

'You know.'

'Probably. There's perverts everywhere.' Raelene sounds unconcerned. Yawning, she turns on her side and is asleep within minutes.

Essie lies awake for what seems like hours. She can hear the cane whispering beneath Raelene's snores and she remembers the stories. Not the ones she reads in her social studies textbook about the explorers and the settlers, but others she has picked up here and there.

Once, at the Creadies' place, she heard old Mr Creadie and his friend Arthur Mulligan talking about the Aboriginal people who lived where the cane now grows. How they were driven away so the land could be cleared. When Arthur's wife Dot saw Essie listening, she poked him in the ribs with her elbow and said, 'Little pitchers have big ears.'

In the nearby national park, there's a 'site of interest' where a baby survived after its mother jumped off a cliff rather than be taken by the Native Police. A noticeboard marks the spot where the child was found in the arms of its dead mother.

Other tales have filtered through. About the Islander families in Quala and those in Kaliope. When people want to be mean they call them Kanakas. Her mother has told her not to use that word, but when Essie asks her why, she can give her no satisfactory explanation.

FOUR

THE CANE'S SO bloody rife up this way people have no clue what was here before. Those plains, they were once meadows of blady grass. And the coastal wetlands, carpets of sedge and spikerush mainly. All gone now. Not to mention the groves of myrtle, protea, boronia, wattle and grass trees that were burnt and torn out of the ground. And almost no one around here is old enough to remember the open woodlands of blue gum, swamp box and tea tree. All laid to waste over the years with axes and great toothed saws. Most of the lowland rainforest went the same way.

Of course, when the forests went, so did the birds and the beasts. Red-cheeked dunnarts and pebble-mound mice—you hardly ever see them now. And most people have forgotten the numbers of koalas you used to be able to find, because, no surprise, once the trees were felled, they disappeared. Birds too. Gouldian finches, gorgeous bloody things, the colours of them—purple, green, yellow, red—lucky to see one now. Not to mention the olive-backed sunbirds. Graceful as all get out with curved bills and building these strange, suspended nests. Keep your eyes peeled if you want to catch a glimpse of one of them around these parts.

Bugger-all consideration was given to preserving habitat back when they were clearing the land. Same all over the state, I guess. But up here, all that effort of clearing and destruction was so that the country could be sown with sugar cane. Acres of it. Swathes of it. As-far-as-the-bloody-eye-can-see of it.

I've got a bit of a love–hate thing going on with the cane. I've made my living from it, after all, and so have my kids. Still, when you think what was lost. But no time to dwell on it now. The weather's cooling, the rain's moved south and the crush is underway. Almost all the farmers have begun burning and cutting their cane. The sugar mill is fired up and you can smell molasses day and night.

~

The box, packaged in nondescript brown paper and addressed to Eamonn Sullivan, arrives at the Creadies' snug with the rest of their mail. When Jean trips over it for the second time later in the morning, she throws her hands up, appeals to Vince. 'Would you drop this off at the old house? I'm going to break my blessed neck.'

'I've told those young blokes to have a word to June. I don't know why she keeps dropping their mail off here,' Vince grumbles. He takes a felt-tipped pen from the drawer of his desk in the office next to the kitchen and scrawls a note on the side of the box. *Left at the snug. Perhaps let June Ryan at the post office know she can deliver any mail for you at the old house. V. Creadie.*

'Oof.' Vince hoists the box up to his chest. 'I'll run it up now and leave it on the verandah. John wants me to go into town to pick up something for him at the mechanics anyway.'

'The old house' is what the Creadies call the cottage they rent to Eamonn Sullivan and Peter Parslow. 'The big house', about a third of a mile away and obscured from view when the cane is high, is where Vince's son John lives with his family. Now that John has officially taken over the running of the farm, Vince and Jean have moved into 'the snug', a small modern bungalow that's been built on the track running between the big house and the old house.

The Creadies charge a modest rent for the old house, a two-bedroom cottage perched on absurdly high stilts in a small depression and surrounded by acres of sugar cane in every direction. It's only a twenty-minute drive from Kaliope and in good enough condition for a couple of young single blokes like Eamonn, who's a teacher at the high school, and Pete, a local lad who works as a clerk in the Kaliope council offices.

When Vince's father, Walter, was laying the foundations for the cottage in the 1890s, a huge flood had come down the river, inundating the site of the planned house. Rather than find a new site, Walter had chosen to simply increase the height of the stilts the house rested on. Its aspect means that you can see the ocean from the verandah when the cane isn't too high. On a really clear day, the hazy outlines of the coral islands flicker on the horizon. Now, with the Creadies delaying the start of their harvest, the cane crowds in around the cottage, tall and thick and almost impenetrable, blocking out everything. At night, the wind rustling through it sounds like a great creature stirring.

In a normal year, John Creadie and Cam Tranter would have begun harvesting by now, like the other cane farmers already have. Every evening you'll see fires lighting up the sky. Vince has told John they can't hold off much longer, but John reckons they should wait for things to dry out a bit more. Nonsense. John has a tender heart—made more so by the death of his sister ten years ago. He's been moved by Barbara McClymont's pleas to hold off burning the cane until her daughter's remains have been found. But they can't wait forever. Their cane is ripe and ready to burn.

~

'Maybe it's more singlets from his mother,' muses Vince as he carries the box addressed to Eamonn Sullivan out the door.

'Oh, don't!' Jean claps hands either side of her face.

'Or underpants.'

'Vince! Don't remind me.' Jean chuckles. 'I thought his ears would catch fire they were that red.'

The first time a package for their tenant had been delivered to the snug, Vince had waved Eamonn down on the track to tell him that a parcel had arrived for him. Eamonn had ripped it open right there on the Creadies' kitchen table, with all the excitement of a small boy at Christmas, Jean later remarked to Vince. Out of the torn brown paper and curls of snapped string spilled a copy of *The Catholic Leader* and several singlets. ('Doesn't Eamonn's mother realise her son is living in the tropics?' Vince said to Jean later.) These were followed by two pairs of very brief, fire-engine-red underpants with cartoon imps grinning and brandishing tridents on their nylon folds.

Eamonn, blushing furiously, bent over the table, his long red hair failing to screen his crimson face, and attempted to stuff the parcel's contents back into the torn packaging. In his haste, he swept one pair of the jocks onto the floor. Vince bent to retrieve them, held them out to Eamonn. The product tag swung, posing the question: *Devil enough to wear them?*

'Oh yes,' said Jean, darting a glance at Vince. 'All the young men are wearing those Jockettes now, I've heard.'

'Suppose it gets cold in Toowoomba up there on the range,' Vince said, avoiding Jean's eye. 'Not that them undies would do you much good in that respect. They'd scarcely cover your privates, by the looks of them. The singlets compensate, I expect. That's where you're from, isn't it? Up on the Downs?'

Eamonn snatched the jocks from Vince's hand, agreeing that yes, he was from up that way, and then fled.

Vince and Jean managed to hold their laughter until their tenant had escaped the kitchen and was well down the stairs.

From its weight and feel, Vince guesses this latest parcel addressed to his tenant contains books rather than underwear. Out of curiosity, he looks for a return address, but nothing apart from a Brisbane postal mark gives any indication as to who sent it. He climbs the steps to the old house's verandah, and as he reaches the top, a cat, an orange tom, low-hipped and furtive, slips through the gap between the slightly ajar front door and its warped frame.

Vince has already seen a few strays lurking about the place. Jean hates them because they hunt the birds. Pete Parslow complained that he'd come home the other week to find one—probably this moggy—in his bedroom and that the place had smelt of cat's piss for days afterwards.

'Psssht! Get out of it, you dirty thing,' Vince hisses, then steps back, teetering on the top step as the cat scurries between his legs and bolts down the stairs. Vince puts a hand out to steady himself and the box tumbles out of his grip. The tape securing the flaps crimps, pulling off the cardboard, and several books, scarcely more than pamphlets with red covers, tip out. When he recovers his balance, Vince stoops to pick up the scattered volumes. Examines the title on them: *The Little Red Schoolbook*. The box is full of them. *How did Eamonn Sullivan get hold of these?* he wonders. *And what's he planning to do with them?*

When Vince walks back through the gate of his own place, Jean looks up from where she's kneeling, weeding the front garden bed. He tells her about the books. 'Dozens of them, he's got.'

'Is he a communist, then?' she asks.

'Just a young leftie, I reckon.'

'Did you read any of it?'

'No.' Vince shakes his head vehemently. 'What would I want with that rubbish?'

'Should we tell the police?'

'No, woman! They're only a bit of piss and wind. The bloody things look like comics. Bill Wren and those detectives from down south have got enough on their plates at the moment without worrying about a young ratbag with a few banned books. To look at them, you'd hardly take them seriously.'

'Well, I hope he keeps his head pulled in.' Jean grasps Vince's hand and he hauls her to her feet. 'What with everything, no one's got much of a sense of humour around here at the moment.'

~

With his long red hair and cheesecloth tunics, Eamonn Sullivan is enough of an odd bod to draw attention to himself in Quala, even in the most settled of times. Vince sees no need to add to his notoriety by putting it about that he's got hold of a couple of dozen copies of *The Little Red Schoolbook*. People are antsy enough in the wake of Janet's disappearance, and they won't have forgotten that the coppers looked at both of the Creadies' tenants pretty hard after Janet went missing. Mind you, the coppers also grilled John and Vince, as well as every other adult male within cooee of Quala. No one was above suspicion. It was bloody alarming for a week or so.

Eamonn and Pete were able to provide alibis. In fact, it was Vince himself who told police that the young men had left the property in the early afternoon to go to the football match in town and he hadn't seen Eamonn's car pull up to the old house until well after eight.

There'd been a few murmurs at the pub one evening several days after Janet went missing, John told Vince. Suggestions were mooted that the Froome boys might pay Eamonn and Pete a visit, not a particularly friendly one, to see how their story of being at the footy held up under a bit of forceful questioning.

It was Eamonn, being a blow-in, who they were most leery of. Calmer heads prevailed, thankfully, and the Froome boys were persuaded to have another beer rather than indulge in a bit of argy-bargy with Eamonn Sullivan.

Vince suspects that Eamonn won't be in Quala very long. Shortly after he moved into the old house, Eamonn told Vince about his hankering to live in London. 'The only thing holding me back,' he said, 'is that I'm bonded to the Education Department. The only way I could afford to go to university was by training as a teacher and going wherever the department chooses to send me for the first few years after graduating.' After eighteen months teaching in Toowoomba, he'd been sent to Kaliope West High School, so his life was on hold for another twelve months at least. That's how Eamonn put it to Vince. It was either work out the time on his bond or pay off his debt.

Vince can't fathom why anyone would want to move to London, but Eamonn reckoned Australia was a backwater and lots of young people were heading over there. Perhaps if Vince was Eamonn's age, he might think differently, but the war extinguished any semblance of itchy feet for Vince. After that business, he's never wanted to leave home again. In his opinion, Australia is God's own country and a man would be a fool to want to leave.

FIVE

I'M NOT KNOCKING the local coppers. Although they got a bit of stick from other people in Quala and Kaliope. They did the best they could, but they had no clue what happened to Barbara and Ted's girl or who might have taken her.

The poor bastards got bombarded by people claiming they'd seen something suspicious or knew of someone dodgy who'd been acting strange. 'Course, police stations across the whole country were taking phone calls from people telling them to look into this or that. And mostly the police followed up these so-called tip-offs no matter how malicious, foolish or ill-informed they were. It's their job, the unfortunate buggers. Wet-behind-the-ears constables were sent out to poke at cow bones bleached white from the years they'd lain in the sun, or knock on doors and scare the shit out of young blokes with long hair or dark skin. Loners and alkies, broken old men, blokes with reputations as kiddie fiddlers or for breaking their girlfriends' teeth were invited down to the Kaliope cop shop or were given to understand that if they knew what was good for them they'd step aside and let the coppers have a poke around in all the rooms and the sheds out the back and the boot of their car. Not that it's done one blind bit of good.

It took a few days before detectives from Brisbane got here. Blokes who knew how to do these things properly. The local boys took it hard. They looked a bit like idiots.

If you want the truth, I reckon most of us had our noses put out of joint when the detectives arrived from down south. We all felt like we were suspects, for a start. A week or so after the girl went missing, Gary Blenheim's dog ran behind his tractor as he was backing out of the shed. Gary held off burying it because he was worried the disturbed ground would look suspicious. He thought about dumping it up in the bush somewhere but that might look odd too. He ended up taking it to the police station wrapped up in a hessian bag. He dumped it on the front counter and told them to dispose of the bloody thing themselves. That's how bad it got.

Even after the Brisbane crew turned up, one of the Kaliope coppers swore he wouldn't go home until they found that little girl. I know she was sixteen years old, but she was still a little girl to her parents and anyone else with a daughter that age. Anyway, the copper was as good as his word. He didn't sleep in his own bed or sit down once at his kitchen table with his family for ten days straight after Janet went missing. His wife brought him food and clean underwear and socks, took his shirts home to wash and came back with them pressed and starched. Then one morning, early, she turned up at the station before anyone else, carrying a plate of bacon and eggs on toast, covered with foil to keep them warm. She walked in and found him dead at his desk. Heart attack. He was the size of a brick shithouse, admittedly, and never said no to a beer, but still, bloody poignant.

At least the coppers from out of town were a bloody sight more polite than the journalists and reporters who turned up here like a bunch of crows hanging around a lump of roadkill. Quala and Kaliope were full of them for weeks. Impertinent and up themselves. Swanning around like they owned the joint. They traipsed through private property, took photos of whatever they liked—even of poor bloody Barbara McClymont looking as mad as a cut snake.

They stood in front of cane fields, sometimes nowhere near where the McClymont girl disappeared, holding microphones in their city-soft hands like they were something precious. They'd be as happy as Larry, joking and carrying on with the cameraman or whoever, then as soon as the cameras started rolling they'd suddenly be as sorrowful as anything. Two-faced bastards. The *glee* on their mugs to be covering a story like that. It'd make you sick.

Though it's died off now, at first the story was being screened and talked about all over the country. Maybe the world. Sometimes it felt like the whole of Australia was looking at us and judging us. And sometimes I felt like they were right to. How could we have allowed one of our own, a young girl scarcely more than a child, to be taken from us, probably violated and almost certainly murdered? That we couldn't see that there was someone in our midst, maybe someone we drank with at the pub, who was capable of doing something like that and we didn't even know. How useless must we be?

I tell you what, it makes a bloke feel half a man. Like someone has taken a cane knife to the ball sacks of every man from Quala to Cairns.

There's only one of the Brisbane coppers left up here now. The others have given up and gone home—no, I lie. In actual fact, a new female officer, Carmel something, has just arrived to join the investigation. Now I come to think on it, she looks like she might be pretty handy with a cane knife and all.

~

The heat and humidity hit Carmel Maitland as soon as she gets off the plane in Kaliope. The weather back in Brisbane has started to cool and there's been hardly any rain this year. It's still warm, but the humidity is falling and the city has been easing into balmy winter. Up here, the sun continues to radiate summer.

Carmel's been seconded to an investigation into the disappearance of a teenage girl. She'd wondered why it's taken so long to get a woman officer involved. Then a mate who'd previously worked under Detective Sergeant Patterson, the lead detective she'll be working for, told her that it probably hadn't even occurred to him that it might be a good idea to call in a female cop.

'He's a bit of a dickhead, actually,' he warned her.

'What sort of dickhead, exactly?' Carmel asked.

'Well, when a female officer was transferred to our unit, he reckoned we'd work more efficiently because now we'd have someone to make tea for us.'

'Oh, great. That sort of dickhead.'

When Carmel arrives at Kaliope Police Station, Patterson keeps her waiting for half an hour, before bringing her up to speed on the investigation—disappointingly few leads and even fewer suspects. 'Your role is less as an investigator and more as a liaison with the women in the district,' he tells her, stirring his tea. He doesn't offer her a cup of anything. 'They might tell you things they wouldn't mention to us.' He leans back in his chair and takes a slurp of the milky liquid in his cup, his lips forming a spout. 'You'll also be the main point of contact for the McClymont parents,' he adds.

'How are they holding up?' Carmel asks.

'About as well as you'd expect,' Patterson says. 'Ted McClymont joined the searchers every day after his daughter disappeared. He's kept it up even now that we've called off the official search. He and whatever mates he's got left have been going back over places that have already been searched with a fine-tooth comb. He tears off every time someone tells him they've found a bit of clothing or they've seen a light at the end of some deserted road. He's convinced himself she's still alive. Won't hear a word about any other possibility.' Patterson drains his cup. 'Bit of a heads-up, Ted turns up here at seven o'clock sharp almost every morning asking about our lines of enquiry. Giving us updated maps of where he's been looking. You wait. He'll be back again tomorrow.'

'And Mrs McClymont?'

'Mental,' Patterson says. 'Understandable, really,' he adds.

Carmel nods, phrases her next question carefully. 'Why do you think the missing girl's body hasn't turned up yet?'

Patterson gestures at the window that looks out onto a riot of vegetation growing over the chain link fence enclosing the yard around the station. 'Have you looked outside? Once you're out of town, it's like a bloody jungle. The rainy season was late this year. Every pothole and ditch from Cairns to Rockhampton was filled with muddy water the first couple of weeks after she disappeared. Every patch of open ground is still covered with weeds and guinea grass. Thankfully, the weather's been relatively dry since and the crush has started. I'm hopeful that once the fields have been burnt near where she disappeared, her remains will be found. That's if Barbara McClymont stops insisting the cane cockies who own those paddocks keep holding off.'

'Why . . .' Carmel begins.

'Don't ask. Some rubbish about wanting to find her daughter's body intact. After all these weeks? She's out there every day for hours at a time, crawling through the fields near where the girl disappeared looking for her body. Anyway, enough chitchat.'

Patterson leaves Carmel to go through the case file. After that she checks the girl's tooled-leather shoulder bag, the one her mother found in the cane field, which is currently the only piece of evidence they have. The one thing the mother identified that might be missing from the bag and the things scattered around it was a tube of strawberry lip gloss. She said her daughter always had several of them on the go at any time, and always the same flavour and brand.

The local coppers conducted a search of the girl's room in the days after she was reported missing. They were looking for clues—bus tickets, a diary, cigarette papers—anything that might indicate why she'd vanished: had she been pregnant, planned a trip, used drugs, or been involved in anything else that might explain her disappearance? They found nothing useful, but Carmel's surprised the Brisbane blokes didn't bother to take another look.

Carmel decides she'll start with another search through the girl's bedroom, but she has to work hard to convince Patterson it would be a worthwhile exercise.

'As a woman,' she hears herself say, 'I might have a better idea of what to look for.'

She hates herself for doing it—playing up being female in a man's job—but she didn't deal the cards, she just has to play the hand she has.

On most of the farms Carmel passes on the drive out to Quala, mechanical harvesters and men wielding formidable-looking knives are working their way through drill after drill of burnt cane. When she pulls up outside the McClymonts' home, though, it's obvious the fields closest to their house are untouched.

It's around four-thirty in the afternoon. Numerous administrative tasks Patterson insisted she do have made her later than she planned.

Patterson even asked her to make him a cup of tea at one point, but she laughed it off as if he'd said something hilarious. In what she interpreted as a sign of support, Bill Wren, the local cop who'd taken over the running of the station since the other bloke keeled over with a heart attack, gave her a subtle nod. As he turned away, she caught the half-smile on his face.

When she leans forward to grab her bag off the floor in front of the passenger seat, the cloth of her jacket peels off the back-rest where her sweat has stuck it to the vinyl. Carmel would have preferred to wear a cotton shift, but the pantsuit gives her a more professional look, more masculine too, which she knows translates to authority. At least Patterson hasn't insisted she wear a uniform.

As Carmel climbs out of the unmarked Q car in front of the high-set house in Rosella Street, a sandy-haired woman wearing a sleeveless floral house dress, buttoned down the front and falling to just above her knee, walks out of the gate and towards a parked station wagon where two young girls wait. Something about the woman makes Carmel wonder if she's not a local. Perhaps it's her hairstyle, feathered in layers that frame her face, or just something quick and sure about her movements, a contrast to the low-geared ambulation she associates with country people. The woman pauses when she sees Carmel, then looks her up and down as Carmel approaches the path leading to the McClymonts' front steps. Carmel feels for her name badge, reassures herself she remembered to pin it to her jacket pocket and smiles a greeting.

'Are you the lady police officer from down south?' the woman asks.

Carmel nods and holds out her hand. 'Senior Constable Carmel Maitland.'

'Connie Tranter,' the woman says, shaking Carmel's hand as if she's out of practice, before swinging her gaze towards the McClymonts' house, and then back to Carmel. 'Look, Barbara's in a pretty bad way. She's been out searching for Janet's body all day. I've left a casserole for their tea, but you won't get anything useful out of her. Her husband Ted isn't even there. He won't be back before dark.'

'You're probably right,' Carmel says. 'But I'm here now.'

The woman, Connie, lingers.

'Are you a neighbour?' Carmel asks.

'More or less. Our farm is on the other side of the highway.' Connie bites her lip and then, almost as if she's blurting out something she promised herself she wouldn't, says, 'Janet used to babysit our girls for us.'

'I'm so sorry. It must be dreadful for you.'

'Nothing compared to what it's like for Barbara and Ted.' Connie Tranter's eyes redden, but she doesn't turn away, and nor does she look like she's leaving.

Carmel realises that she is waiting for an indication that she, Carmel, will be turning her car around and heading back to Kaliope. 'I'll just pop in for a few minutes. Introduce myself.'

The woman sniffs. 'You lot should be out there.' She jerks her head in a gesture that takes in the land beyond the town. 'The McClymonts can't tell you anything more than they've already told the other officers. There has to be dozens of creeks and dams that no one's dragged yet.'

'Her body would have floated long before now if she'd been dumped in the water,' Carmel replies. She doesn't mean to be brutal, but she doesn't want Connie Tranter following her into the McClymonts' house. When she sees the girl's room and the rest of the house for the first time she wants as few distractions as possible.

The woman's face suddenly twists with the effort of trying to quell a sob, but she fails and it tears out of her throat. The sound startles them both. Connie shoots a glance towards the station wagon, where the girls, her daughters, Carmel guesses, are avidly watching them.

Eventually, Connie sighs. 'Well, I hope you can do better than the other detectives they've sent up here. No one in Quala can take much more of this.'

'I'll do my best,' Carmel says. 'I promise.'

The woman wipes a hand beneath her nose. 'Good luck.'

The girls in the car stare at Carmel as their mother drives off, her station wagon travelling slightly faster than is warranted given the narrow, potholed road.

A steep flight of stairs leads up to a wide verandah that surrounds the McClymonts' house on three sides. When she reaches the top step, Carmel surveys the cane fields stretched out behind the house to the west. They carpet the landscape as far as the hazy blue hills in the distance. To the south-east is a view of the inlet and the mangroves hugging the coast. Beyond, the afternoon sun reflects off the surface of the ocean.

Barbara McClymont comes to the door at the sound of Carmel's tread. Of course she looks wretched; as white and hollow as a wraith. She barely says a word when Carmel tells her she's there to search her daughter's room, merely indicates the direction with a limp hand. As she passes the bathroom, Carmel notices a box of sedatives on the vanity through the open door.

Either the Kaliope police who searched Janet's room did a lousy job, or Barbara, or someone else—Connie Tranter perhaps, wanting to be helpful—has returned it to its current tidy state. Everything appears to be in its place. The bed is made, and two pairs of shoes—white strappy sandals with a heel and a pair of brown school lace-ups—are on the floor beneath it. All the girl's clothes are either folded neatly in the chest of drawers or hanging in the wardrobe. On the wall above the bed is a poster of David Cassidy in a paisley shirt, looking sweet and not at all dangerous, with fussily styled hair.

On the bedside table is a copy of *Jonathan Livingston Seagull* and a well-thumbed edition of *Love Story*. Ornaments and grooming items are carefully arranged on the dressing table. The centrepiece is a small white vase decorated with the Holly Hobbie girl in an oversized bonnet and a patchwork apron holding a spray of wildflowers. The words 'Start each day in a happy way' bracket the figure above and below. Two bowls—one pottery and containing ribbons and bobbled hair ties, the other crystal and holding several pairs of earrings—sit either side of it. A small woven basket contains a few items of makeup—a mascara, a lidded tray of eyeshadow, and a tube of strawberry-flavoured lip gloss.

Carmel looks through the girl's things, carefully placing everything back where she found it. There is nothing that strikes her as out of the ordinary, no letters or notes that give any indication that something was amiss. Although anything obvious, she presumes, would have been picked up in the initial search.

A school port sits on a wicker chair in the corner. After briefly rifling through it, Carmel decides to ask Mrs McClymont if she can take it back to the station to examine it more closely. There might be an overlooked comment or name in a pad or a textbook that will shed some light on Janet's disappearance. A diary is inside, but apart from a large heart outlined in red biro enclosing the initials JC, it appears to contain only prosaic reminders of when homework was due or netball games scheduled.

Hanging in the hallway outside Janet's bedroom is a large canvas. Dark green, almost black, foliage crowds around the trunks of trees, their crowns invisible. Here and there, bright splotches of colour—tropical birds, perhaps, or flowers—shimmer in the gloom. Carmel pauses for a moment in front of it before stepping out onto the back verandah, where Barbara stands smoking. At the far end, through an open door leading onto an enclosed sleep-out, Carmel glimpses several other large canvasses propped against the wall. Through the sleep-out's windows, the sea rocks uneasily.

'Thank you, Mrs McClymont. I'll be heading off now. Do you mind if I take Janet's school port? I'll be sure to return it.'

Barbara doesn't even turn her head, an almost imperceptible nod the only indication that she is aware that Carmel has spoken.

'I'll leave my card on the sideboard. You can reach me at Kaliope Police Station if you need me for anything.'

When Carmel pauses at the top of the front stairs and looks back along the hall that runs through the house, Barbara McClymont hasn't moved. She is gazing out over the cane, a long column of ash trembling on the end of her cigarette.

~

Carmel arrives at the station first thing the following day, unlocking the front door on her way in. She has just boiled the kettle in the kitchenette when she hears the bell that announces someone's arrival. She goes out to the front counter, a teabag seeping colour into the mug of hot water in her hand.

The man holds his hand out over the counter. 'Ted McClymont, Janet's father. You must be the new policewoman. Barbara told me you'd been out to the house. You'll get things moving, I've no doubt. Janet's out there somewhere and I'm sure we'll find her.'

Ted McClymont exudes a ghastly cheerfulness, stretched thin over insomnia and chin stubble. The smile plastered on his face is a rictus of grief hiding beneath his blustery optimism that his daughter will be found safe and well.

Carmel can only guess at the mental energy it must take to stop his mind from continually looping images of the likely fate of his daughter. If he admitted to himself what almost everyone else believes is the case, that his daughter is dead and unspeakable things were done to her, Carmel imagines his face would fall from his skull, piece by brittle piece.

Ted is keen to hear if any reports have come into the station overnight, whether anyone has followed up on the bloke he heard on the telly saying he'd seen a girl matching Janet's description in Mount Isa, or if Carmel came across anything of note in Janet's school things. 'Barbara said you'd taken her port from the house.'

As Carmel is telling him that there is no new information, she hears someone entering the police station through the back door that opens onto the yard where the police park their cars. The knob on the door behind her turns and the door opens briefly before softly closing again.

She promises Ted that she will look through Janet's schoolbooks this morning and tells him that she has arranged to visit the school in a couple of days. 'I know her friends were interviewed before,' she says, 'but I'd like to speak to them again.'

'Good thinking.' Ted tucks his unwashed shirt into the loose waistband of his shorts. 'A smart young woman like yourself, you'll know what questions to ask.' He leaves the station with a wave and a cheery 'Hooroo'.

In the desolate silence left after his departure, Patterson puts his head around the door. 'Has he gone?' He looks at the cup in Carmel's hand, but if any thought of asking her to make tea for him crosses his mind, he thinks better of it.

~

It seems incredible to Carmel that, well over a month since the girl went missing, the investigation has turned up so little. No body, no witnesses, no likely suspects. Initial enquiries have, not surprisingly, focused on the men closest to Janet McClymont. It's a tried and tested way to proceed in such crimes, and in the vast majority of cases, it bears results. But in this case, Janet's father

Ted was cleared almost immediately. He had been drinking with several other people five miles away when his daughter disappeared. Her boyfriend, Joe Cassar, was with his extended family. Although, if it's up to Carmel, she'll be looking harder at the boy's alibi. It was a large gathering, by all accounts, easy for someone to slip away and not be noticed, and a family's natural instinct is always to protect one of its own.

Moving outwards, one had to consider other male friends and, perhaps, teachers. Patterson has mentioned Eamonn Sullivan, who teaches at Kaliope West, and his housemate Peter Parslow. They live near to where the girl disappeared, and Sullivan has ruffled a few feathers by talking to his students about his political activism when he lived in Brisbane. But again, they both had alibis and have been excluded as persons of interest.

The district always has itinerant workers passing through, particularly during the crush, but Carmel thinks it's unlikely one of them is responsible for the girl's disappearance. The population of Quala is small. An unfamiliar vehicle, a stranger hanging about—these would have been noticed by someone. And the track the girl would have taken on her way to the Tranters' is only used by locals. Nevertheless, she has to consider the possibility that it was a purely opportunistic crime by a complete stranger.

Patterson has elaborated little to Carmel on his theories as to what might have befallen Janet McClymont. He believes she's dead, she gathers. 'The crushing season lasts about six months,' he told her. 'Sometime over the next few weeks, her body will be discovered in a cane field. That might be the thing that prompts someone to come forward with the information we need.'

'So we just wait?' she asked him.

Patterson looked at her with a paternal expression. (*If he tries to pat my head, I'll deck him*, was the thought that crossed her mind.) 'When you've been in the job as long as I have, love, you learn that sometimes time can be your friend.'

There is another scenario that Carmel hasn't dismissed entirely. The girl may have engineered her own disappearance, either alone or in concert with someone else. Another boyfriend? She and her family moved up from Brisbane not that long ago. Perhaps there's someone in Brissie the girl is still in love with. Could she have decided to run away to be with him? It seems unlikely, but the fact that Carmel keeps coming back to is that the girl's remains have not been located. She makes a note to ask Barbara McClymont about any letters her daughter might have received or whether there'd been any long-distance phone calls to the house.

But first things first. There's Janet's school port to go through and she wants to go over the case file again to familiarise herself with the names and descriptions of the Quala locals she might come across tonight. Patterson has asked her to accompany him to a meeting at the town's Memorial Hall, where he is slated to give the residents and the local farmers an update on the investigation. He also wants to introduce Carmel as part of the investigative team. No doubt most of the town will turn up. It will be a good opportunity to cast an eye over the men of Quala. If whoever is responsible for Janet's disappearance is a local, Carmel is confident he will be there tonight.

SIX

SUGAR CANE IS basically bloody big grass, and with plenty of sun and water, it grows like the clappers over coastal plains and along river valleys all the way from Mossman to Grafton. No need to bother with germinating seeds and coddling sprouts, just lop a length of cane from a full-grown plant, drop it into a furrow and cover it with dirt. Each of those jointed lengths is called a sett, and at each joint, buds swell, and within a few days, weeks at most, up to a dozen shoots will erupt. Now, that cluster of shoots when they bust through the soil, that's called a stool.

As it grows, the cane takes sunlight and converts it to sugar—it's like bloody magic. And it stores that sugar in the stalks, almost like blood in a body. It takes between nine and sixteen months for the cane to ripen, by which time it'll be anything from twelve to twenty-eight feet tall with tasselled flower heads, called panicles, on long stalky necks.

Up round here, the crush starts in early June, when the weather starts to cool, and goes through to November. But this year, with the time spent searching for Janet McClymont, things were a bit delayed. Most of the local farmers dropped everything to help with the search, but when she wasn't found and the sugar mill was about to fire up, they had to put aside the grief, the unsettledness, the sense of things not right, and get stuck into the harvest.

Now the mill is operating twenty-four hours a day and everyone's more or less on track. Except for the Tranters and the Creadies. Barbara's still traipsing through their fields most days.

Usually in the weeks leading up to the crush, everyone gets caught up in the anticipation of it all. There's something special about that first burn of the season. Something about the flames and the dusk, all the kids waiting for that moment when the low line of fire around the edge of the field lets rip. It races through the cane, throwing scraps and embers into the sky that will fall to earth dozens of miles away.

Not everyone loves it, of course; some kids, well, they're just born fearful of the flames. Others can scarcely stop themselves from setting a struck match to just about anything that will combust. You've got to keep a close eye on those ones. They're pretty easy to spot. They're the kids always standing a little too close to the flames—the ones who are always looking to hide a box of matches in their pocket. At the drop of a hat, they volunteer to help, just for the thrill of being as close to the fire as possible.

They hare after the floaters, those scraps of embers that swirl up on the eddies of air created by the fire and drop into the unburnt drills; calling over their shoulders not to worry, they'll chase them down before they can set the field alight. And when they fail to reappear, their mothers track them down quick smart. They'll find them crouched beside a breakaway ember, feeding it with leaves and bits of paper they've got stashed in their pockets. Old hands look out for these ones. They're trouble, alright.

In the days after a field's been burnt, teams of cane cutters move in and start slashing. Although, more and more often these days, its mechanical harvesters that roll up, shearing off the stalks at the base, slicing them into billets twelve inches long and funnelling them into the haul-outs driving alongside. Those tramways you'll have seen meandering across the countryside transport the billets to the mill, where they're crushed and the juice is extracted.

Back in the paddock, within days the nodes on those roots left in the soil, they're already starting to swell.

~

Principal Ern Shaw is satisfied with how the two newly qualified teachers, Marie Jarvis and Eamonn Sullivan, have settled in at Kaliope West. Marie's almost a local. She trained at the Townsville Teachers' College and has taken to teaching maths and science to the Grade 8s and 9s like a duck to water. She's a feisty young woman with an interest in women's lib. Not that she thrusts it down anyone's throat—unless she's provoked, that is, which Allan Carmody (PE and woodwork) is happy to do. Ern may need to have a word.

Eamonn, a red-headed beanpole, trained in Brisbane. He's had a bit of a rough trot with some of the rowdier boys at the senior levels. Ern has thrown him in the deep end by getting him to teach English and economics to the Grade 11s and 12s, and he's not making a bad fist of it. Ern's also roped him in to taking some of the younger grades for sport, although it does seem cruel to make someone with his complexion go out in the sun on a hot afternoon. His freckles have almost joined up on his face and arms, even though he's taken to wearing a large straw hat with a toggle, like the ones the cane farmers wear. The moustache he's grown shields his lips to some extent, although they still flake and peel after lunchtimes on yard duty. Ern doesn't mind that he keeps his red hair long— he understands fashion is important to young people—but why Eamonn wants to draw further attention to his colouring in this way is a mystery. The students call him 'Fantapants', usually behind his back.

It was tough for everyone at the school, students and teachers alike, when Janet McClymont disappeared. Especially for her friends, of course, but also for Marie and Eamonn, who are not that much older than the missing girl. It was a big ask, given their lack of experience, to walk into classrooms of weeping girls and defensive, tough-talking boys, and attempt to guide the students through their grief and outrage without the emotion teetering into hysteria or an excuse for creating chaos.

More than a month later and the students are still jittery—
the girls nervous and tearful, the boys torn between their
competing impulses to comfort their female classmates with
protective gestures and to whip up the already febrile atmosphere percolating in the school into a fever of misrule and
rabble-rousing.

Ern has counselled the male teachers to ensure that they
are never alone with any of the female students and to resist
the completely understandable instinct to put an arm around
a distressed girl or allow her to cry on their manly shoulders.
He has noticed, though, that many of the girls, particularly
the older ones, rather than looking to their male teachers for
consolation are almost hostile towards them. Well, who can
blame them?

Janet McClymont's close friends are still permanently on
the verge of tears. Even though she'd only been at the school
since the beginning of the year, Janet had slipped into a friendship set easily. Ern understands her friends' need for rites and
demonstrations of mourning, but he sometimes feels that there
is something performative about their grief, particularly from
those who weren't overly close with Janet.

In the days following Janet's disappearance, a ritual devel-
oped in which a group of girls from her grade would sit on
the floor around her homeroom desk every lunch hour and
sing songs from Carole King's *Tapestry*. There are at least six
of them there every day, although, prompted intermittently by
some intensification of mood beyond Ern's perception, the group
sometimes swells to more than twenty. Some of the boys from
Janet's grade and the one above often hover around the group.

Whether they are genuinely concerned for the grieving girls or simply aping solicitude, Ern isn't sure. Sometimes he views them as being like sharks lurking around a pod of dolphins, hoping to pick off the most vulnerable. For the most part, the girls regard the boys warily, even angrily. A couple of the girls earned the contempt of the rest of their clique the Friday after Janet disappeared by pashing off with two of the boys outside the classroom. Inside, the other girls sang 'So Far Away'.

It is well known throughout the school that Joe Cassar was Janet McClymont's boyfriend. Largely, Joe has kept himself at a distance from her tearful friends. They, almost ostentatiously, have closed ranks against him, when previously several of them were friendly with him. The girls are jealous of their grief, unwilling to recognise that others share their sorrow and fear.

~

Ern is in the kitchenette off the staffroom spooning granules of International Roast into a cup when the teachers file in at morning recess. Eamonn is complaining about his nickname, the way the students focus on his appearance. 'Why do people always go on about red hair?'

Marie is unsympathetic. 'Now you know how women feel. We're always getting comments about our appearance. Maybe it'll make you more aware of what we have to put up with, encourage you to take our side.'

'I am on your side,' Eamonn says. 'I've read *The Female Eunuch*.'

'It's the personal experience of oppression that raises consciousness, Eamonn, not reading books.'

He reminds her that he was at the anti-Springbok tour demo on Wickham Terrace in Brisbane. 'I've experienced police brutality.'

'You weren't even arrested,' Marie scoffs.

Allan Carmody has followed them into the staffroom. 'If you're going to burn your bra, Marie love, don't feel you can't still wear those clingy T-shirts. We'll support you, and your tits too if you like.'

Marie gives him the forks. Mrs Pocock (home ec and ancient history), who already has a cup of tea and an Iced Vovo from the biscuit tin she keeps on her desk, tuts.

'No need for that sort of language, Allan.' Ern pokes his head through the kitchenette door. He's a big man, but quiet.

'Jesus.' Allan ducks his head. 'I mean, jeez, Mr Shaw. You'd give a man a heart attack.'

'Just keeping you on your toes, Allan.'

Ern settles himself on the couch in the corner of the staffroom with his cup of coffee, spreads the newspaper on the low table before him.

'Have you really read *The Female Eunuch*, Sullivan?' asks Allan, white shorts riding just a little too high on his muscular legs.

'Of course.'

'Well, blow me. I hope you're not taking discussion of that kind of rubbish into the classroom. You'll be handing out copies of *The Little Red Schoolbook* next.'

Eamonn pauses on his way to the urn in the kitchenette. 'Why not? I think the students would be grateful for some unbiased information about sex, drugs, and how society's inherent structures keep them ignorant and oppressed. The ones in the older grades are mature enough.'

'Did you hear that, Mr Shaw?' says Allan, hands on hips, feet apart. 'We've got a commie agitator in our midst.'

~

Joe Cassar is in Mr Sullivan's Grade 12 English class. Recently, Fantapants gave them an assignment where they had to mount an argument either for or against protesters breaking the law to demonstrate against an issue they deemed immoral. Joe suspects Fantapants is partly looking for an excuse to skite yet again about demonstrating against the Springbok rugby tour. He's always bringing it up—the hundreds of protesters on Wickham Terrace; the country cops in their khaki uniforms wielding their specially made batons; the way the cops took off their identity badges before they started thumping the shit out of the demonstrators; how he'd only escaped being arrested or beaten to a pulp because a Black Power activist pulled him into one of the old water reservoirs across the road from the Tower Mill Hotel.

When Fantapants talks about it, Brice Kable and a few of his dickhead mates pile it on thick. 'You don't look like much of a shit-stirrer, sir, but good on you, giving the pigs some stick.'

They egg him on, laughing at him behind his back when he accepts their admiration as if they mean it, deliberately misinterpreting him when he insists his civil disobedience was about trying to achieve positive social change, not attacking the police. Brice and his mates aren't that interested in the finer points of resisting tyranny versus violent agitation. 'About time the cops got some of their own medicine. Hey, sir, can you show us how to make a Molotov cocktail?'

They hoot and toss their schoolbooks like missiles.

Joe wouldn't have pegged Fantapants as a soldier for social justice. He looks too soft, too girlish to put up much of a fight or even stand his ground in the face of an onslaught of baton-wielding police officers. Joe has some sympathy for the protesters, though most of his mates would think they're all communists and dole bludgers.

'You shouldn't mix sports with politics,' Martin has said more than once, repeating something his mum has probably said a million times at the Zammits' dinner table.

In class, during the discussion about the right to protest, Brendon asked Joe what he thought about the tour. 'You know, given your mum's an Islander.' It was a serious question and Brendon wasn't meaning to put him on the spot, but Joe didn't want to talk about it. Joe loves rugby, loves playing it, loves watching it. The Springboks are one of the best teams in the world. Part of him would give anything to see them play. But then, when he imagines what his life would have been like if he had been born in South Africa, with his mother, his sisters and himself looking the way they do with their brown skin, it all becomes too confusing and troubling to think about.

Joe doesn't want to consider himself as being different from his friends, even when dickheads like Brice Kable make that impossible. Like the time last year when on the Monday after a working bee at the school, Brice made a crack. 'Bloody hell,

Cassar, your mum works like a Kanaka. Oh, that's right. She is a Kanaka.'

Joe had gone him. It was Mr Shaw who pulled them apart, but not before blood was streaming out of Brice's nose and he was crying like a baby.

Later, Mr Shaw called Joe into his office. Not to punish him, just to talk to him. 'He's jealous of you, you know,' Mr Shaw said. 'The Kable boys don't have much. Both your parents work hard and do everything they can for you and your sisters. I can't say the same for Brice and Darren's parents.'

When Fantapants gave them the essay assignment on the ethics of protesting, Joe took it seriously. He asked his mother what she thought. Her family are mainly Seventh Day Adventists, but she'd converted to Catholicism when she married his father.

'Consult the New Testament, Joseph,' she said, directing him to the story of Jesus throwing the moneylenders out of the temple as an example of an act of righteous civil disobedience.

He also came across a book in the school library that had a reference to JFK quoting someone called Edmund Burke who said, 'The only thing necessary for the triumph of evil is for good men to do nothing.' He put that in his essay too.

In their essays, almost everyone else in the class came back arguing on the side of upholding the law no matter what the circumstances or the issue at stake. Joe recognised the language of the local Country Party politicians and outraged letters to the newspapers. His own father used it: *Protesters are usually longhairs and dole bludgers. Most don't even believe in what they're protesting against. Blocking traffic in street marches inconveniences drivers and they should be punished with the full force of the law. They're troublemakers who should get a haircut and a job.* Pretty predictable, really.

Mr Sullivan took him aside after the class where he'd handed the essays back. He'd given Joe a pretty good mark for it, although he'd written 'apocryphal' in the margin beside the Burke quote. Mr Sullivan told him that if he wanted to learn more about activism for social change he could lend him some books.

~

The afternoon their essays were handed back, Joe, Martin and Brendon are sharing a quick durry after school behind the sports shed. Martin has just lit up when Fantapants appears with a tennis net in his arms. The satchel he always carries that looks as if it's been made out of a hessian sack is slung across his body.

'Joe, Martin, Brendon.'

Martin throws the cigarette into the dirt and grinds it out with his foot.

'Sir,' the boys say in unison.

Joe sees Fantapants register their resentment at making them waste Martin's last smoke, but he makes no mention of the ground-out durry, just walks past them and into the shed to stow the net he's carrying.

'See ya,' Brendon says to his two mates, hoisting his school port onto his shoulder and sprinting off towards the school gate where the bus to Quala waits.

Joe and Martin scramble to gather up the pads and textbooks, the pencils and pens and lunch boxes that spilled onto the ground when they upended their ports to look for a ciggie and a lighter. They're only a couple of yards into their escape when Sullivan emerges from the shed and says, 'That was a really interesting discussion yesterday about social justice and the right to protest.'

The words hit them in the back like a handful of poorly tossed ball bearings. Joe and Martin pause mid-step, look over their shoulders, unsure whether to engage with his overture. Thoughts tacitly pass between them: what, if any, consequences will follow if they simply ignore Fantapants or tell him to fuck off? Probably none. He's so eager for them to like him, to appear different from their other teachers.

Joe supposes that, to a degree, he is different from other teachers. He attempts to engage them in discussions about things that are happening in the real world, encouraging them to think like adults, to make up their own minds about issues that are sending cities into turmoil, about unjust wars and even stuff like women's lib. If only he wasn't so needy, didn't so patently crave their approval.

Martin has made his decision, he turns to move off, and Joe follows suit.

'Hey.' Sullivan swings his embarrassingly girlish bag around to the front of his body. 'I've got something that you boys . . .' He stops, corrects himself. 'That you guys might be interested in.'

Martin gives Joe a sideways look, his mouth twisted sceptically. 'What would that be, sir?'

Sullivan coughs as if to relax his vocal cords, and lowers his pitch. 'You guys seem pretty switched on.'

'Switched on, sir?' Martin feigns incomprehension.

'I mean, you can see what's what.' Sullivan is attempting a tone of man-to-man.

'What's what? What *is* what, exactly, sir?' asks Martin, merciless.

Fantapants digs his hand into his bag. Joe turns his head away, bites his lip in an effort not to laugh.

Sullivan has grasped whatever it is in his bag that he wants to show them. For a terrible moment, Joe fears he's about to hand them a stick magazine. Fantapants' arm becomes entangled in his bag's long strap, before he finally manages to give a book to Martin.

Martin widens his eyes, adopts a childish lisp. 'My mum told me that I shouldn't take anyfing from strange men.' He hands the book back to Sullivan.

Joe snorts, kicks the ground. Martin is cruel, but fuck he's funny.

'I've got to go, sir,' says Martin. 'Dad's expecting me home to help with the boat. See ya tomorrow.'

Martin thumps Joe on the shoulder and lopes towards the fence, leaps over it in one easy motion. Joe follows Martin with his eyes for a moment and turns back to find Sullivan holding the small red book out to him.

Joe remains where he is. What keeps him here now that Martin has gone? he asks himself. Is it that he feels sorry for his teacher, wants to help him avoid further humiliating himself?

'Thanks, sir.' Joe holds out his hand and Sullivan, in his eagerness, drops the book on the ground. Joe makes a move to retrieve it, but Fantapants has already bent to pick it up. They almost bump heads, bobbing awkwardly around each other until, finally, Joe is able to yank the book out of his teacher's hand and read its title.

So, this is *The Little Red Schoolbook*. The dangerous publication looking to corrupt young minds like Joe's and turn them on to sex and drugs. For such a potent object the small red volume is flimsy and insubstantial. Joe guesses that the simple, almost childish font of the title is supposed to come across as subversive and wry, but in his hand, up close, it appears fatuously cartoonish.

'It looks like something for a kid,' says Joe, looking at the unprepossessing cover. From reading the letters railing against it in the paper, he'd expected something more sophisticated.

'Well, yeah,' Sullivan says. 'It's meant for kids.'

Joe thinks about dropping the book back in the dirt. If he runs, he can still catch up with Martin.

'It's for young people your age,' Sullivan clarifies hurriedly. 'It has lots of information about questioning authority and how you don't have to conform all the time, stuff about drugs and sex without the bullshit.'

Joe looks up into his teacher's face and, encouraged, Sullivan adds more confidently, 'It's got some really interesting things to say about teenagers like you taking control of your lives, you know, standing up to the man, changing stuff that sucks. About finding out about what you really need to know, not just what adults want to tell you, stuff that will help you make decisions about important things in your life.'

After Sullivan's little speech, there is an uncomfortable silence.

'Thanks, sir.' Joe stuffs the book into the pocket of his shorts, picks up his bag. 'I have to go now.'

'I'd be really interested to hear what you think about what it has to say. And, uh, Joe?'

Joe pauses, adjusts the strap of his port where it lies across his shoulder.

'Technically, the book is banned from schools. You may not want your parents to see it. They might not understand. I mean, it's not pornographic or anything, but, well, you'll see what I mean.'

Joe feels his face flush. Jesus. It's getting embarrassing now.

'And Joe, you don't have to call me "sir" when it's just the two of us.' Fantapants thrusts another book into his hand, makes an attempt at a blokey, conspiratorial grin. 'Here, take one for your girlfriend. You'll thank me later.'

Joe stares into Sullivan's face. He doesn't feel anger, just disgust. What the fuck does Sullivan mean by that?

Sullivan looks confused and then, when comprehension dawns, stricken. 'Sorry. I forgot. God, Joe. Shit.'

But Joe is already jogging away.

~

Joe's friends never talk to him about Janet, not anymore. When she first went missing, there was a bit of gossip around the school that he could have had something to do with her disappearance, that he possibly knew where she was. Brendon and Martin actually took him behind the sports shed, ostensibly for a ciggie, but actually to ask him if he knew what had happened to her. Joe told them to fuck off, that of course he didn't know where she was. They've never asked him again, just stuck close, almost like his own personal bodyguards. They monster any of the fuckwits, like Brice Kable, who make a crack about darkies, how you can't trust them around white women.

For a couple of weeks afterwards, wherever Joe went, whenever he entered a room or walked past a group of students, conversation would stop and people would look at him. He was in such a fog of shock and disbelief he couldn't read whether their expressions were of distrust or compassion. None of it seemed real. Not Janet's disappearance or the likelihood that she was dead. Or that some people actually thought he might have hurt her.

There were a couple of girls in his grade who tried to swoop on him, as if now that he was all wounded or some shit he was somehow more attractive or something. They'd coo and try to pet him like he was an orphaned puppy. One of them even tried to pash him off. Weird. But since he rebuffed their attempts to console him, most of them just ignore him. Some of them smile pityingly at him, which just gives him the shits. Those girls who were closest to Janet just seem angry at him.

Ox—Mr Shaw—called him into his office on Joe's first day back at school after Janet disappeared. He was all overly gruff and hearty, telling Joe to keep his chin up. Joe likes Mr Shaw, and he knows he was trying his best, but fuck, he was crap at whatever he was trying to do. Comfort him, maybe? To be fair, nothing anyone said to him about Janet penetrated. It was all just words that bumped up against him like annoying flies that he wanted to swat away.

Even his parents are terrible at it. He knows they're trying to help him, but his father seems more concerned with what people will think of them as a family and Joe as a person rather than Joe's pain or even what happened to Janet. His mother is better. She says less, but she is kinder, cooking his favourite meals and just giving him some space. When he takes off on his bike or wanders around the farm by himself she leaves him be, not calling after him the way his father does. A couple of days after Janet disappeared, she asked him if he wanted to talk to Father Moran, but Joe couldn't imagine the priest would have anything useful to say to him. Joe has actually tried to pray. He retains an uninterrogated belief in God, but apart from asking that Janet be returned safe and well, it seems kind of pointless.

Mostly he's glad that people don't try to talk to him about Janet. He would probably just start crying like a girl, and if that happens he doesn't know if he will be able to stop.

SEVEN

IF I HAD a dollar for every time I've heard someone come out with some bullshit like 'Kaliope's innocence has been stolen', I'd be living high on the hog, I'll tell you that much.

People have short memories. Some people, anyway. Not Dusty Orkins. The stories his grandmother told him. She was only a kid when it happened, but she reckoned two hundred of her people were killed by the Native Police. Men, women, children shot or forced to jump off the cliffs in the national park just up the road. 'Dispersals', the authorities called them. More like massacres. Bloody brutal stuff.

Or talk to Nola Cassar—Nola Tanna that was. She was only born in this part of the world because her grandfather and his brothers were brought here from Vanuatu by blackbirders to work in the cane fields. Women were brought over to work too, and kids. Not just from Vanuatu but from the Solomon Islands, Fiji and Papua New Guinea.

Too bloody soft to swing a cane knife, the white landholders were. Not too soft to deliver a few thrashings, of course, or to turn a blind eye to the fact that most of the so-called 'Kanakas' had been kidnapped or given some bullshit promise about good wages and conditions. A couple of bob a week and sleeping in a tin shack after working their guts out ten or twelve hours a day, more like. People say Australia never had slavery. Well, I guess it depends on how you define slavery—or how prepared you are to face facts.

And don't tell me the Islander women were treated with kid gloves. Not that the coppers or anyone else would have been too worried by white blokes taking advantage of brown-skinned girls back then. Some might say not now either.

And then, after all that, to add insult to bloody injury, after they'd been here for a couple of generations, made homes and lives for themselves as best they could under the circumstances, the government sent most of them back to the islands they'd come from. Forcibly deported. White bloody Australia policy bullshit. As if being white in this country is the natural way of things.

Doesn't sound so innocent to me.

Dot gives me an elbow to the ribs or a kick under the table whenever I start going on about this stuff to other people. Most of the locals don't want to hear a bar of it. Makes them feel 'uncomfortable', Dot says. Well, they can stick their head in the sand if they want to. Me? I reckon this stuff is better out in the open.

And there's more recent goings-on, too. Janet McClymont's disappearance is just the latest in a long line of tragedies. Whether those dispersals set the tone or whether it's always been like that, I don't know, but this country, it doesn't rest easy. It's like the dirt can't forget the taste of blood. It remembers and wants more. You'll think I'm cracked for saying it, but there's parts around here that give me the willies. That stretch of road after Ingleton? Bad stuff has happened along there. Murders, car accidents, suicides. You name it. You'll barely see a light at night on either side of the highway, no one lives in cooee of it. I don't like driving it day or night. The young blokes who used to work for me during the crush, I'd tell them when they were travelling south on their way home, if you need a toilet stop or a soft drink, wait till you reach Rocky. They might have laughed at me, but they didn't stop. Not if they knew what was good for them.

~

Connie is stationed by the urn in the Memorial Hall's supper room with a large aluminium teapot in her hands. The Brisbane detectives and the Kaliope police officers have arrived for the information session to update the community on the investigation into Janet McClymont's disappearance. They're due to begin speaking in a few minutes. Essie is on the other side of the room. She's with Raelene, of course; they move as a unit. Connie watches as Raelene, her chin on Essie's shoulder, trickles words into her ear as they wind their way between the adults drinking tea, eating triangles of curried egg sandwiches or juggling thick slabs of lemon slice in their hands.

Essie's expression is rapt, her face wide open as she swims in Raelene's flow of words. Usually, Connie feels an urge to protect the motherless girl. She has no doubt that Raelene has been exposed to things unsuitable and perhaps damaging for a child her age. But tonight, something avidly sensual in the girl's face, the lips too plump, the eyes too knowing, fills Connie with unease. She has already noted that Gordon Mason, Raelene's father, isn't in the hall. What can he be thinking letting his daughter roam around at night by herself?

The shape of Essie's name is in Connie's throat, but before she can call out to her, to lasso her to her side, an unexpected touch makes her arm jerk back in surprise. Tea sloshes out of the spout of the overfull pot, the hot liquid splashing onto the skirt of her cotton dress and searing her skin. She squeals automatically at the shock and the pain. Heads swivel towards her. The teapot is lifted from her hands and she pulls at the wet cloth of her dress, peeling it off her skin. In a few quick steps, the policewoman who was so intent on bothering Barbara the other day, whose touch has now caused Connie to scald herself, relieves her of the teapot and moves around to the serving side of the counter where she stands. Carmel Maitland grips Connie's arm, steers her over to the sink against the wall.

'Ooh, lovey.' Bev Zammit, who has been cutting up cake, meets them with a saucer of butter. 'Quick, put some of this on your legs.'

'No, no.' Carmel brushes away the proffered butter. 'Cold water's the best thing.'

She turns on the tap above the sink, pulls up the hem of Connie's dress. Connie slaps at her hand and they tussle over her skirt, before the policewoman abruptly lets go, takes a step back. A tea towel lies on the bench. She picks it up and thrusts it under the water gushing from the tap. When it is thoroughly wet, she holds it out to Connie. Connie takes the sopping cloth, turns her back to the woman and hitches up her skirt, pressing the wet tea towel on her smarting skin. Instant relief. She catches Bev's questioning eye, shrugs.

'I'm really sorry,' Carmel says. 'How bad is it?'

Connie looks at the woman properly. Outside the McClymonts' place the other afternoon, she was too upset and unnerved by Barbara's decline to take in the details of the policewoman's appearance. She is tall, athletic looking, almost mannish. A largish nose with a slight bump on it means she'll never be considered pretty. She's wearing a fawn pantsuit—a short-sleeved jacket with breast pockets and another two at hip level, and trousers, slightly flared. A shoulder bag, large and practical, is slung across her body, and her hair is layered in a fashionable cut. Her lips are tinged coral.

'Who are you, love?' asks Bev, her arms folded across her generous bosom.

'Carmel Maitland.' The policewoman holds out her hand, the gesture making her seem even more masculine.

Bev looks at Carmel's hand for a long moment before extending her fingertips for a brief touch. 'You that lady copper up from Brisbane?'

'Yes. I've been seconded to help in the investigation into Janet McClymont's disappearance.'

'Well, you've not been much help so far, have you, love?' Bev smiles broadly.

'Carmel?' calls a man in a suit, the detective whom Cam pointed out to Connie earlier. He signals from the door to the main hall. 'We're about to start.'

'Off you go, love,' says Bev, giving Carmel an encouraging prod. 'Now, Connie. How about some butter for those burns?'

Connie scans the crowd filing from the supper room into the main hall, looking for Essie, but she has slipped from sight.

～

In the main body of the hall, huge canvas fans swing to and fro. Their rhythmic movement disturbs the heavy air, giving some relief from the humidity. The smell of dust, raised when the women swept the hall earlier in the day in preparation for the meeting, lingers. The children have been ordered to stay in the supper room, the older ones given instructions to make sure that no one ventures outside now that it is dark. One of the double doors between the two rooms has been shut and the other left slightly ajar in an attempt to prevent the children from hearing unsavoury details while still permitting the adults to keep an eye on them. A few babies remain in the arms of their parents gently swaying their hips to soothe them to sleep.

The buzz of conversation and clatter of bodies settling themselves onto metal seats arranged in rows subsides when the detective appears in front of the stage and clears his throat. Stragglers, nursing unfinished cups of tea and wiping crumbs from their lips, emerge from the supper room. The detective is a city type with a smooth, shiny face and a comb-over. Looking around, Connie sees two police officers from Kaliope sitting in the back row. She recognises one of them as Bill Wren. The other is a young constable she hasn't met before. She and Cam went to Bob Cronin's funeral, the officer who died shortly after Janet went missing, and who coordinated the search before the Brisbane detectives arrived.

By the time Connie, the skin on the front of her thighs still stinging and shiny with butter, finds Cam and the empty chair he has kept for her, the detective has begun speaking.

'As most of you already know, I'm Detective Sergeant Doug Patterson. I'm based in Brisbane, but this case falls under my remit. This young lady beside me is Carmel Maitland. Carmel's also from Brisbane and has been seconded to give us a hand. Ladies particularly, if you have any questions or things you might be more comfortable talking to another woman about, well, Carmel's available. Now, you blokes, Carmel's pretty good-looking for a copper, I know, but she's all business, aren't you, Carmel?'

Guffaws greet Patterson's sally and Connie sees the police-woman give him a tight-lipped smile that fails to reach her eyes. Connie wonders if Patterson knows how much his colleague resents him and, if he does, whether he cares.

~

Standing beside Patterson, Carmel scans the faces of the forty or so Quala locals who've turned up for the community briefing. Apart from Connie Tranter, seated beside a man who is handsome in the sunburnt, skin-roughened way of a farmer, she's yet to meet any of them. She didn't catch the name of the woman intent on buttering Connie's scalded legs. Neither of the McClymonts is here.

Sitting a couple of rows behind the Tranters—she assumes the bloke's Connie's husband—is a woman with the tightly curled hair and brown skin of an Islander. Even sitting down, her height and ampleness are apparent, partly because the man beside her is relatively small. Carmel recalls her review of the case file and concludes that they're George and Nola Cassar, the parents of Janet's boyfriend, Joe. There don't appear to be any other mixed-race couples in the hall.

There are no teenage girls present, at least not in the main room. The two girls she'd seen roaming in the supper room earlier appear to have been deemed too young to hear the discussion about to take place. The girlfriends Janet had made at school all live in Kaliope. For whatever reason—something in the water?—most of the teenagers around Janet's age in Quala are boys.

At the back of the hall, spurning the chairs provided, are a group of boys in their late teens. Carmel guesses their ages as being between sixteen and nineteen. At the centre of the pack, surrounded as if by flunkeys, is a tall lad with tousled blond hair and the tan and muscled arms of an outdoor labourer. Even in analytical mode, Carmel objectively notes his pure, youthful beauty. He catches her looking at him and holds her gaze, his mouth twitching up into a one-sided smile. She breaks the connection, sweeps her keen regard across the four other young men who are arranged around him, the top dog. Three are grinning, taking their lead from him and insolently returning her stare. A fourth, at the edge of the pack, keeps his head down, his eyes on the floor.

None of the group could possibly be the son of the Cassars. It was probably a sensible decision for him to stay away, given some of the talk Carmel has already heard in relation to him and Janet. She does another sweep of the room, but she sees no one matching the description of Joe Cassar.

~

Essie peers into the hall through the gap between the supper room doors. She can't see much, and the swish of the canvas fans makes it hard to hear anything the detective is saying. She catches sight of her mother at the same moment as Connie, somehow sensing that Essie is doing something she shouldn't, spies her. How does she do it? Her mother frowns and flicks her hand. *Go away.*

A sharp jab between her shoulder blades.

'Come on,' Raelene hisses in her ear, hooking her arm through Essie's, and they sidle away from the ten or so other children intent on the bowls of ice cream Mrs Zammit handed out just before the detective started to speak. Mrs Zammit is now standing at the door between the supper room and the hall listening to the detective. She doesn't see them as Raelene, with Essie close behind, gently eases open the door that faces onto a strip of grass between the hall and the toilet block.

For a moment, Essie resists. She looks back at Helen spooning chocolate-chip ice cream into her mouth. 'We're supposed to stay inside.'

'We'll only be outside for about five seconds,' Raelene says. 'I want to hear what the police are saying.'

Essie follows Raelene. A single light globe above the door only deepens the surrounding shadows, making everything outside seem strange and scary. As they run the short distance past the toilets to the back of the hall where another door leads onto rooms behind the stage, the darkness encases them like a sleeve. Essie glances up at the starry sky. The Milky Way flows across its pillowy blackness like a river. A sound, the *thunk* of the door to the outside dunnies, makes her jump.

Essie tugs at Raelene's arm. 'It's probably locked.'

'Don't be a baby. What are you scared of?'

'You know.'

'The pervert?' Raelene blows air through her lips like a horse. 'He'd be no match for the two of us. I'd kick him in the nuts and you could go for his eyes. Anyway, it's not locked. They opened it earlier today to bring in extra chairs for tonight.' She points to the chain hanging loose and the unsecured padlock.

Essie is familiar with the hall's backstage layout. The primary school presents its end-of-year concerts in the building and it's also used as a venue for the regional arts performances that tour a couple of times a year. Every few months, old-time dances are held here. The adults waltz and dance the Pride of Erin, while the kids play games of hide-and-seek or occasionally kiss-chasey, with only the main hall out of bounds. An exception is made for the Mexican hat dance, when the children and any teenagers who've been persuaded or forced to come are allowed to take over the dance floor.

The room behind the stage is mainly used for storage. It takes a few seconds for Essie's eyes to adjust to the gloom.

Wooden benches and folding tables are stacked against one wall, music stands are clustered together beside another, piles of large cloth banners are folded and dumped in a corner. On either side, doors open onto narrow corridors that lead to the stage. Raelene guides Essie up one of these passages. The heavy curtain hanging from the top of the proscenium arch effectively blocks the light from the hall, although here and there, where the cloth has worn, tiny slivers of light stream through, and there's lots of dust. When Essie turns away to sneeze, her foot kicks against a large empty metal vase. It teeters on its too-small base, causing something inside it to rattle against its sides.

'Shh.' Raelene grabs Essie, holds her close.

They clamp their hands over their mouths, swallowing down laughter. The murmur of the Brisbane detective's voice is audible, but his words are indistinct. Raelene takes Essie's hand, leads her up a short flight of stairs onto the stage. The dusty curtain puddles at their feet and they push themselves into its folds, Raelene pressing up behind her. Within seconds, Essie is too hot, the air trapped in the heavy cloth warm and stifling.

Raelene locks her arms around her. 'Keep still.'

⁓

Someone interrupts Detective Patterson from the back of the hall. Connie recognises the voice of Jimmy Froome, and along with most of the seated listeners, swivels in her chair to look at him. Unlike most of the men here tonight, he hasn't removed his hat. He gets to his feet to ask about a report circulating in the local press that a girl answering Janet's description was seen in the back of a car with four Aboriginal men in Longreach, over four hundred miles away.

'Have you coppers checked that out?' he asks, combative.

'All leads are being followed up.' It is Carmel Maitland who answers. Connie notices Patterson purse his lips in displeasure. Carmel notices too and is grimly amused, Connie sees. No doubt she's the one who's having to sift through the dozens of helpful and not-so-helpful tip-offs the police are probably still receiving every day.

'What the bloody hell does that mean?' Froome turns to the two local policemen, offers his palms to the ceiling.

They shrug, nod in the policewoman's direction. *It's her show.*

'We're in contact with the Longreach police,' Carmel says. 'So far they haven't been able to substantiate that claim.'

'Jesus. Have they been kicking heads in? That's how I'd bloody substantiate it.'

Patterson cuts in before the policewoman can respond. 'I can assure you, Mr Froome, that all information we receive is being taken seriously.'

'How serious are you coppers taking it when you send a bloody sheila up here? Just because she's wearing a safari suit or some bloody thing doesn't mean she's up to doing a man's job.'

Froome swells at the ripple of laughter that meets his last remarks.

One of the men beside him, his brother Frank, nods vigorously. 'Good on ya, Jimmy.'

'It's a disgrace,' Froome goes on. Several other men standing behind him mutter encouragement when he points out the amount of time it's been since the girl has disappeared. Why hasn't she been found? he wants to know.

Patterson outlines all that has been done, lists the areas that have been searched, the tip-offs that have been received. People from Weipa to Adelaide have reported seeing Janet—hitchhiking, buying a carton of chocolate milk, staying in a caravan park with a bunch of hippies. He understands that everyone is concerned, that no doubt all the men here tonight—and a few of the ladies—were involved in the initial search. It's been an impressive effort, he says, listing the helicopters and horsemen, the four-wheel-drive vehicles and those on foot who scoured the bushland, cane fields, beaches, back roads and sidetracks. Hundreds of square miles have been thoroughly searched, he says. He mentions the heavy rain in the lead-up to Janet's disappearance. 'It was a real bastard, excuse the language.' The grass had grown like nobody's business, water lay everywhere. He details the many dams, creeks, rivers and swamps that have been dragged in case Janet's body was weighed down. Water police have been over every inch of the inlet, the detective adds before pausing for breath.

'You're not telling us anything we don't already know.' It's Froome again. 'Most of us have taken time away from our work, the start of the bloody crush was delayed because the farmers were searching for that girl. The Tranters and Creadies still haven't been able to harvest their cane. Our wives made mountains of bloody sandwiches. We can all see what the weather's doing without your help. Is she dead or alive?'

'There's always hope. Apart from the fact that she's missing, we've found nothing that indicates she's come to any harm.'

The detective pauses, glances towards the half-open supper room door. 'But after this amount of time, it's fair to assume the worst.'

'If the bastard has still got her, she'd be better off dead,' says Froome.

With Jimmy Froome's bald statement, images Connie usually manages to keep at bay cram into her mind. Around her, she senses a similar intrusion has afflicted everyone else in the hall. There is a collective drawing in, as if a thin noose has been looped over them as a group and tightened ever so slightly.

'As I said, it's unlikely that she's still alive,' the detective says. 'But we have to consider all possible scenarios. Perhaps there's a boyfriend involved or some lad out there who took a shine to her. Maybe she's too scared to come home.'

The teenage boys at the back of the hall tighten into formation, their faces hardening. Several people glance at the Cassars. Nola Cassar stares straight ahead. George appears to be attempting to wring non-existent water out of the hat he holds in his lap.

For an instant, Patterson's gaze settles on the Cassars. 'If she's no longer daddy's little girl, if you understand me.'

There are murmurings. They do understand him.

'You fellas,' says the detective, directing his attention to the handful of young men. At his addressing of them, they relax their aggressive stance, resume lounging against the back wall, hands in their pockets, legs crossed at the ankle in exaggerated insouciance. 'If you've got a mate, or you know a mate's mate who's a bit on the nose, don't be afraid to come forward out of some misplaced sense of loyalty. It could be your sister next time.'

Within the group, their glances flick from one to another, and a couple of them nod in the Cassars' direction. Connie is watching Carmel, who is eyeing the young men closely. The policewoman catches Connie looking at her, tilts her chin up in a question that Connie doesn't know how to answer.

The detective alters his stance, hitches up his trousers to indicate a change of tack. 'Now that the crush is underway, I'd like you men to be on the lookout for anything which may assist in the search for Janet McClymont. Those of you who've already begun burning and cutting your cane . . . If you come across anything . . .' Patterson pauses, adjusts his tie, 'anything unusual, call the Kaliope Police Station.'

'What's likely to remain if her body is lying in one of the cane fields, what will be left after the fire goes through? Just bones? Or what?' asks John Creadie, somewhere between embarrassed and hostile.

There is a long silence.

John looks around the room. 'I mean, what's the point of beating around the bush? It's been over a month already, so with decomposition and that—I just want to know what to look for. What to prepare myself for.'

'If the girl's body has been dumped and left in a cane field, you'll see it,' says Patterson. 'The temperatures needed to reduce a body to ash are far higher than anything likely to be generated by burning cane.'

Another long silence follows.

Up on the stage, with Raelene's breath in her ear and the muffling effects of the heavy black curtain, Essie can hear very little. People are asking the police questions; some of them sound angry. Raelene is pressed up behind her, pushing her face into the thick material, and it feels suffocating. Her feet are tangled in the curtain pooling at her feet. Essie tries to step back, to disentangle herself from the curtain, but Raelene, rigid behind her, pushes her hard in the back and she is buried deeper into the folds. Essie can't breathe. She scrabbles with her hands, tries to locate the edge of the curtain, to push it aside, desperate for fresh air. She ignores Raelene's warning pokes and urgent commands to stop moving, finds the hem of the curtain under her fingers, snaps her head back, pitches sideways, crunches down on a foot. She is rewarded with cool air, and Raelene is no longer behind her. But before she can untangle herself completely, a hand, large and male, is on her shoulder. Just like in her dreams.

EIGHT

HOT TEARS SPRING into Connie's eyes. It's unbearable, the thought of sweet little Janet, her white pedal pushers reduced to ash, her skin scorched and blackened, her flesh and her tender eyes shrivelled, her hair singed. Let alone what torments she may have suffered beforehand, if she is indeed dead. Of course she's dead. What other possible explanation could there be for her disappearance?

Connie can't tolerate listening to this discussion of bones and burnt flesh. She focuses instead on a point above and beyond Detective Patterson's head. Through blurred vision she sees a movement at the left of the stage. Something is struggling within the folds of the heavy curtain. A small pale hand appears at its edge. Patterson is responding to a question about whether the police believe Janet was snatched by a local or someone outside the community. Connie glimpses her daughter's face, hears a shriek. The curtain swings back, Essie's face disappears.

Before anyone else can move from their chairs, before even the detective in front of the stage and the policewoman beside him have time to react, Connie sprints forward, hauls up her dress, vaults onto the stage and drags back the edge of the curtain. Standing behind Essie is the red-headed teacher from the high school, the one living in the old house on the Creadies' place. He is looming over her daughter, his hand on her shoulder. He is like a large ungainly bird, some kind of carrion eater, dim and ruthless. Raelene, beside them both, is grinning hugely, hopping from foot to foot.

'Let her go.' Connie tears Essie from the teacher's grip and holds out her other hand to Raelene, her fierce protective impulse swamping her dislike for the girl. 'Come with me, Raelene.'

She pushes both girls through the gap in the curtains and directs them off the stage, clambers after them with more decorum but less agility than her earlier leap. Everyone in the hall has fallen silent, their attention moving from Connie and the girls to the teacher. Connie sees Cam go to stand and forestalls him with a quick shake of her head. The two Kaliope policemen are making their way towards the stage. She turns around to face the teacher, who is standing still, looking awkward and gormless.

Carmel appears at Connie's side. 'Is everything okay?'

'Into the supper room, you two. Now.' Connie follows the policewoman's gaze back to the teacher.

Blushing furiously, his thin, pointed face almost glowing, the teacher has sprung down from the stage. He is flanked by the Kaliope officers, who look unsure as to what the hell is going on and whether their presence is required.

Connie jerks her chin in the direction of the teacher. 'Why don't you ask him?'

~

Carmel sees understanding dawn on the red-headed man's face. Everyone in the hall—Patterson, the Quala locals lined up on the rows of metal chairs, the two Kaliope cops beside him—is watching him. He can see they are drawing conclusions.

From the back of the hall, someone shouts, 'You dog, Fantapants!'

Laughter and bellowing in response.

Connie Tranter, shepherding the two girls before her, has now reached the supper room. The red-headed man has managed to evade the police officers and is striding after them. Carmel beats him to it. She crosses the threshold before him, bars his way. Behind him, she can see that several of the Quala men have got to their feet. Even with the steady swing of the canvas fans, the atmosphere in the hall has stilled.

Jimmy Froome, the big man with the terry towelling hat squashed on his head, cracks a knuckle. The ruddy skin of his big square face is evidence that his hat's narrow brim does little to protect him from the sun. His hands are large and rough from hard work, the fingers thick and ingrained with grease and dirt. Patterson has told her that he and his brother have an earthmoving business based in Quala. Hiding a girl's body would be easy for him. Perhaps his questions for Patterson were a ruse to divert any suspicion away from himself.

'It's okay,' Carmel says, dragging her gaze away and projecting her voice to reach all of those watching. 'I'll sort this out. Continue, Detective Patterson.'

She puts a hand on the red-headed man's elbow, propels him into the supper room, waves off the Kaliope cops and closes the door behind her. Connie Tranter still holds the taller of the girls by the hand and has put an arm around the other. The smaller, younger-looking girl's mouth is slack, her face blank.

'We were scared, Mrs Tranter.' It is the taller girl, her straight black eyebrows framing a face that looks anything but frightened.

'Yes, I'm sure you were, Raelene,' Connie says. 'You're safe now. Why don't you both get yourselves something to drink? I think there's some cordial left.' She ushers the girls towards the kitchen, returns to stand beside Carmel.

The dozen or so other children in the supper room, their mouths smeared with ice cream and cake, look up from their play.

The red-headed man attempts a jolly smile. 'No harm done. They were just curious, I think. Spotted them going in the back when I was coming out of the toil . . .' His voice falters as he says the last word and he gestures towards the opposite door.

'You were following them?' asks Carmel. Mentally she is going through all the case notes she's read and she comes up with a name. Eamonn Sullivan. The teacher.

'No. I just thought . . .'

'What?'

Sullivan shifts his smile from jolly to delighted. He addresses himself to Connie. 'I don't think we've met. I'm Eamonn Sullivan. I live in the Creadies' old house. Your neighbours?'

He turns to Carmel. 'I'm a teacher at Kaliope West High School,' he adds, throwing out the word *teacher* like a lifeline.

Carmel chooses not to catch it. They both watch it sink. She stays silent so that the teacher is compelled to keep speaking.

'I saw the girls leaving the hall. I followed them to see where they were going. It was dark . . .'

In the face of the distaste that twists Connie's features, Sullivan tries again. 'I was going to bring them back to the supper room. What with everything that's happened, I was worried that . . .'

Carmel almost feels sorry for him.

'I'm a teacher,' he says again, plaintive.

Connie swings around to face Carmel, points an accusing finger at Sullivan. 'He's a troublemaker. Filling the students' heads with all sorts of dangerous rubbish. Promoting socialism, boasting about participating in demonstrations and bashing police . . .'

'Wait!' Sullivan's prominent Adam's apple is jumping in his long, freckled neck. He appeals to Carmel. 'I have never, ever . . .'

'I'm a good friend of Martin Zammit's mother. He's one of your students, isn't he? I've heard about the sorts of things that go on in your classroom.' Connie turns back to Carmel. 'What right does he have to expose young minds to that kind of left-wing . . .'

Sullivan appears to make a decision. He draws himself up to his full, not inconsiderable height. 'I apologise if I've frightened you or your daughter and her friend. I was trying to *protect* them. I'll be off home. I've got essays to mark.'

Carmel follows Sullivan through the supper room's external door and around the side of the building to the wide street in front of the hall. He climbs into a green Hillman Hunter and turns the key. Carmel reaches the vehicle before he can drive off. She leans into the driver's window. 'I'll be visiting Kaliope West High School tomorrow to speak to Janet McClymont's friends, Mr Sullivan. I'd appreciate it if you could make some time to see me while I'm there.'

Sullivan is breathing rapidly. He keeps his hands on the steering wheel, stares out through the windscreen. 'Of course.'

As Carmel steps back from the car, Sullivan turns his head to look up at her through the window. 'I want you to know that I have never advocated violence against police and I have certainly never *bashed* anyone. And, just for the record, I would never under any circumstances hurt a kid or . . .'

'Or what, Mr Sullivan?'

Sullivan has returned his gaze to the windscreen. 'Or touch them inappropriately.' He slaps the gearstick into reverse and backs the Hillman in a wide arc before grinding the gears into first. The car jerks forward, stalls. Sullivan starts the engine again, revs it. This time he successfully manoeuvres the car down the street and towards the highway. Belatedly, the Hillman's headlights snap into life, the beams piercing the darkness of the road ahead.

~

'Let's go.' Raelene grabs Essie's hand and tugs her down to crouch behind a trestle table. They scuttle out of the kitchen and along the supper room wall until they reach the door onto the main hall. Essie risks a glance over her shoulder. Her mother is standing on the grass just outside the supper room, facing the road, her back to them.

'Come on.' Raelene pulls Essie after her and they stumble into the hall, almost colliding with a handful of women who are chatting while they stack chairs.

One of them, Bev Zammit, scolds them. 'Steady on, you two. Don't go causing any *more* trouble.'

They ignore her. Essie sees her father among a knot of men on the other side of the room, and ducks behind Gladys Jensen and her husband, who are talking to one of the local policemen.

'Do you think she's going to arrest him?' whispers Essie. The thrill of being swept up in events—the policewoman grilling the teacher, her mother's steely accusations—fills her with a giddy excitement.

'Let's go watch.' Raelene links an arm through Essie's and they thread their way through the gnarl of people milling near the door that opens onto the hall's verandah. Before they can skip over the threshold, a male arm descends like a boom gate in front of them, barring their way. It belongs to a tall blond teenage boy who Essie recognises: Kenny Connolly. He is surrounded by his mates, some of whom she also knows— Brice and Darren Kable, and Martin Zammit—and one or two other young men.

'Hey, you're the girl from the pub,' the blond boy says to Raelene. 'Your dad's running it now, yeah?'

Raelene returns their accoster's stare. 'Yeah. So what?'

'Nothing. Just making conversation with a couple of good-looking girls.' He grins at his mates, who smirk back at him. 'Gidday, Essie,' he says, turning to her.

Essie is surprised he remembers her name. It's been years since he's deigned to speak to her. When she was younger, her parents and his, Chester and Gloria Connolly, were friends. At least, her father and Chester would sometimes go out fishing together with a couple of other men from the district. Chester was a little older than her father, but they'd known each other since they were kids. Essie and Gavan, Kenny's younger brother, ignored each other while the families socialised, Mrs Connolly barbecuing the fish the men caught out on Mr Connolly's boat. But something changed, Essie isn't sure what, and the barbecues with the Connollys stopped. She knows her mother doesn't like Mr Connolly, remembers hearing her complaining to her dad sometimes about the way Chester Connolly touched her. But before Essie can think of how to answer Kenny, Raelene rolls her eyes, guffaws and ducks under his arm, pulling Essie after her. 'See ya, Romeo.'

Essie sees Kenny turn to his mates, arms spread, palms facing outwards. Brice punches him on the arm and they wrestle, Kenny driving him into the wall with his shoulder.

At their mocking laughter, ashamed fury curdles in Essie's stomach. She curls her hands around the verandah rail, her fingernails digging crescents into the soft, splintery wood.

'Who's that?' Raelene leans into her.

'Kenny Connolly. Gavan's older brother.'

'The one that works as a brickie's labourer?'

'Who cares?' Essie points at the green Hillman Hunter speeding towards the main road. 'Look, he's going.'

The policewoman in the pantsuit stands on the bitumen, watching the teacher drive away.

Raelene bumps her hip against Essie's. 'The lady police officer and your mum scared him off.'

Someone is standing behind them.

'Who's this friend of yours, little Essie?' comes the booming voice of Chester Connolly. Essie looks over her shoulder to see him peering down at Raelene. 'Well, blow me. If it isn't the new barmaid.'

Essie leans into the verandah rail so that his leg is no longer brushing against her bottom. 'Hello, Mr Connolly,' she says into the weathered wood.

Chester Connolly pushes himself between her and Raelene, tucks each of them under an arm, presses them against his body. His khaki-coloured work shirt is open at the neck. Coarse dark hair peppered with strands of white sprouts forth. He smells of sweat and beer.

'I saw you talking to my lad,' he says to Raelene, a hand resting on each girl's hip. 'You watch out for him. He's got an eye for the ladies, if you know what I mean.'

His chuckle is mean and fake, like that of a TV baddie.

Essie is trapped, unable to get out from under his heavy arm, or to escape the fingers kneading her flesh. His maleness and that he is an adult render her passive.

'Get your hand off my bum,' says Raelene loudly enough that there is a lull in the buzz of conversation around them. She escapes his grasp and turns to face him, hands on her hips.

Connolly pretends to be scared and steps back, his arms raised. 'Aren't you a little wildcat.' He laughs comfortably, turning to Essie. 'Don't worry, Essie, it won't be long before you'll be wrapping the boys around your little finger like your friend here.' He replaces his arm around her. 'And growing in all the right places.'

'Time to go, girls.' Essie's mum appears in front of them.

Despite the dislike in her mother's voice, Mr Connolly doesn't shift his hand from Essie's hip. 'Nice pair of pins you've got there, Connie. That scramble of yours up onto the stage really gave us an eyeful.'

Essie is familiar with the various moods of her mother's face, but this coldness, the refusal to smile and play along with Mr Connolly's jokes is new. She is astonished when her mother raises her hand, plants it on Mr Connolly's chest. It is little more than a tap, but he staggers back, releasing Essie, as if her mother had shoved him with all her strength.

'Nice to see you, Chester. Say hello to Gloria for me.' Despite her friendly words, her mum's face remains stony. She propels Essie and Raelene towards her dad, who is waiting for them with Helen near the verandah steps. John Creadie is standing beside him. Essie sees the glances exchanged between her parents and John.

'We'll give you a lift home, Raelene,' her father says, just as the girls catch sight of Kenny Connolly propped against a motorbike near the bottom of the stairs.

'I'm alright, Mr Tranter. I'll walk.'

'Not tonight, Raelene.' Her father passes Helen, sleepy and quiet, into her mother's arms. He says goodnight to

John, and then guides Essie and Raelene towards the station wagon, opening the back passenger door. 'Hop in.'

As they drive off, Essie sees that the policewoman, Carmel Maitland, is still standing on the road. She is looking back at the Memorial Hall, staring at the men from the town of Quala.

~

Carmel watches the young man, the blond boy king, leaning against his motorbike with such arrogance, eye Raelene as Connie Tranter's husband manoeuvres her and his daughter past him and into their car. She sees Raelene dart a look at him, bold and curious. He stares back, directing a slow wink at her as she passes. She ducks her head and whispers something to the Tranter girl before they both begin giggling.

'You'll have work tomorrow, won't you, Kenny?' Tranter says as he shuts the car door after his daughters and Raelene have scrambled onto the back seat. 'You should be heading home for a good night's sleep.'

The young man, Kenny, grins broadly. 'I'm not an old bloke like you, Cam. I can party all night and still work like a black-fella the next day.'

Carmel sees Tranter's face harden. In a rural community like this one, she knows, someone Kenny's age would generally be expected to address a man of Tranter's generation as mister, unless invited to do otherwise.

'Yeah? Well, mind how you go.' Tranter slides onto the station wagon's driver's seat. His wife is already in the car, her seatbelt fastened. He turns over the car's engine and in backing out, slides the fender closer than necessary to Kenny's motorbike.

Kenny who?, Carmel thinks. Another name to check back for in the file on Janet McClymont's disappearance. He catches her looking at him and performs the same well-practised wink that he'd bestowed on Raelene, before scooping his helmet off the seat of his bike.

'You heading off home, son?'

The query comes from the man leaning on the hall verandah's rail whom Carmel saw getting short shrift from Connie Tranter. Chester, she'd called him. The name is singular enough for her to recall his surname from a list of locals recorded in the files: Connolly. Carmel can see a family resemblance. The older man would have once been as handsome as his son.

'Couple of rums at the pub first,' Kenny says. 'See you there?' He grins broadly at Carmel and adds, 'I mean Cokes, of course.'

'Too right,' Chester says. 'Just gotta have a word first with Jimmy.'

The big man with the towelling hat and the earthmoving business—Froome—is standing beside Chester. 'You still working down at Bowen, Kenny?'

'Gidday, Mr Froome. Nah, finished a couple of weeks ago. Got a local job on at the moment, other side of Kaliope.'

'Yeah? Well, don't work too hard.'

Kenny rides off in the same direction as the Tranters' station wagon and Carmel watches as Jimmy Froome and Chester Connolly walk to the far end of the verandah. She quietly opens the door of the Q car she and Patterson had driven out from Kaliope in and slips into the passenger seat. They had parked beneath a tree earlier, and in its shadow and with the interior light off she has an excellent view of the Quala locals as they gradually leave the hall, while she remains almost invisible. Froome and Connolly are deep in a discussion that looks serious. Connolly seems to be making a case for something. Froome looks sceptical.

A group of teenage boys clatter down the steps. They were the ones clustered around Kenny Connolly earlier. Two of them, with identical haircuts—long at the back and a dead-straight fringe—and the same ski-jump nose, look like brothers. The older of the pair, Carmel thinks, was the one who called out 'Fantapants' when Sullivan was revealed behind the curtain. The third, dressed like Kenny Connolly in KingGee work shorts and with limbs muscled from outdoor labour, might be an apprentice tradesman. He derisively farewells his companions— 'Better go and finish your homework, boys'—before climbing into a battered Holden one-tonner ute and driving off in the direction of the pub.

Carmel scans the last of those leaving the hall, looking for the fifth member of the group, who had kept himself slightly separate, his eyes on the floor, not completely at ease. She sees him at last, following Bev Zammit down the stairs and carrying a couple of empty Tupperware containers. He has her colouring—dark eyes and straight, almost black hair—and a similar stocky build. She recalls the name Martin Zammit from the police files, a mate of Joe Cassar's. That fact could account for his uneasiness. Another observation to file away and examine later.

Essie rests her chin on her hands and looks out the station wagon's open window. The warm, humid night air clings to her face. She had gone to climb out of the car with Raelene when they pulled up, but her father told her to wait with her mother and sister. Raelene has asked her over to play on the weekend more than once, but Essie has never been inside the pub. Her mother will only say that a hotel is no place for children.

'Raelene's a child,' Essie replies whenever her mother utters this judgement, but her mum won't be drawn into an argument. The pub is a place of and for men. Essie has only glimpsed the interior from the outside. The high wooden bar, the companionable stools, the smell of beer and working men possess an exotic pull. Raelene, who passes between this masculine, adult realm and that of the schoolyard, carries the knowledge and power of both.

At the threshold to the public bar, her father pauses, standing in the glare of the bare light globe above the door. He ushers Raelene ahead of him with one hand while the other bats at the insects careering in frenzied circles around his head in the cone of light. He directs a wave to someone inside and shakes his head. 'Wife and kids in the car,' she hears him say.

When they're back on the road, her father keeps one easy hand on the steering wheel, an elbow resting on the window frame. He doesn't swerve to hit the cane toads that appear in the beam of the headlights, nor does he try to avoid them. Helen is already nodding off, her head thrown back against the seat, her mouth agape like a stranded fish.

'So,' her mother says brightly, turning around to look at Essie.

Essie recognises this tone as the one her mother uses to hide the hungry need to know. Before the coming question is even asked, she is resolved to deny her mother whatever it is she wants to learn.

'What were you and Raelene doing behind the stage?'

'Nothing.'

'Nothing?'

Essie shrugs, her gaze fixed on the cane fields that line the road. 'Raelene wanted to hear what the police were saying.'

'I don't want you creeping around in the dark at any time, but especially not at the moment,' says her mother. 'You know why, don't you, Essie?'

Essie nods, but keeps her eyes focused on the darkness outside the car, the cane growing beside the road blurring into an unbroken wall of shadows and vegetation.

'Look at me, Essie.'

Essie drags her eyes back to her mother.

'You're still a child. There are things you don't need to know yet.'

'Raelene says Janet was murdered by a pervert who did it to her and then chopped her up into little pieces,' Essie says in a rush.

Her mother looks stunned, blinks rapidly. 'Well, no one knows for sure what has happened to Janet. But Essie, please, be good. Be patient, okay?'

As her mum sinks back against the seat with a tight, exasperated sigh, Essie sees her father glance at her mother. Keeping one hand on the wheel, he reaches across the space between them with the other, his hand below the level of the seat back. Essie sees the tension in her mother's neck and shoulders ease and the smile her parents exchange. Her father lifts his arm so that it lies along the top of the bench seat. 'Slide over here, old girl.'

Her mother raises her chin, smiles. Her father cocks an eyebrow, twitches one corner of his mouth, a caricature of a suave movie star. Essie feels somehow reassured as her mother laughs, unfastens her seatbelt. Shimmies across the vinyl seat to lean against him.

'You know,' Essie's father says, 'I reckon your mother could represent the state in high jump after seeing the way she leapt onto that stage tonight.'

The headlights illuminate a tunnel wending between the fields of cane pressing in on either side of the car. In the distance, orange flames colour the sky above the horizon.

NINE

WHEN THEY PULL up outside their house, Cam eases Helen out of the back seat and carries her inside, her head limp against his chest. Connie stands beside the car waiting for Essie. Does her daughter dawdle like this expressly to drive her mad? Even while she is telling herself to be patient, Connie can't stop herself. 'Get a move on, Essie. I'm waiting for you.'

A mumble reaches Connie through the car door, ajar.

'What?'

'Nothing.'

Connie clenches her teeth. 'Don't be infuriating. What did you say?'

'I said, I. Don't. Need. You. To. Wait. For. Me,' says Essie, over-articulating every word, each one a bullet.

Connie restrains herself from reaching into the car and hauling her daughter out. Just. She opens the door wide. 'Out. Now.'

Essie slouches out of the car and Connie smacks the door shut. The edge of it scrapes against her daughter's arm.

'Ow!' Essie clasps her shoulder to herself. 'You hurt me!'

'Oh, don't be ridiculous. It scarcely touched you.'

'Look, there's a big scratch.'

Cam has switched on the light at the back door on his way in. Its faint halo barely reaches the foot of the stairs.

Connie's rage at her fractious daughter deflates. 'Come inside and I'll have a look at it.'

Mollified, Essie allows Connie to place an arm about her shoulders. Doesn't shrug it off.

Once the bedtime routine has been completed, Connie sits on the edge of Essie's bed. 'That man, the high school teacher, has he spoken to you before?'

As Connie thinks of him again, looming over Essie and Raelene on the Memorial Hall stage, a flush of something violent and primeval grips her. If he had made another attempt to touch them, Connie would have fought him, punching and kicking and scratching. She would have wielded anything within reach as a weapon. Nothing he could have done would have been able to counter the maternal fury firing her limbs, her heart.

In the bed on the other side of the room, Helen utters a small, sighing sound. She is lying in the same position as Cam left her after easing the sandals off her grubby feet and pulling the sheet up to her chest. Connie glances over at her younger daughter. Will she learn the contrary, surly ways of her sister as she grows older? Lately she and her elder child are constantly picking at each other's tender places. They cannot be easy together. Essie is always pulling away, the cord of their connection constantly taut and twanging.

The soft light from the globe in the recess of Essie's bedhead softens her older daughter's sulky expression. Like this, in her rose-patterned seersucker shortie pyjamas, Essie looks younger than she does in her school uniform or in the T-shirts she wears around the farm that cling to her developing breast buds. A recent growth spurt has transformed her once sturdy little body into something alarmingly coltish and awkward, but she is still a child, not so far removed from the baby for whom Connie held such fierce, uncomplicated love. Connie misses the purity of that emotion, unsullied by ambivalence. She strokes Essie's thick hair, dark like Cam's, still crimped from the plaits Connie wove it into that morning.

Essie hasn't answered, and Connie asks again, gently, 'Has he? Spoken to you?'

'No.'

'Does Raelene know him?'

Essie shrugs. 'She's seen him at the pub sometimes, I think.'

Connie tries to keep her tone light. 'Tonight, behind the curtain, before I saw you . . .' she begins, then consciously slows her breathing before asking, 'did he touch you anywhere private or ask you or Raelene to touch him?'

Essie screws up her face. 'No!'

Her daughter's incredulousness at the question gives Connie comfort. She straightens the sheet, pulling it up until it lies beneath Essie's chin.

Essie, irritable, shoves it back down. 'It's too hot.'

'Was he one of Janet's teachers, do you know? Did she ever speak to you about him?'

Essie turns her body towards the wall, hauling the sheet over her shoulder and dragging her hair out of her mother's reach. 'I don't know.'

'So Janet never said anything about him? Whether she liked him or not?'

'No.' Essie sounds as if she is speaking through clenched teeth.

Sadness clutches so swift and tight at Connie's throat that she has to stand in order to breathe. She bends and kisses her daughter's hair. Before she can leave, Essie, her eyes screwed shut, grabs her mother's hand and squeezes it tightly before tossing it away.

~

Connie clutches Cam's hair in her fingers. He has let it grow longer, and with her hands full of his dark locks and her arms clasping his head to her breasts, she is almost carefree. Like this, his weight on her is sweet and heavy like molasses.

~

When Essie wakes it is still dark, and the wind is causing the lace curtains to flutter, then collapse, only to leap up when another gust rattles the window sash. The cane, too, is restless, chattering to itself in whispers and sighs. Essie remembers the weighty blackness of the stage curtains. How it stopped her nose and throat, the trapped dust acrid and thick. She takes a great gasp of air, sitting up in her bed and opening her mouth wide to feel the cool air rush down her throat. She is panting.

A tremor that begins far away judders through the house and vibrates through her bed's wooden frame. She leaps up to stand by the open window, and in the light thrown by the late-risen moon she can see a ripple of movement, as if something large and swift is striding through the cane.

She pads over to Helen's bed. Her little sister is lying on her back, her arms flung above her head.

'Move over,' Essie whispers, and Helen rolls onto her side.

~

The following day, Connie's disquiet and suspicion regarding Eamonn Sullivan are unabated. She woke repeatedly in the night fleeing anxiety dreams where she watched helpless as her daughters—babies again—were stolen from her by creatures, strange melds of beasts and men, or because of a moment of distraction were whisked out of her arms by storm or flood.

When she returns home from dropping Helen and Essie at school, Connie channels her agitation into cleaning and baking.

In the afternoon, Cam wanders into the kitchen in his socks, having left his workboots outside. He gives her a kiss and leans against the pantry door, his forehead marked with a horizontal line left by his hat. His hands, black from investigating the harvester's engine, toss a piston ring back and forth. Connie immediately sweeps him into the conversation she's been having with herself about Eamonn Sullivan.

'You know that the police questioned Sullivan and the Parslow boy over Janet's disappearance?' She opens the oven, checks the biscuits browning on a tray.

'Of course they did. They questioned everyone in a ten-mile radius of Quala. They were up here, remember, asking where we were and what we saw.'

'Jean told me the police have been through the old house more than once.'

'Like I said, I'm not surprised.' Cam puts the piston ring in his pocket, wipes his fingers on the front of his work shorts. 'But Vince told me that Sullivan and Pete were seen in Kaliope before Janet would have left her house.'

Connie pulls on an oven mitt, lifts the tray of biscuits onto the bench beside Cam. 'Let them cool,' she warns him. 'And wash your hands.'

Cam holds a cake of soap under the tap and lathers it. 'If you want to know what I think, I reckon whoever took Janet is long gone by now. It wasn't anyone local.'

Connie wheels on him. 'Really, so what do you think Sullivan was up to with Essie and Raelene? Why was he behind the curtain with them?'

Cam agrees that it looked a bit off. 'But honestly, I think he was doing what he told you and that policewoman—he saw them running around in the dark and wanted to make sure they didn't get themselves into any strife. John Creadie said he spoke to Sullivan later that night on his way home. He said Sullivan was that embarrassed. John and Vince vouch for him. So does the principal at Kaliope West, Ern Shaw. John said Shaw wrote a character reference for Sullivan when he and Pete wanted to rent the old house.'

'You know he told his students they could call him by his first name.' Connie tosses the oven mitt on the bench beside the biscuits.

'Most of those Grade 12 boys are practically men. Where's the harm?' says Cam.

Connie stares at him. 'You can't have students thinking their teachers are equals. Where's the respect, the structure? You weren't that keen when Kenny Connolly took a similar liberty with you last night.'

Cam shakes his head, regards her with a half-smile.

'What?'

A snort of reluctant laughter escapes him. Before Connie can snap at him, Cam holds up his hands as if to ward off a blow. 'It's just that when I first met you, I thought you were such a sophisticate, a real city girl with modern ideas.'

Connie is not amused. 'Motherhood changes you. Children need rules, clear boundaries. It was how I was brought up.'

'Connie,' Cam says softly, taking her in his arms. 'Our girls will be alright. They are alright. We'll keep them safe.'

When Cam goes into the hallway to call his mechanic, Connie sits at the kitchen table and re-reads a list in the morning's newspaper. She gets a pen and copies out the list, underlining the word *never* wherever it appears. Then she rummages in the drawer where she keeps the scissors and finds a roll of sticky tape. Cutting out the list from the newspaper, she sticks it to the wall beside the calendar and then sits back down at the table.

'What's this?' says Cam, looking at the list on the wall then reading the copy over Connie's shoulder. '*Never talk to strangers. Never accept offers of lollies or presents from strangers. Never accept offers of a ride in a strange car.*' He looks at her.

'The police minister says all children should know how to stay safe,' says Connie. 'I'm going to put this up in the bedroom.'

Cam taps the clipping beside the calendar. 'You've already got it stuck to the wall here, love.'

'It won't do any harm to have it in their bedroom as well.'

'Essie and Helen know all this. *All* the kids do. The police were at the school two days after Janet went missing lecturing them about all this stuff. There's no need to make them more terrified than they already are.'

Connie pushes back the chair, stands. 'Are you picking the girls up from school?'

Cam watches as Connie leaves the kitchen, the sheet of paper and the roll of sticky tape in her hand. He picks up the keys to the station wagon from the table and takes a biscuit from the rack. It is still hot and he has to juggle it in his hands.

~

It's true that Connie's years in Quala have made her a more conservative person, but they have also, she thinks, made her more realistic. She has become a wife and mother, her professional ambitions put aside. The prestigious Catholic boarding school where her parents had sent her for her secondary education in Grades 8 to 12 was run by an order of nuns who valued girls' education—to a disconcerting degree in the opinion of some in staid 1950s Brisbane. The school, housed in a grand building boasting Gothic arches and wide sweeping balconies overlooking the city below, was a world away from the local state primary school that Connie had attended until Grade 7. The nuns championed the importance of a rich intellectual life for their students and placed great emphasis on the study of art in all its forms.

In her final year at the school, Connie realised that her parents were only vaguely aware that the school was preparing her and her fellow students to take up professional lives. Connie, encouraged by the principal, Sister Elaine, sat the public service exam at the end of senior year. Her typing speeds were very good. Perhaps she might be offered a position as an assistant to a department head.

'Are you sure?' her parents asked Connie when she announced her plans to live and work in Brisbane after she finished school. They'd expected her to come home when she matriculated, maybe get a job in a doctor's office in Stanthorpe and work there until she got married, perhaps to one of the MacGregor boys.

They were anxious when, after spending a few months living at home, Connie secured a job with the Queensland Arts Council and moved to Brisbane. They insisted that she board with a Catholic family. To pacify them, she agreed. Three months later she moved into a flat with a female colleague.

Connie's job with the Arts Council was only an administrative position, but she had hopes for advancement. Living in Brisbane, she took advantage of all the cultural offerings available to her—such as they were—with subscriptions to the opera, the ballet, the Queensland Theatre Company. It was expected, given her job.

After a year or two in Brisbane, she began contemplating a move to Sydney. There was a job going with the Art Gallery of New South Wales that she thought she might be qualified for. Nothing senior, of course. That was never really going to be a possibility for a woman. And then her school friend Alison invited her to her wedding to Cam Tranter's cousin.

In the end, after all her parents' misgivings about her ambitions, Connie complied surprisingly closely with their expectations by marrying a farmer and moving to the country. Sometimes, when she is in her kitchen baking chocolate slice or cutting up sandwiches to take out to Cam working on the tractor, Connie thinks back to her days living in the city, earning her own money, doing a job she enjoyed. To think that she gave it all up to be a farmer's wife.

No, she reminds herself, not a wife to some anonymous farmer, but wife to Cam. Nevertheless, she does, on occasion, find herself thinking, Damn you, Cam Tranter. Damn your golden forearms and that smile that promised to give me exactly what I wanted. And at that time, when she met him, it was sex she wanted. The nuns at her boarding school had had a lot to say about the girls under their care fulfilling their intellectual potential and meeting their spiritual needs. They'd had precious little to say about the body, about satisfying one's carnal desires. That area of knowledge and experience definitely hadn't been part of the curriculum.

Cam helped remedy that gap in Connie's education. The sight of his forearms can still make her reach across the table to brush his skin with her fingertips.

Back then, even if she'd married a doctor and lived in the city, she would have still had to give up her job. Not now, though. Barbara is right. Things are changing for women.

She tears up at the thought of Barbara, who's stopped painting since Janet's disappearance. Stopped wanting to do anything or see anyone. Connie misses her friendship terribly. Her heart aches when she imagines the anguish Barbara is going through, but Barbara won't allow Connie to comfort her. She has frozen her out. Barbara has been emptied of everything except her despair.

When Barbara and Ted moved to Quala with Janet, Connie was eager to meet them. She was delighted when Barbara threw a party within a fortnight of moving into their house. Connie gravitated immediately to Barbara with her loud laugh and her extravagant clothes. She admired Barbara's standing as an artist, her bohemian style and her intellectual curiosity. She was envious, too, that Barbara had been able to go to art college when Janet started school. She told Connie that the people she'd met there had changed her, opening her eyes to feminism and the possibilities for social change.

'I love Ted,' she said to Connie, 'but our politics have moved further and further apart.'

Connie was surprised that Ted managed to persuade Barbara to leave Brisbane. It was some deal they had struck between them. Ted had grown up further north and obtained a law degree from the University of Queensland. There was the opportunity for a more senior position in the Department of Primary Industries if he took a job in the regions for a period of time. Barbara agreed to give it two years. After that, the plan was that Ted would apply for promotion and a position back in the Brisbane office in time for Janet to attend university.

Ted didn't chafe against the country-town conservatism the way Barbara did, and her perspective on things made Connie realise how her own outlook on the world had become more conventional since arriving in Quala. Despite that, after thirteen years, occasionally Connie still feels like an outsider. Even now sometimes, someone will laughingly refer to her as a 'blow-in'. Although, she reminds herself, the Creadies, Vince and Jean and John and Meg, were welcoming from the moment she arrived and have become good friends.

Like her, Barbara views Quala with an interloper's eye. Barbara would never take a step back in a conversation with a man and would argue the cause of women's liberation at the drop of a hat, perhaps a little too stridently, Connie sometimes thinks. The nuns from her boarding school would applaud Barbara's intellect, but they would disapprove of her tone. Yet, Connie was pleased when Barbara passed on books to her that she thought she would like, or more accurately, thought she should read: *The Left Hand of Darkness* by Ursula K. Le Guin, *The Golden Notebook* by Doris Lessing, *The Bell Jar* by Sylvia Plath.

'Read these as a warm-up. I'll give you *The Feminine Mystique* and *The Female Eunuch* next,' she said, making sure that Cam heard their exchange and grinning conspiratorially at Connie when he groaned.

Connie has found some of the ideas raised by these books challenging, their framing of women's experiences troubling even. But her conversations about them with Barbara rekindled that sense of stretching her mind and her understanding of the world she remembered experiencing under the tutelage of her most demanding teachers in her later years at school. It was thrilling.

Connie still tries to get to Brisbane a couple of times a year. She catches up with school friends and she and her sister go to the ballet or attend a concert. Locally, there is an amateur theatre company in Kaliope as well as a small chamber orchestra of weekend musicians that a retired professor from the Queensland Conservatorium of Music conducts. She attends their performances whenever she can, sometimes with Cam, sometimes alone. And at least there is a decent library in town.

Barbara made the world of Quala seem larger and more open. Now it is shrunken and claustrophobic. She imagines Barbara and Ted both wish they'd never come north.

⁓

From the bedroom, Connie hears the ute pull up in front of the house and then the familiar sounds of the screen door slapping shut, the thumps of the girls dumping their school ports on the kitchen floor, footsteps along the hall. She recognises Essie's tread in the girls' room and goes to see her. Pausing at the bedroom door, she watches Essie stand side-on in front of the full-length mirror on her wardrobe door, one hand resting on a jutted hip. She looks over her shoulder at her reflection, pulls out the elastic band securing her plait and flicks her hair, bats her eyelashes.

'How was school?' asks Connie.

Essie ducks her head, flushes crimson, shoots a glance tinged with annoyance at her mother.

'Did you see the list on the wardrobe door?'

'Yes.'

'What do you think?'

'About what?'

'About keeping safe.'

At Essie's shrug, Connie's exasperation tips into anger. 'It's important, Essie.'

'I know, I know. They talk about it at school all the time. I'm not stupid.' She runs down the hall, past the kitchen door, out onto the verandah and down the stairs.

Connie resists the urge to run after her, to tell her to come back, to not grow up too quickly.

The sensuality that Connie sees Essie aping is, she has no doubt, a result of her friendship with Raelene. In Essie's performance it is pantomime, but Connie senses that Raelene's flirting and flaunting is based in experience and an early awakening. She leaches an adult sensuality. There were girls at Connie's boarding school who, like Raelene, came to an early appreciation of the power of sex and the force of their own desire. Connie's awareness came much later, but when it hit, it almost knocked her off her feet.

Connie doesn't want Essie to be like Raelene. The world is cruel to girls who parade their sexuality like a prize. Cathy

Creadie had been a little like that—brazen and ripe. Janet had not. But she'd been punished anyway.

~

In the kitchen, Helen is waiting expectantly at the table. She launches herself at Connie, full of joy.

'Hello, sweetheart.' Connie clasps her youngest to her, lifting her up so that their faces are level, and kisses her damp, hot forehead, savouring her little-girl smell of grass and Vegemite.

A scuffling sound makes her turn. Essie is leaning on the doorframe.

'Come here, sweetie,' says Connie, releasing Helen and holding out her arms to Essie, who allows herself to be kissed on the top of her head.

Cam appears behind her. 'Kettle on?' he asks, smiling at the image of all his girls together and happy. He pulls his chair back from the table.

Connie's unease lifts. When they are all here in the kitchen sitting around the table eating the biscuits she has baked, she can believe it is possible to keep them all safe from perverts and predators, from communists and long-haired bludgers.

TEN

'A SENSIBLE GIRL. Thoughtful. Sure of her opinions and happy to express them. Settled in very quickly. Made friends.' Ern Shaw, Kaliope West High School's principal, leans back in his large oak swivel chair until its springs complain. 'I told the detectives all this just after Janet disappeared. And Janet's friends, I'm reasonably sure, will have nothing more to add either.'

'You're probably right, Mr Shaw. But I'd still like to speak again to the girls who were closest to her. I already have their parents' consent,' says Carmel, briefly worrying for the wellbeing of the principal's chair. Then again, from the scratches and dents on its surface it looks like it's accustomed to the rough treatment that comes with bearing the substantial bulk of Ern Shaw on a daily basis.

'Please just call me Ern,' he says, projecting himself upright. 'You can use my office. You have a list of names, I presume? I'll ask them to come in one at a time, shall I?'

'No. If it's possible, I'd prefer to speak with them as a group,' says Carmel.

'Of course, whatever you think is best,' Ern replies, re-tucking his shirt tails into the belted waistband of his dress shorts, and straightening his purple-and-gold-hued, geometric-patterned tie.

Carmel locates the list of three names in the inner pocket of her bag, hands it to Ern. 'They're all in Grade 11, I think?'

Ern scans the paper Carmel has given him. 'Yes, that's right. They'll be about to go on morning recess, so we'll waste no more time. I'll have them rounded up in a jiffy.' Ern exits his office with the speed of a migrating wildebeest, but with considerably less dust.

~

Janet McClymont's three closest friends are scrunched together in front of Carmel on the battered couch in Ern Shaw's office.

'What do we call you?' asks the middle girl, the tsarina of the group, Carmel assesses. Her eyebrows are plucked to one hair-breadth wide, her fringe dyed peroxide blonde.

'Carmel's fine.' She lets them settle for a moment. They ineffectually tug the hems of their school uniforms down towards their knees and pull at their socks.

'Which of you is Michelle?'

The girl in the middle tosses her bleached bangs. 'I prefer Shelley, actually, Carmel.'

'And Katrina?'

The girl on Shelley's left, who has large grey eyes in a pale, pretty face, lifts her hand from her knee in a kind of salute.

'Then you're Andrea,' she says to the other girl, who is thin, almost skinny. She peers out at Carmel with a worried expression beneath two curtains of dead-straight, dark brown hair that fall to her elbows.

Carmel guesses their group is middle order in the Grade 11 social hierarchy, perhaps enjoying a temporary bump in status due to their friendship with the missing girl.

'First of all, I am so sorry about what happened to Janet. It must be very sad and distressing for you.'

Shelley nods, turning her head away and staring hard out the window. Katrina pulls a handkerchief out of her pocket and presses it to her eyes. Andrea takes in a shuddering gasp of air, her shoulders folding in around her narrow chest.

Carmel waits. 'This won't take long.'

Shelley swings her gaze back towards her. Carmel thought the girl was fighting back tears, but she sees that Shelley is, in fact, furious. 'We've already spoken to the police. We don't know anything about what happened to Janet. Why are you even here? Why aren't you out there looking for her?'

Katrina pulls her head into her shoulders, glances at Shelley, grimly admiring of her friend's hostile insolence. Andrea too, Carmel sees, is prepared to be antagonistic. She can't find it in herself to blame any of them.

'I know it must be frustrating—and frightening—that we still don't know what happened to Janet,' Carmel says. 'Nevertheless, I would really appreciate it if you would be patient and answer my questions, even if you feel that you've answered them before.'

The three girls exchange looks, come to resentful acquiescence.

Carmel leads them into a general discussion about their friendship with Janet, what she'd told them about her home life, whether they knew of any friendships she had outside of school, her favourite teachers, the subjects she took, if she'd said anything about what she hoped to do after her senior year.

'Do any of you have Eamonn Sullivan for a teacher?' Carmel keeps her tone neutral, the muscles around her eyes relaxed.

Shelley and Katrina shake their heads, no.

'I'm in Mr Sullivan's Grade 11 English class,' Andrea says.

Shelley snorts. 'Fantapants.'

Carmel holds her pen above her notebook. 'Fantapants?'

'That's what everyone calls him,' Shelley says. 'Because of his red hair.'

'Ah, I see. And Janet?'

'She was in his English class, too,' Andrea says. 'He takes the top Grade 11 class; she's—well, she was—really good at English.'

'Janet told us he was always going on about the demonstrations he went to in Brisbane. Saying stuff about the importance of civil disruption in the face of injustice or something,' Shelley says.

'Disobedience, not disruption,' Andrea corrects her.

'Same diff.'

'Did she ever mention if she saw him outside of school?' Carmel asks.

'Do you think he was the one that took her?' Shelley asks sharply. Her finely plucked brows give her an expression of permanently outraged surprise.

'Mr Sullivan lives quite close to Janet's parents' house in Quala, and to where her things were found. I'm just wondering if she ever mentioned talking to him on the weekends or after school.'

Katrina glances at Shelley, then says, 'Nup. She never said anything about seeing him outside of school.'

'Hanging out with Fantapants?' Shelley smirks. 'Not likely.'

'He drove her home a couple of times.' Andrea's draped hair conceals her face.

'What? That's bullshit.' Shelley glances at Andrea and then looks at Carmel, the toss of her head communicating disbelief.

'Did Janet tell you that, Andrea?' Carmel keeps her voice gentle, the question a casual one.

Andrea pushes back a tress of her long hair. 'She missed the bus to Quala two, maybe three afternoons. Mr Sullivan saw her the first time running after the bus and offered to drive her home. He said to come and see him in the staffroom if it ever happened again.'

'She never said anything to me about it.' Shelley draws herself up, folds her arms across her breasts.

Andrea looks through her hair at Carmel. 'Janet did, though. Get a lift with Mr Sullivan a couple of times.'

'Did she say if he ever did or said something that made her uncomfortable, or that she didn't like?' Carmel asks. Her body is tingling, a cat edging towards a bird.

'Nup. They didn't talk much, she said. Just listened to the radio, mainly.'

'So he is a perv.' Shelley seems satisfied that this fact has been established. 'Maybe he did kidnap Janet.'

'The police interviewed all the teachers after it happened,' Andrea counters. 'They had to say where they were the night when she went missing. Mr Sullivan wasn't even in Quala when it happened.'

'That's what he says.' Shelley sits back and looks out the window.

'Other people said it too. He was still on his way back from the footy match, they reckon.'

'Yeah, that's what they reckon.'

Carmel changes tack. She will need to recheck the notes of the police interview with Sullivan, but she doesn't think he mentioned ever giving Janet McClymont a lift home to Quala. 'Did you ever see anyone strange hanging about the school? Vehicles that regularly drove past or men parked in cars?'

The girls flick their hair like so many skittish ponies. '*All* the time.'

'Really?'

They regard her as if she's simple. 'Yeah.'

'Any ones in particular?'

'There's always devos driving around the school and following the school bus,' Shelley says.

'Devos?' Carmel cocks an eyebrow.

'You know, deviants. They pull out their dicks and stuff like that. Only some of them. Most of them are just perving.'

Katrina scratches at a pimple on her chin. 'The guy in the orange Charger.'

Andrea examines her hair for split ends. 'Those two blokes in the truck.'

Shelley side-eyes her companions. 'The spunks with the motorbikes.'

The three of them hug their ribs and giggle.

'Did any of them have a particular interest in Janet?'

'Not really. The devos mainly hang around town. Janet caught the bus that comes in from Quala—not the town school bus—or sometimes her dad drove her in,' Andrea says.

Carmel circles back around. 'What was Janet doing that made her miss the bus those times?' she asks Andrea.

Andrea glances at Shelley with something akin to compassion, Carmel thinks, before answering. 'She was pashing off Joe in one of the classrooms.'

Katrina bites her bottom lip, her eyes darting from one friend to the other.

With a small curling movement of her little finger, Andrea tugs on Shelley's skirt. 'Janet didn't say anything to you about it because it was before she'd really told anyone she was going with Joe.'

'The boy Janet was "pashing off" with, that was . . .' Carmel pretends to check her notes, 'Joe Cassar? He was her boyfriend?' She doesn't look at them directly, scrawls nonsense in her notebook.

Andrea and Katrina nod confirmation. Shelley inspects her fingernails.

'It started at the concert for the music department,' adds Katrina, then peeks at Shelley, checking that she hasn't gone too far.

'What did you think about Joe and Janet going around together?' Carmel asks the three of them, but Shelley appears to have signalled that she will take it from here.

'It was the biggest mistake Janet ever made.' She straightens her back and her soft mouth transforms into a grim line.

A realisation dawns on Carmel. 'Did you like Joe too, Shelley?'

'It isn't about that,' Shelley spits. Her anger has returned.

'What is it about, then?'

'It's Joe's fault.' Shelley's voice is constricted, forced out through held-back tears.

'What is?' Carmel speaks softly. The room has closed in around her and the missing girl's friends.

'Janet going missing, probably getting killed.'

'Why do you say that?' Carmel asks.

'If it wasn't for Joe Cassar, Janet would've gone straight to the Tranters' to babysit. She wouldn't have been hanging around in the cane waiting for him.' Shelley is openly crying now. 'She would still be here.'

~

Carmel stands as Eamonn Sullivan walks into the room. He removes his oversized straw hat and draws his long fingers through the honey-red hair that reaches his shoulders. His large hands are heavily freckled, as is most of his other exposed skin, despite the hat. His moustache is more auburn than the hair on his head. He's dressed similarly to Ern Shaw—belted dress shorts, short-sleeved collared shirt and knee-length socks in oatmeal colours. His taste in ties isn't as flamboyant as Ern's, however; Sullivan's matches the mission brown of his shoes. He looks to be in his mid-twenties. Tall and thin. Knobbly knees prominent above his socks.

'Carmel Maitland,' Carmel reminds him, holding out her hand.

Sullivan takes it, gives it a brief shake, then, with the same hand, strokes his moustache.

Carmel notes that the skin of his face is damp. She indicates the schoolyard outside the window. 'Hot out there?'

'Not so bad.'

They are both still standing.

'Let's sit.' Carmel takes the chair she was sitting on earlier, forcing Sullivan to lower himself onto the couch. His legs are so long that his knees jack-knife above his waist.

Carmel launches straight in. 'So, Mr Sullivan, can you tell me what you were doing behind the curtain the other night at the Memorial Hall with Essie Tranter and Raelene Mason?'

The skin in the hollow of Sullivan's throat begins to pulse. 'I wasn't doing anything *with* them.'

'Then what were you doing on the stage?'

'As I said at the time, I noticed the girls as I was coming out of the toilets. They were running towards the back of the hall. All the kids were supposed to be inside because of . . . because the person, or the people, who are responsible for Janet McClymont's disappearance still haven't been caught. I was concerned about them being out in the dark by themselves.'

'How long would you say that you were with them before you were discovered?'

'Discovered? What do you mean by that?' Sullivan wipes his palms along the length of his shorts. 'I wasn't hiding from anybody.'

'How long?'

'A minute, maybe less.'

'Had you noticed them before?'

'What do you mean?'

'I mean, had you seen them around Quala? Did you know their names? Were you aware of where they lived?'

'No. I mean, yes. Vaguely.'

'Vaguely?'

Sullivan expels air audibly, as if reminding himself to relax. 'I didn't know their first names. I'd seen the older girl sitting at the front bar of the Quala pub. Her father owns it. The other one, the Tranter girl, her family live on the farm next to the Creadies' place where I rent a cottage.'

'So you've never been alone with either of them before?'

'No! Listen, Constable Maitland . . .'

'Senior Constable.'

'What?'

'It's Senior Constable Maitland.'

'As I'm sure you know, Senior Constable, I was interviewed shortly after Janet McClymont went missing. So were all the men who live in Quala, as well as all the teachers here at Kaliope West. I'd been to the football that day. At the time she disappeared I was driving back home with my housemate. I've told your colleagues all this before.' Sullivan leans back in the couch, crosses his arms over his chest.

'You've got a reputation as a bit of a rabble-rouser.'

Sullivan shoots her an irritated glance, with something else beneath it. A touch of pride that he is regarded as a provocateur. 'I don't know what you mean.'

'Oh, you know, impressing your students with tales of demonstrations, marches, agitating.'

'If you mean I've encouraged discussion in my classroom about social injustice and this country's willingness to participate in acts of American imperialism, then yes, I have.' A bell rings in the corridor outside Ern Shaw's office. 'And now I really have to get to my next class.'

'Okay, but before you go, just one more question,' says Carmel. 'How many times did you give Janet McClymont a lift home from school?'

⌒

Carmel hasn't been back from the high school for more than five minutes before Patterson calls her into the office he's commandeered at Kaliope Police Station. The ceiling fan above his desk spins frantically, riffling the papers—reports, copies of statements, newspaper clippings—lying in trays or stacked in piles on his desk. The more precarious arrangements are weighted down with half-empty mugs, teabag tags dolefully hanging from their rims.

'Why've you got a bee in your bonnet about Eamonn Sullivan?' asks Patterson.

How he heard so quickly that she's spoken to the red-haired teacher is a mystery to Carmel. News—and gossip—travels quickly around Kaliope, obviously.

'We looked pretty hard at both him and that bloke Parslow who he shares a house with, as well as her boyfriend, and they all checked out,' Patterson continues. 'Besides, you're supposed to be concentrating on the females. Anything they can tell us about dodgy blokes who've been sniffing around. Those schoolgirls you spoke to, they tell you anything interesting? Any of them been banging a fella on the sly who likes a bit of rough stuff?'

The mustard-yellow dial telephone on Patterson's desk suddenly rings, its shrill, hectoring tone boring a hole in the bone above Carmel's ear.

Patterson holds up a finger, dismissing her. 'Write up anything you think's important and I'll take a look at it.'

Carmel pulls the door to his office closed behind her. Through the glass panel, she sees that Patterson is on his feet, animated, smiling hugely, already reaching for his jacket.

'I knew it would be a bloody darkie,' says Patterson, beaming as he comes out of his office, briefcase in his hand. 'Carmel, love, you can drive me to the motel and then to the airport. Looks like our colleagues on the Southern Downs have had a stroke of luck.'

The call was a heads-up from Warwick police. A uniform had pulled over a male of South Sea Islander appearance driving a car with an out-of-date rego sticker and with his licence showing a Candleford address. The uniform had done a cursory check of the vehicle. In the coin tray was a hairclip in the shape of a butterfly.

'He says it belongs to his daughter,' Patterson crows, 'but what are the odds, especially given Candleford's only thirty miles from Quala?'

At the door, Patterson pauses, swings back to face the two local officers, Bill Wren and the wet-behind-the-ears constable who's manning the desk. 'Now, not a bloody word to anyone—and I mean *anyone*—about this. I'll fly back to Brisbane to interview this darkie, then I'll talk to the bosses before issuing a statement to the press. Alright? Just sit tight.'

'Ah, Detective?' It's Bill Wren. 'What about the McClymonts? We should tell them something before they hear it on the news.'

'Good thinking, Bill. Carmel, you can call in on them after you drop me at the airport. I'm looking forward to getting my hands on this bloke, I'll tell ya that for nothing.'

~

When Carmel mounts the McClymonts' front steps, she can see Barbara sitting on the back verandah, smoking. She glances over her shoulder at Carmel's knock, raises her hand holding the cigarette in a gesture of admission.

Carmel walks down the long hallway to stand beside Barbara's chair. 'There's been a possible development,' she says gently.

Barbara pushes herself halfway out of her chair. 'Have they found her?' she asks, an urgent quaver in her voice.

'No,' says Carmel, her stomach plummeting.

Barbara collapses into the chair, her back to the ocean, her gaze fixed on the cane. She takes a long drag, exhales smoke through her nostrils. 'Then why are you here?'

Carmel fills her in on the phone call from Warwick.

'So, nothing except that a brown-skinned man has been unlucky enough to be found in an unregistered car?'

'His driving licence shows a Candleford address.'

'And?'

'The officer who pulled the car over found a girl's hairclip in the ashtray similar to the one Janet was wearing, though Sergeant Patterson didn't get a detailed description of it.'

Even though Barbara is sitting down, Carmel is afraid that she might topple out of her chair. She sways forward and Carmel springs to catch her, but Barbara clutches the armrests to prevent herself from falling. Her cigarette drops onto the floor, ash scattering at her feet.

When Carmel is satisfied that Barbara isn't going to faint, she goes to the kitchen and returns with a glass of water. 'Drink this. Slowly. Small sips.'

Barbara obeys, grasping the glass in two trembling hands. 'I'm terrified,' she says eventually.

'Of what?' Carmel asks.

Barbara coughs out a sound harsh enough to hurt her throat. 'That this man will tell the police he killed Janet and where her body is.' She pauses, lights another cigarette. 'Or that they'll find he had nothing at all to do with her disappearance.'

'I'm sorry,' Carmel says. 'It must be unbearable.'

'And yet here I am,' Barbara says, 'being forced to bear it.'

She refuses Carmel's offer to remain with her until her husband returns to the house.

'Can I call someone to ask them to sit with you, then? Connie Tranter?'

But Barbara shakes her head. 'No. I'd prefer to be alone.'

On her way back through the house, Carmel is struck by a smell, sour and sharp, the odour of grief. Another smell lingers beneath it. The smoke of last night's cane fires.

Back at the Q car, Carmel leans on the roof, her head on her hands.

At the turn-off to the highway, the Crown Hotel stands out from the thicket of sugar cane surrounding it. Suddenly, a beer seems like an excellent idea. Carmel swings into the empty block beside the pub that serves as a carpark. At the entrance she takes off her sunglasses and pauses for her eyes to adjust to the dimness of the bar after the blindingly bright afternoon sun. Out of habit, she checks the name of the licensee above the door: Gordon J. Mason.

Apart from the huge stuffed cane toad on the counter wearing a top hat and holding aloft a tiny walking stick, and the pair of cane cutters mounted on the wall behind, the Crown is largely indistinguishable from the dozens of country pubs Carmel has had cause to enter over her years in the force. On the walls, the framed photos of the local football team; the head of a dead animal—in this case a huge, black-bristled boar with curving tusks; and the cartoon on yellowing newspaper skewered by a thumbtack featuring a large-breasted woman in a short skirt being harassed by two jokily leering men, are almost reassuringly familiar. There's only one other customer, a man propped at the far end of the counter. A lazily circling ceiling fan fails to disturb the fug of beer.

The only barman, who Carmel assumes is the proprietor, Gordon Mason, nods when she orders a drink. He's in his early forties, she guesses, with a shrewd, thin face. He is clean-shaven, with a crewcut he probably touches up once a week with a pair of clippers. There's a murmur from the other customer, and an answering rumble from the publican before he puts a seven-ounce glass of beer on the counter in front of her. She blinks at it and then at Mason. 'I asked for a pot.'

Mason points to the other drinker, who wears khaki work shorts and shirt and a wide straw hat with a hole worn through the crease at its peak. One elastic-sided workboot is propped on the slops tray that follows the curve of the bar where it meets the floor. She recognises Chester Connolly from the community meeting at the Memorial Hall. He raises his glass, a pot of beer.

Mason wipes the counter in front of her. 'He's paying and he said you'd take a pony.'

'He's that tight?'

'Hate to see a woman drinking out of a pot.' Connolly adjusts the front of his shorts. 'Makes her look a bit rough, I reckon.'

Carmel pushes the glass to the side, finds a handful of coins at the bottom of her bag and places them on the counter. 'I'll have a pot and I'll pay for it myself.'

Mason takes a ten-ounce glass from a tray and fills it. He picks up a few of the coins, placing a couple in front of Chester and tossing the rest in the tray of the cash register.

'Not often we see ladies in the front bar, Gordon.' Connolly puts both elbows on the bar, leans in to where Mason is restocking the stand of beer nuts. 'Mind you, wearing that pantsuit and in a dark corner, hard to tell if she's male or female.'

Carmel estimates the number of mouthfuls in her fresh glass. Almost regrets not accepting the pony.

'Whatya doing out this way, love?' Connolly says with a sideways smirk at Mason, who ignores it. 'Following up a hot lead?'

Carmel takes a swallow; not too much froth and the beer is fresh and hoppy. 'Just checking in on the McClymonts.'

'Terrible business with their girl.'

Carmel nods agreement.

'Mind you, not entirely surprising that she ran into trouble.'

A cold, hard fury almost makes Carmel gag on her beer. Here it comes. She should walk out now. She knows it. There is no point engaging with this dickhead. Still, she can't stop herself. 'Oh? And just what do you mean by that?' She turns, one elbow on the bar, to face him.

Connolly takes a long pull from his glass, swallows. 'Maybe it's different down south, but up here? Well, a white girl that'd go with an Islander would go with anybody.'

Before Carmel can take the two strides to toss what's left of her beer in Connolly's face, before she can tell him what a foul, rancid arsehole he is, before she can have his great ugly head on the counter and his arm twisted to breaking point behind his back, something clatters against the metal slops tray at her feet. A girl in school uniform scrambles up on a barstool between her and Connolly. It's Raelene, who was with Connie Tranter's daughter during all that fuss at the community briefing.

'Gidday, Raelene,' Connolly says. 'Maybe your dad'll let you drink that pony of beer the lady copper turned her nose up at.'

Mason puts a bottle of cola on the bar in front of his daughter, levers off the lid with an opener attached with a chain to the bar. Tosses the contents of the beer glass into the tray beneath the beer tap. 'How was school?'

'Good.'

'You got homework?'

'A bit. Not much.'

'Drink that up, then off upstairs. Come down for your tea about six. There'll be a pie for you.'

Raelene turns her head to look at Carmel. Straight black brows, thick hair like the bristles of a broom. Bold as brass.

Carmel tosses off the rest of her beer. 'Nice to see you again, Raelene,' she says to the girl, before tapping the bar in a farewell salute to the publican.

She hears Connolly's last jibe before she reaches the door. 'You know, Gordon, some married bloke's out of a job because of her.'

Back at the Kaliope cop shop, Carmel writes up her notes on her interviews with Janet McClymont's school friends, Eamonn Sullivan and Joe Cassar, who she'd also managed to have a conversation with. He struck her as a decent kid whose grief for his missing girlfriend seemed genuine. She digs out and re-reads the record of the interview the dead policeman did with Sullivan and his housemate Peter Parslow in the days after the girl's disappearance. Although she finds nothing that contradicts anything Sullivan told her, he'd failed to mention anything about driving Janet home from school. He'd kept that to himself. His story of being at the football that day and driving home with Parslow at the time she went missing seems to check out. Still, she'd like to look a bit more closely at him.

She takes down the names and addresses of those who said they'd seen him and Parslow. Decides to wait until she hears back from Patterson on the result of his interview with the man of interest in Warwick before talking to the people on her list. It's dark when she leaves the station, and she stops at the Chinese restaurant in Kaliope for a chicken chow mein.

When she opens the door of her room on the upper level of the Kaliope Motor Inn, the hot, stale air that has been trapped inside all day washes over her. When she breathes in, she tastes plastic and Mortein. She pulls out the swimsuit from her suitcase, puts it on and tucks a towel around her waist before walking barefoot down to the motel's thirty-foot pool. The floodlights that normally illuminate the pool area at night have been switched off and the gate is locked. The sign on the steel fence advises pool hours are from 8 am to 9 pm sharp. Carmel checks her wristwatch: ten-thirty. She puts her towel on the top of the fence and boosts herself up and over, then swims lap after lap in the warm oily water.

~

With Patterson out of town and given what she thinks may be his misplaced confidence that the Janet McClymont case is about to be closed, Carmel allows herself a sleep-in. She walks into Kaliope Police Station at nine-thirty the following morning.

Before she has a chance to ask if Patterson has rung, Bill Wren gives her the news. 'Turns out the car was registered but the bloke hadn't got round to changing the sticker. He and his family have been living in Warwick for the past eighteen months; he's employed at the meatworks. Being paid cash in hand. Patterson didn't even have time to get a car assigned to make the drive to Warwick.'

'The butterfly clip?'

'He really does have a daughter. There was one that matched it in her bedroom.'

It is enough to categorically eliminate him as a suspect.

Carmel doesn't bother putting down her bag. 'I'll drive out to the McClymonts'.'

Bill nods. 'Patterson said he wouldn't be coming back up north immediately. So I guess we've been left to our own devices for the next little while.'

ELEVEN

THINGS GOT STIRRED up a bit after that detective flew back to Brisbane all of a sudden. That young constable at Kaliope likes big-noting himself by blabbing stuff he should keep mum about. There was more talk and gossip, but it died down when no arrest was made.

Right from the outset, as you'd expect, there'd been plenty of theories about who was responsible for what might have happened to Janet. Like anywhere, there are a few men around the place who are a bit odd. Drinkers and loners or those who are a little simple. Not surprisingly, any of the Islander men who were anywhere within cooee of Quala or Kaliope that Saturday she disappeared were hauled into the police station for questioning. John Creadie's name was even mentioned, but that was shut down pretty quickly. John was one of the first people who turned up to help search and one of the last to stop looking. Well, he would've been, wouldn't he, given what happened to his sister?

Of course, after the police found out that red-haired teacher who sounds like a bit of a shit-stirrer had failed to mention he'd driven Janet home a couple of times, and after that kerfuffle at the Memorial Hall, he drew a bit of renewed attention. His alibi was solid, though.

There was talk about the Kable boys, too, come to think of it. The lads that live next door to the pub. They catch the same bus to school that Janet used to. The way those two talk to their mother, swearing and saying terrible things right to her face, is disgraceful. If my kids had ever spoken to me or Dot like that, they would've got their arses slapped.

Some people got hot under the collar about young Joe Cassar, who plays footy with my grandson, Grant.

It got ugly a few days after Janet disappeared when Jimmy Froome, who's a bloody fool if you ask me, took it upon himself to go out to the Cassars' place. Jimmy was half full, of course. Not that that's any excuse.

Anyway, when he turned up, Joe was out at footy practice. I'd picked him up with Grant a couple of hours earlier. Jimmy storms up their front stairs and George wouldn't let him in the house. He's half the size of Jimmy, but a hothead, that's for sure. Jimmy started going on about how everyone knew that Joe was keen on Janet, how he was a bit wild and that. All bullshit, of course. Joe's pretty fierce on the footy field, but he's a good kid otherwise.

Well, George would have gone him then and there, except Nola—George's wife—steps out onto the verandah and stares

Jimmy down. She's a bloody big sheila, but calm, you know. Works as hard as George and Joe on their farm, and they do alright. She tells Jimmy to piss off. Well, not in those words. Nola's never been one for bad language. But it got Jimmy's goat, and he starts going on about George being a wop and Nola being a Kanaka, saying that Joe's got the McClymont girl stashed away somewhere hoping he'll get her to marry him. He made some crack about Janet being no better than she should be. That's when George bangs the door open and takes a swing at Jimmy. He misses by a mile, but Jimmy steps back and falls down the bloody stairs. Like most of the houses around here, the Cassars' place is built up on stilts and Jimmy fell about ten foot.

Just as he hits the deck, I drive up with Joe and Grant. Just as well too. If we hadn't of been there, I reckon Jimmy would have tried to do George some serious damage. He likes a bit of rough stuff, and the only thing hurt in his fall down the stairs was his pride. I managed to convince Jimmy to head home. Bloody idiot.

It does make you think, though. About people. About people you think you know. That cop I mentioned who died, Bob Cronin, he reckoned it was probably someone passing through that took her—killed her, almost certainly—and that they were long gone by the time the search began in earnest. But I don't know that I believe that. Sure, this time of year, with the crush happening, there's lots of blokes, some of them odd bods, looking for work. But it could have been anyone. People can have terrible dark thoughts, and maybe that evening someone just acted upon thoughts they'd had for ages and that poor girl was in the wrong place at the wrong time.

But yeah, ugly stuff.

~

'Is this that banned book?' George Cassar holds the flimsy crimson volume between two pinched fingertips as if it is something foul he's peeled off his shoe. It doesn't look like much—barely more substantial than a pamphlet. He reads the title aloud: '*The Little Red Schoolbook.*'

Joe looks at his feet, sullen and defiant. 'Yes.'

'Where did you get it?'

'I found it.'

'Found it where?'

The boy shrugs.

'Tell me where you got it.'

'I found it lying in the grass behind the sports shed.'

'Bullshit. Have you read it?'

'Most of it.'

'Your head filled with sex and drugs now, is it?'

Joe doesn't answer. Toes the leg of the kitchen table with his grimy foot.

George waits; can't contain himself for more than a few seconds. 'Well?'

The boy murmurs something.

'What?'

'Nothing.'

'Don't give me that shit. What did you say?'

Joe sighs heavily and then, when his father takes an impatient stride towards him, says, 'It's not all about drugs and sex. There's other stuff too.'

'Like what?'

Joe utters a strangled sound, as if his throat is blocked.

'Spit it out.' George is bent forward at the hips. His son, head down, kicks at the table leg.

'For God's sake, Joe, stop destroying the bloody furniture, would you? What's in that filthy little book that could possibly be of interest to a young bloke like you?'

Joe opens his mouth, tries again, shakes his head. 'You wouldn't understand.'

The man's face contorts with the effort of restraining himself from seizing the boy's shoulders and shaking him. 'Jesus, Joe. Just answer a question like a normal person.'

Joe doubts there's anything to gain in having this debate with his father, but he resolves to have it. 'It says stuff that's true, that adults just want to control everything. I don't want to end up like you and Uncle Dan and the rest of them—doing donkey work, never questioning anything, just doing what you're told, day in and day out.'

'Donkey work?' The fury in his father's face sets Joe back several steps. 'Is that what your mother and I do? Putting food on the table for your sisters and you? Is that donkey work? You ungrateful little bastard.'

But Joe ploughs on, telling his father he wants to go to uni in Brisbane next year.

'And who's going to pay for that?' George demands.

'There are scholarships,' Joe says. 'I might be able to qualify for one.'

'No son of mine is going to live off the government tit. Bloody scholarship be damned.'

'I've already decided I don't want to work on the farm when I leave school. I want more than that.'

'Do you now? Well, mate, I'll let you into a little secret. We all do, we all want more.'

They stand facing each other, the man and the boy. The air in the kitchen is thick with their breath.

'You're playing with fire, Joe. You should know how quick things can turn.'

There is a moment of silence between them. They both understand what he's talking about.

'I was nowhere near her place that evening. You know that. The police know it too. They said so.'

'It doesn't matter. Your mother's a Kanaka.'

'Don't call her that.'

George sees that Joe has clenched his fists, continues, 'And your father's a wop. You have to be more careful than the white kids. People know you two were keen on each other.'

Joe makes a noise, an expression of disgust or despair.

'All I'm saying is, if people think you're a troublemaker, things won't be easy for you.' His father waits a beat. 'Or for the rest of your family, either. It's not just about you, Joe. Do you really want Jimmy Froome turning up here again, scaring your sisters? He may not be on his own next time.'

His son shoots him a look, tortured and resentful.

George juts out his chin. 'I'm going to nip this in the bud. I'll be talking to Ern Shaw. He should know this commie rubbish has made its way into his school.'

'Leave it, Dad, please? Mr Sullivan's alright. I don't want to get him into any trouble.' Joe realises his mistake immediately.

'Sullivan, eh? Thought you found it in the grass behind the sports shed? Did he give one to anyone else?'

'Not that I know of,' Joe says.

George swears under his breath. At least that's something. 'It's the teacher's fault. That's where the blame lies and that's where it's going to land.' George sees Joe struggling with this. 'Leave it with me, Joe. I'm handling this now.'

The muscles in Joe's jaw tighten. He holds out his hand. 'Can I have it back?'

'Not bloody likely. Now piss off.'

The boy passes his father with a whisker of space between them, clipping a chair and knocking it over. He doesn't stop to pick it up, but leaves the kitchen through the door onto the verandah, and continues down the stairs, his weight and speed shaking the house on its stilts. George is intensely aware of his son's size, his bulk; almost a man and he knows it. His display wasn't an outright physical challenge but a barely disguised taunt. *Not long, old man; not long before I'm bigger and stronger than you.*

Old bull, young bull. That's what Nola calls it when he and Joe engage in mock fights, wrestling and shoving each other, mostly in a good-natured way. But in the past six months, the stakes have been raised. Both sense the approach of a tipping point. George feels equal pride and resistance at the thought of his son besting him, but it is not within him to yield. Not in their battles of strength and not in this more nuanced, complicated struggle for Joe to become a man—not physically, but in his awareness of himself, his independence of thought and belief. It is for the son to push through to dominance, not for the father to allow himself to be vanquished.

George has almost forgotten the sorry scrap of a book that he still holds. He flicks through the pages. Stapled together on cheap paper, it looks like something a child might have designed, the headings and occasional illustrations crude even to his farmer's eyes. He runs a finger down the contents page. *How to have influence*; *How to make a complaint.* George skips over the next few entries—they look harmless enough—then, here we go: *Cheating or cooperation?*; *Demonstrations or strikes.* Bloody reds. Oh yes, here it is: *Sex*; *Masturbation*; *Orgasm.* Strike me pink, they didn't mince words. *Intercourse and petting*; *Contraception*; *Menstruation.* Well, that would have been an eye-opener for the boy. *Homosexuality*; *Abortion.* Jesus wept. Joe better hope his mother doesn't get wind of this. Then: *Drugs*; *Tea and coffee*; *Tobacco*; *Alcohol.* His eyes seek out the dangerous words: *Marijuana and hashish*; *LSD*; *Amphetamines*; *Heroin*; *Cocaine.* So a cup of tea and a few beers are on the same scale as those poisons, then. *Discrimination against girls.* Of course the women's libbers would be all over it. *Solidarity*—yep, another one for the bloody reds.

George tosses the book onto the kitchen table and rights the chair that Joe upended. Leans on it, his hands on the top rail. Little more than two months since that girl disappeared;

the whole of Quala, not to mention Kaliope, Candleford and all the little places up and down the coast still in a state of shock and outrage. And then, into the midst of this violation, the sense of things being so badly out of kilter that nothing could ever be right again, that teacher, that red-headed streak of pelican shit, has brought this filth into contact with their precious young ones.

Ern Shaw sighs inwardly as George Cassar waves the red scrap of a book in his face. He thought he'd shut that particular stable door, but perhaps the horse had already bolted. He'll just have to hear George out, allow him to let off some steam.

'Where the hell would Sullivan have got something like this?' George says, bouncing on the balls of his feet, a little bantam of a man. 'I thought this bloody thing was supposed to be banned. Everything's a bloody shambles. It's no wonder young girls are being abducted by perverts when we can't even uphold the laws of the land. If this young bloke, this school-teacher, has got his hands on this filth, who's to say he's not handing out drugs to our kids? Have you seen the stuff this book talks about? Abortion, for God's sake, bloody birth control and drugs. No wonder the boy can't keep his mind on anything, let alone his schoolwork.'

'Janet McClymont's disappearance is distracting everyone, George. Especially her schoolmates. They're bound to be disturbed and acting up.' Ern pauses. 'And I know that Joe was fonder of Janet than most. He'll be alright. He's got a good head on his shoulders, and a good heart.'

'Well, I used to think so.' George looks ready to shred the book now twisted in his hands. 'Have any other kids been given a copy?'

'Nothing has come to my attention,' Ern tells him, 'although I understand that Martin Zammit was there when Mr Sullivan gave the book to Joe.'

George's bluster deflates, his hands on his hips. 'Terrific. Well, that's that then. If Bev bloody Zammit knows about this, then the whole of bloody Quala *and* Kaliope will have heard my boy's a troublemaker and a communist and everything will be stirred up again. Jimmy Froome came looking for Joe at our bloody house, accusing him of hiding Janet somewhere. Our house, if you don't mind.'

Ern is reassuring. He'll have a quiet word with Eamonn Sullivan. Straighten him out.

'May I?' he asks, holding out his hand.

George slaps the book down onto his palm. 'You're welcome to it. I'll be glad to have the filthy thing out of the house.'

George turns to go, stops when he reaches the door of Ern's office. 'Why the hell did he single Joe out? God knows his mother and me try to keep him on the straight and narrow.'

'Joe's curious about the wider world, George. Maybe Sullivan sees that.'

George still has his hand on the doorknob, his gaze inward. 'Are you positive he didn't give it to any of the other Islander kids?'

'Leave it with me, George. I'll handle it.'

In Ern's massive hands, *The Little Red Schoolbook* looks ludicrous, a joke.

Joe had noticed Janet right back in first term when she started at Kaliope West. There was a bit of interest in her because she'd moved up from Brisbane and her mum was an artist. Janet wasn't up herself at all, though. She and his sister, Angela, were in the same school netball team and Angela liked her, said she was great. The netball team were playing Candleford High one Wednesday afternoon when there happened to be a bye in the cricket competition, so Joe and some of his mates went to barrack for them.

Angela was a terrific goal defence, dogged and not giving the Candleford goal attack—one of those blonde hard-faced bitch types that Martin and Brendon were so keen on—a look-in. Angela intercepted a pass and had the ball down in her team's goal circle before the opposition knew what had happened. At the next centre pass, the goal attack got right up in Angela's face. Joe didn't hear what she said; didn't have to. He heard similar taunts practically every time he played a game of footy. *Kanaka, darkie, coon*. Angela just kind of crumpled. The goal attack was all over her after that for the next couple of points. But Janet, who was playing wing defence, put her hand on Angela's shoulder and said something to her. Angela laughed, and after that they had the game won. He even saw Janet give the goal attack a hip and shoulder at one point. She was called on it by the umpire and given a penalty. But that look she gave of 'who, me?' Jeez, it made him laugh.

When he got to know Janet she was really nice. Not that he ever said that to anyone. Martin and Brendon would have given him all kinds of shit back then if he'd told them that was why he liked her. Not now that Janet was missing and probably dead, of course.

Janet was pretty ordinary looking, really. At least, that's what he'd thought before he got to know her a bit. But she seemed to get prettier and prettier the more time he spent with her. She had these amazing blue eyes; kind, but also they just *blazed* when she was fired up about something. And she didn't have that knowing hardness of the girls Martin and Brendon went after.

He and Janet had ended up in the same ancient history class even though she was a grade below him. Because there'd been so few Grade 11s interested in taking the subject, the school had combined the two levels. They were both pretty good students and found the Roman Empire and all that shit interesting, so Mrs Pocock allowed them to sit together in the back row and didn't complain if they talked as long as they kept it down.

They'd got together towards the end of first term. The music teacher, Mr Murphy, had been putting on a concert in the rec hall on a Friday night to raise money to buy new instruments and stuff. He'd asked Joe and a few of the other Grade 12 boys who weren't performing if they'd mind staying after school to set up a stage using rostra. They'd strung a big curtain in front of it that went the width of the hall.

Joe had offered to stay on to stage-manage the show. His parents were attending the concert anyway because one of his sisters was singing 'Day by Day' from *Godspell*. Janet and two of her friends did a medley of songs from that Carole King album. They were always singing songs from it, even just walking between classes. One of Janet's friends, Andrea Borg, played guitar. Pretty well, actually. And Janet and the other girl, Katrina Dunn, had really nice voices. Not big or anything, but clear and sweet.

As stage manager, all Joe had to do was move chairs and mike stands about mainly. When Janet and her mates came off, he helped one of the Grade 8 kids carry his electric organ onto the stage. When Joe returned to the wings, Janet was there by herself, and they both watched the kid play 'House of the Rising Sun'. He kept messing up the beginning and it took a while for him to get through the whole thing. Janet was standing close enough to Joe that he could smell her—clean and fresh like Sunlight soap. He was working up the guts to make some kind of move when he felt her hand brush his, and just really naturally their fingers entwined. His blood was thumping so loud in his ears he wondered if she could hear his heart beating. His thumb stroked hers.

There was an interval next and Joe had to do a big set-up. Martin and Brendon and a couple of their other mates who fancied themselves as musos were doing two Bee Gees songs. They were all in costumes that Martin's mum had made. Joe had to lug out a drum kit, a couple of electric guitars and a bass, as well as several amps. It took about twenty minutes, and the audience got up from their chairs to get a cup of tea and a sandwich from the supper that the P&C had put on. He saw Janet with her parents at the back of the hall, and a bit later he caught a glimpse of his mum and Barbara McClymont talking together while they waited in line to get hot water from the urn.

When the interval was over, Janet came back to watch at the side of the stage. She took his hand again and leant against him so that their shoulders were touching. Martin and Brendon's band performed 'Spicks and Specks' and 'Lonely Days'. They tried to sing the harmonies at the same time as doing a bit of fancy footwork, which all kind of fell apart. The audience didn't seem to mind and clapped along. During the second song, Janet turned her head towards him, and they kissed. A full-on pash. It was brilliant. He stroked her hair at one point and the butterfly hair slide that was holding her fringe back came off in his hand. He put it in his pocket and she didn't ask for it back.

Janet was gone when he got back after he'd moved all his mates' instruments to the rear of the stage. As the final act, the junior choir, sang 'Imagine', Joe looked out through the curtain and watched Janet sitting with her parents. They were an odd pair, Mrs McClymont with her crazy hairstyle and weird caftans and Janet's dad in his pale blue safari suit. Janet wasn't really like either of them, although she had thick, wavy brown hair like her mum.

On Monday morning when the Quala bus pulled up in front of the school, he was sitting on the fence waiting for her. She walked right up to him and he took her school bag and they walked over to assembly. At the end of the day, he walked her back to the bus. When he kissed her goodbye, he put the butterfly hair slide in her hand. Martin and Brendon gave him shit, but he didn't care; he could still taste strawberries.

They were pretty low-key at first. Janet said her friend Shelley would be cut about them being together, but it wasn't long before everyone knew. They didn't see a lot of each other outside of school. Joe lives out of town on the other side of Quala closer to Kaliope and usually rides his bike to school. It's a bit of a grunt, but it's good exercise and keeps him fit. And apart from the evening he has training and on Saturday when he plays footy, he has to help his parents on the farm in the afternoons and on weekends. Two or three times he took the old ute and drove the back roads to meet her on the track between the cane fields behind her house.

They actually talked on the Friday before the night she went missing about meeting on her way up to the Tranters' to babysit. He told her he probably wouldn't be able to make it because the crush was on and his dad was going off the deep end about all the work they had to do. There was also the family party for his uncle's birthday that he didn't think he'd be able to get out of. Janet told him not to worry. She'd leave home a bit early and if he was able to meet her it would be good, if he couldn't, it didn't matter. That was one of the things he liked about her, she was easygoing and didn't make a drama about unimportant stuff. There were no games between them.

At about five-thirty on Saturday, Joe knew there was no way he'd be able to get away. They were still pushing firebreaks through the cane when his mother came to tell them it was almost time to leave for his uncle's place.

He didn't hear that Janet was missing until Sunday morning when he and his family went to 8 am mass in Kaliope. They didn't wait for communion, leaving his two younger sisters with his uncle Dan while he, Angela and his mum and dad went to help with the search. He couldn't believe the number of people who turned out. The cops got them to join the group of searchers who were moving through the mangroves down at the inlet.

Everyone turned out again on Monday. Mr Shaw closed the school for the day, out of respect for Janet, he said, and so that the teachers and the older students could join the search. Janet going missing was all anyone could talk about. A few days later, back at school, that dickhead Brice Kable made some smart-arse comment about darkies or some shit. About the lengths some girls have to go to to let blokes know they're not interested. Brendon told Brice to shut the fuck up. Threatened to punch the shit out of him, but Ox came out of his office and told them all to get to class. Even Brice shuts his mouth when Mr Shaw tells him to.

For days it felt so unreal. Joe was numb. He kept thinking if only he'd been able to get away to see Janet that evening. And he kept expecting to find her keeping a seat for him in ancient history, or he'd turn up to meet her at the shady place beside the rec hall where they ate lunch together. Then he'd remember seeing Barbara McClymont on that Sunday when they were searching for Janet. How she looked after she found Janet's bag. Her skin almost transparent. Swaying on her feet. Her eyes wild. Then he'd know it was true, and the loss would hit him like a fist to the solar plexus.

It's still like that: an endless loop of wishing he'd been able to make it that Saturday and feeling as if he's walking through someone else's dream. His body feels like it's made of a completely different substance to everything else around him. And then suddenly, out of nowhere, the shock of Janet's disappearance hits him again. It's like getting creamed by the biggest full forward he's ever played footy against.

TWELVE

ERN SHAW SCANS the corridor above the heads of the students churning around him in a rolling boil. He catches sight of Eamonn Sullivan on his way to the staffroom for the morning break and begins wading through the throng towards him. The students part before him like the Red Sea before Moses, and he catches the moment when Eamonn sees him coming. Eamonn's shoulders bunch closer to his ears, a tortoise drawing into its shell. He knows what's coming and is expecting a bollocking.

As Ern nears Eamonn, the expression on the younger man's face transmits his internal reaction of *Oh fuck*, but he recovers quickly, smiling brightly at Ern. 'Good morning, Mr Shaw.'

'Fancy a walk around the oval, Eamonn?'

'Of course. I'll just drop these off in the staffroom,' says Eamonn, gesturing with the books he's carrying.

'No need. Margaret will take them for you, won't you?' says Ern, snaring the shoulder of one of the younger students trying to push past them. He takes the books out of Eamonn's hands. 'Just pop these in the staffroom, dear.'

He steers Eamonn through the students seething in the corridor and out the door that leads to the schoolyard. 'You know, son, we prefer our staff to confine their teaching to the subjects relating to the textbooks on the syllabus. We've had a complaint.'

'Oh?' Eamonn's voice climbs an octave.

'I'm not going to ask you how you got your hands on a copy of a book that is banned in schools, let alone what could possibly have induced you to give it to a student,' says Ern. 'But I would strongly, *strongly* . . .' he squeezes Eamonn's shoulder in emphasis, '. . . urge that you destroy any other copies you might have in your possession.'

Eamonn doesn't have time to draw breath before Ern continues. 'You're a young man, Eamonn, not much older than our senior boys and girls. I wouldn't want to tarnish the career of a young and gullible fellow such as yourself—but that first-name foolishness, and now this?'

Eamonn opens his mouth to speak, but Ern holds up a stoppering hand, drills him with a hard look. 'I trust it was only the one? But regardless . . .'

He cuts off Sullivan's response again. He doesn't want to know. 'Pull your head in, there's a good fellow.'

With a pat on the back, Ern farewells Eamonn and strides off into the melee of the schoolyard. Two eighth graders are going the thump against each other on the asphalt and Ern pauses to pull them apart before knocking their heads together and dumping the pair on the ground. He heads towards the main school building, students running before him in a mob, peeling off in twos and threes like zebra fleeing a lion.

For all their sakes, Ern hopes this will be the end of it.

~

Helen has already spotted her mother and is running down the path towards her. She tosses her port onto the back seat of the station wagon before throwing herself at Connie. Her mother braces herself for the impact as Helen flings her arms around her waist and buries her face in her stomach. Connie swoops to kiss her younger daughter's head and folds her arms around her shoulders.

Raelene waits beside Essie on the school verandah while Essie arranges her books and her lunch box in her port. As Gavan Connolly runs past them on his way to the steps down to the schoolyard, he deliberately barges into them. Raelene punches him on the arm. 'Watch it.'

He swings about to face her, his mouth loose and red. 'Hey, Raelene, what did one girl say to the other?'

She doesn't answer him, just performs an exaggerated eye roll directed at Essie and shoulders her bag.

'Lez be friends. Get it?' says Gavan.

'Yeah, I get it, Gav, you big spastic. And by the way, you're the fourth person who's told me that joke today. It wasn't that funny the first time.'

Gavan puts on a high-pitched voice, turns his attention to Essie. 'Ooh, Essie, lez be friends.' He grabs his chest at nipple level and rubs his shoulder up against hers. 'C'mon, feel me bozies.'

'Nick off, Gavan.' Essie shoves him off with both hands, grimaces at Raelene.

Danny Pine and Tim Froome jostle up against Gavan, and the three boys charge past, knocking Essie's port out of her hands. 'See ya, lezzies,' Gavan yells over his shoulder.

'They're so annoying,' Essie says, affecting weary exasperation, but Raelene smiles as she watches the boys career across the schoolyard to the fence where they left their bikes in the morning. They fling themselves onto the bike seats before pedalling madly out of the gate, narrowly missing the group of parents waiting for their children. One of the fathers barks at them to watch the bloody hell where they're going, and they cackle out an apology—'*Sorry, sorry*'—before racing each other down the hill.

'Hey.' Raelene swings around to face Essie, bathes her in the sunlight of her undivided attention. 'Ask your mum if you can walk home. Tell her I'll come with you all the way.' She links her arm through Essie's and pulls her towards the steps.

Essie chucks her port on top of Helen's and lets Raelene drag her towards the huddle of adults. Connie, with Helen still pressed against her, is listening to one of the parents who farms on the other side of Quala. The talk is of the crush. Who has begun harvesting their cane, who is yet to begin.

Raelene nudges her. 'Go on.'

Essie sidles up to her mother, Raelene close behind, her finger poking Essie's back like a magpie's beak stabbing the ground looking for worms. 'Mum?'

'Just a minute, sweetheart.'

The pokes in Essie's back harden, become painful. Raelene hisses in her ear, 'If we go now, we can catch up with Gavan and them.'

The boys have dumped their bikes on the road and are mucking around at the turn-off; Danny's *Get Smart* lunch box has become a football.

'Mum?' Essie tugs on her mother's arm. Helen frowns. Essie pinches Helen's arm and she squeals and lashes out at her, hitting Essie in the shoulder.

'Stop that, you two.' Connie attempts to peel Helen's arms from around her waist, but she resists, pressing closer to her mother. 'Go wait by the car, girls.' She succeeds in extricating herself from her younger daughter, pushes her gently away. 'Off you go, sweetie. I'll be there in a minute.'

Raelene is now pulling on the back of Essie's school uniform.

'Tell your mum me and Essie are walking home to your place,' Raelene orders Helen. 'Come on.'

Together, Essie and Raelene run down the road towards the boys. Essie glances back to see Helen glowering.

'You've busted it, ya dickheads,' Danny is saying as the girls near them. He's trying to straighten the lunch box's metal lid, but the dint isn't coming out and the catch is twisted. There's a scratch right through Agent 99's head.

'Ya big sook.' Gavan snatches the lunch box from Danny, flinging it further up the road so that it bounces on the bitumen.

Danny looks ready to cry. He aims a kick at Gavan's ankle before sprinting up the road towards the tin box. Tim and Gavan scramble after him.

Raelene is laughing, but Essie feels sorry for Danny. She remembers him telling her that his aunty who lives in Adelaide had given him the lunch box for Christmas. Tyres crunch on the gravel beside her.

'Hop in, Essie.' Her mother waves at the boys, nods at Raelene, who beams back at her.

'It's okay, Mrs Tranter,' says Raelene. 'I'm going to walk with Essie back to your place.'

'Not today, I'm afraid. Come on, Essie. You'd better be getting home too, Raelene.'

'I'm alright, Mrs Tranter, my dad doesn't mind if I walk around by myself.'

'In you get. I'm going in that direction anyway.'

But Raelene, in the bare-faced way she has of ignoring adults' orders, simply smiles, shakes her fringe out of her eyes and walks off towards the boys, swinging her port. Gavan and Tim are throwing the lunch box to each other over Danny's head in a game of piggy in the middle. At Raelene's approach, they stop their game and watch her. Danny takes advantage of the lull, snatches the lunch box from Tim's grip, clutches it to his chest and races back to his bike. Essie waves from the car as it passes Raelene, Gavan and Tim, but none of them is looking in her direction.

~

Bev Zammit is making a dress for Connie to wear to Cam's brother's wedding later in the year. When she tells the girls they will be stopping at Bev's on their way home to drop off the pattern and the material, Helen complains from the back seat.

'Don't whinge. We won't be long,' Connie says.

Bev, surprisingly, given her thick fingers and plump hands, is a talented dressmaker. Her services are in demand even among the doctors' wives in Kaliope who drive out to see her each year in the months leading up to the mayor's ball. For the wedding, Bev is making Connie a long, sleeveless shift with a round neck and a front slit that goes up above the knee. Bev is also making the wide belt that will cinch the dress in at the waist, although Connie will have to buy the buckle from the haberdashery department at Hogans' in Kaliope.

'It's a lovely shape. More a tunic than a dress. Very smart and modern.' Bev turns the Vogue sewing pattern envelope over and skims the description on the back. 'Straightforward enough. When's the wedding?'

'September,' Connie says.

'Plenty of time, then. Now, show me the material.'

Connie pulls the folded swathe of emerald-green satin out of the bag. Bev lifts up a fold, rubs it between her fingers. 'That's a perfect weight and such a gorgeous shade. I've still got your measurements from that pantsuit I made you last year.'

She waves away Connie's protestations that she's put on weight since then. 'You still have a lovely figure. I can make any adjustments at the first fitting. Now, let's have a cuppa.'

Bev puts the kettle on to boil and gives Helen and Essie glasses of orange cordial. They have brought in their school ports and take out their homework to do at the table while the women talk.

Connie asks Bev how Martin, her youngest, is doing in his final year at Kaliope West.

'He's bored,' Bev says. 'Can't wait to finish and join his older brothers at the coal port.' She fills the teapot and brings it over to the table. 'I suppose you've heard the latest about that teacher at the high school? The red-headed one who's living in the old house on the Creadies' place? Sullivan's his name.'

'I know him,' Connie says.

'Of course you do.' Bev leans in, lowers her voice. 'I'm amazed Cam didn't give him a black eye after that business in the hall with Essie and that other little miss from the pub.'

'What's he done now?' Connie shakes her head at Bev's offer of sugar, accepts milk from the jug.

Bev fills her in: the fuss around his telling the Grade 12s to call him by his first name; his attempts to distribute copies of that disgraceful banned book; encouraging the students to petition Principal Ern Shaw for representation on all school committees.

She pours tea into both their cups. 'He told them they were fodder.' Bev nods and takes a sip of tea, leaving a pink lip print on the edge of the cup. 'Oh yes,' she continues in the face of Connie's blank look. 'For the military-industrial complex or some piffle.'

Bev tells Connie how she was one of a delegation of parents who went to see Ern Shaw to complain. 'Apparently Ern knew all about it. Hadn't seen fit to let the parents know, mind. He was trying to keep it quiet to protect Sullivan.' She presses her lips together. 'At first, it appeared that young Joe Cassar was the only one who Sullivan had given a copy to.'

Cassar is a name vaguely familiar to Connie. 'You know, George and Nola,' Bev reminds her. 'She's an Islander. They live on the other side of Quala, nearer to Kaliope. Joe is their eldest. He's a mate of Martin's.' Bev offers Connie another biscuit—store-bought, Connie notices.

Bev shoots a quick look across the table at the girls, turns her face to look directly at Connie, mouths, 'He was keen on Janet McClymont. Of course, she didn't want anything to do with him.' Bev continues in a low voice that steadily rises to a near-normal volume. 'All the kids at the school knew that he was after her, but I can't imagine a girl like that—so much more sophisticated than Joe, who's a nice enough boy, don't get me wrong—would be interested in him.'

Bev takes another biscuit from the plate, dunks it in her tea. 'Anyway, Martin said something to me about this book Joe had and, well, you know me, I didn't let it go until he told me everything. It seems Sullivan told the Grade 12s that he wanted to make the school more *progressive*. Whatever that means.'

Connie waves away Bev's proffering of the teapot. 'So he's just allowed to teach whatever he likes, hand out banned books?'

'Don't worry, our delegation also raised that with Ern Shaw. There's going to be a special meeting of the P&C. Can you believe that Ern was going to let him off with just a warning? Told us there was no need for us to get hysterical. "Listen, Ern," I said, "when I get hysterical, you'll know all about it."'

Connie remembered the night at the hall, the way the red-headed teacher loomed above Essie, his hand on her shoulder.

'I mean, we're not living in Sydney.' Bev glances at Helen and Essie. 'Is it any wonder young girls are being dragged off by perverts?'

In the car on the way home, Helen, who won the battle to sit in the front seat, is telling their mother the joke that has been going around at school all day.

'I don't know,' Connie says, slowing to turn onto the main road. 'What did one girl say to the other?'

Essie interrupts, leaning over from the back seat to ask Helen if the note Mr Day sent home was in her port.

Helen throws off her sister's hand. 'Mum?' She taps her mother on the knee.

'Yes, Helen, I'm listening.' Connie waits to let a caterpillar of haul-outs piled high with billets trundle across the highway on its way to the sugar mill before she manoeuvres the car into the far lane.

Essie can't stop Helen from saying the punchline; doesn't even know, not really, why she wants to, why she feels a little bit sick. She just knows this is not a joke her mother will like.

'Lez be friends.' Helen's face is open, her lips curved upwards, her eyes intent on her mother's face.

Their mother's neck and shoulders stiffen. A slight but unmissable hardening. She keeps her eyes on the road ahead. 'Who told you that joke, Helen?'

Helen's eyes flick over her shoulder towards her sister. Essie ignores her, her face turned to the window, the cane fields filling her vision.

'Who, Helen?' their mother asks again.

'Gavan Connolly.'

'Well, I don't like jokes like that. And stop fidgeting.' Connie takes a hand off the wheel to smack Helen's hands. 'Gavan Connolly is not a very nice boy.' Their mother's voice is cool, her words crisp, cut off. 'Next time he tries to tell you a joke like that, you walk away.'

Later, when their mother kisses them goodnight and turns out their bedroom light, Helen asks Essie why the joke was funny when Gavan told it.

'You'll understand when you're older,' says Essie.

'But what does it mean?'

'Shut up, Helen. You're an idiot.'

~

At night, when the house falls silent, the girls asleep, the radio off, Cam breathing quietly beside her in the bed, Connie hears the cane. It sighs and murmurs. Even with the heaviness of the humid air it is never completely still. The slightest breeze sets it whispering as if it is plotting some nefarious act.

Since Janet's disappearance, Connie avoids lingering by the fields that surround the house. But in fact, from the time she married Cam thirteen years ago and came to live with him on the farm, the cane has made her feel uneasy, hemmed in, claustrophobic. Leery of its burgeoning growth, its thick stalks and impenetrability, the way the fields carpet the landscape in a thick green sameness, she has always had the sense of something lurking within it, hidden and malevolent.

Connie misses the cool, high air of the Granite Belt in the south-east corner of Queensland where she grew up. Its winter frosts and rare flurries of snow such a contrast to the heavy

humid air of the northern part of the central coast. The paddocks
of grapevines and apple orchards set against the massive granite
outcrops and towering angular tors of the Great Dividing Range
had formed the landscape of her childhood. She'd never appreciated how deeply it was lodged within her until she'd come to
live with Cam, had no forewarning of how she would come
to loathe the mould crawling up the walls of the house and
the smell of mildew that, in the wet, permeates the bed linen
and the mattresses; the way her cotton house dresses stick to the
skin of her back as she sweeps the floors.

Cam loves the north, its heat and humidity, and feels totally
at home in the cane. He is forever walking through it, his arms
outspread, letting the stalks spring back against his hands.
Every season, he stands on the verandah exclaiming at how
you can almost see it growing before your eyes. Driving around
the farm in the ute, he hauls on the handbrake and leaps out
of the driver's seat, a cane knife in his hand, to slash a stalk,
turgid with juice, into lengths, for him and the girls to chew
on. If he offers one to Connie, she usually refuses. She much
prefers the crisp, tart apples and sour, under-ripe grapes of her
girlhood over the excessive sweetness of sugarcane juice or the
dense, cloying taste of the mangoes that Cam so loves.

Since Janet went missing, Connie's dread of the cane has
become even more acute. How could she have disappeared so
utterly, leaving no trace but for a few scattered belongings?
The thought of Essie or Helen torn from her in such a way
makes Connie's heart pound against her ribs like a wild bird
ricocheting off the bars of a cage. Images, indistinct but vivid
and breath-snatching, of her daughters' faces, stretched and

distorted, send her scrambling to her feet or leaping up from beside Cam and running across the hall to make sure her girls are still safe in their beds.

Afterwards, hunched over the basin in the bathroom splashing cold water on her face to still her thumping heart, Connie vehemently hopes that Janet is dead. Better a swift death than ongoing tortures. Then the guilt at such a thought—surely it's a sin to wish for anyone's death?—surges thick, stinging and bitter in her throat. But the scenes of violation that spring unbidden into her brain are far worse than imagining Janet's life as already snuffed out.

Since Janet disappeared, Connie has been contemplating the nature of evil and its manifestations. She and Cam aren't regular churchgoers. Connie was raised Catholic and Cam was brought up indifferent Church of England. Occasionally, she will duck into St Margaret's in Kaliope—more frequently since Janet vanished. She and the girls also go to mass at Easter and Christmas and some of the other holy days. The girls were baptised, of course, and Essie has made her first communion, but sporadically Connie worries that she hasn't paid enough attention to her daughters' moral guidance.

Connie fears for both her children, but it is Essie whose welfare concerns her the most at the moment. Helen is still pliable; eager—even before Janet went missing—to be near her mother. She is like a fledgling, always wanting to nestle beneath her wing. Essie, older, mulish, is increasingly sullen and secretive. Impatient with Connie's attempts to draw her in, to keep her close, she is always pulling away, ducking beneath Connie's arms when she tries to embrace her.

Cam continues to maintain that whoever took Janet is, most likely, long gone. With all the attention, the police, the searching, whoever did it is probably in some distant capital city by now. Connie is not convinced he believes it himself, but she understands his decision to imagine that's the case rather than accept that there's a predator living among them. Connie thinks it's more likely that the latter scenario is the reality, and that the perpetrator could well be waiting for another opportunity to act on his dark, urgent desires. He could be a council worker, a neighbour or a teacher at the high school in Kaliope. It could even be someone they know, perhaps someone who has been in their house, eaten their food, touched their children and seen where they sleep. He could strike again in an instant. A turned back, a few minutes late for the school pick-up, and in that moment one of her girls could vanish. If that happened, Connie's life, imperfect but bearable, would be transformed into a gaping wound.

When Connie was about eight years old, her grandfather's favourite dog cornered a big male kangaroo against a fence. The roo seized the dog in its muscular, disturbingly human-like arms, leant back on its thick, sinewy tail and opened up the dog's chest with one almost casual scrape of its clawed toe. She remembers her grandfather cradling the dog, still alive, gasping, its ribs exposed, membranes throbbing with its madly beating heart. In these moments, unable to suppress her fears for her daughters, Connie knows the torment of her grandfather's dog.

THIRTEEN

BUFO MARINUS. What a top idea we all thought that was when the boffins came up with it. If cane beetles are eating the cane, let's bring in something that will eat the beetles. What a bloody cock-up. A cane toad is what they call an opportunistic feeder. It'll guzzle down almost anything it can fit in its mouth—birds' eggs, lizards, spiders, snails, frogs, even other toads. Anything, it turns out, except bloody cane beetles.

It's an ugly creature. Glands bulging on its shoulders ooze venom toxic enough to stop the heart of any animal that tries to eat it. I've seen dead snakes with a toad still wedged in their jaws, stricken before they had a chance to swallow it. I suppose you could call it an irony that a thing so first-rate at eating almost everything is so poisonous that it has no predators.

They brought it in from South America in 1935. And it must have thought, *You little beauty! Warm and wet, just the way I like it.* You know, it doesn't drink. No need. It takes in moisture through its belly skin. And it breeds like all get out. The females lay thousands of eggs in huge, jellied strings. Bloody disgusting. And when they hatch, the water's black with tadpoles. They die in droves, but plenty survive. Numbers of them are always increasing. And they're huge bloody things. Stocky like a pig-dog pup and wide as a dinner plate, some of them. You need two hands to hold the biggest of them—that's if you were so inclined to hold something so pug ugly and noxious.

And filthy! The males'll mount anything—tin cans, piles of cow manure, even other dead toads they find flattened on the road. You might think I'm cracked for saying it, but you see a cane toad and you know there's evil in the world.

Vince has been thinking about using the dowsing rods to search for Janet for weeks. It first occurred to him about a fortnight after Barbara and Ted's girl disappeared. He wonders now why the idea didn't come to him immediately, but in the shock of what had happened, and the way it brought back so vividly and with such awful force those days of freefalling through disbelief and grief after their own Cathy failed to come home, he supposes it's hardly surprising. After Barbara found the girl's bag, there was the frenzy of the search, the hundreds of people traipsing through their fields looking for any sign of Janet, the police wanting to talk to everybody and anybody about who or what they'd seen in the days leading up to that terrible evening. But now, more than a month later, Vince is still hesitating.

People are sceptical, Vince understands that. He had been, too. He still is, particularly about that star-sign poppycock that Jean insists on reading aloud to him from the newspaper. He can't fathom why they waste ink printing that rubbish. The dowsing rods are different. He has seen and felt what they can do. He can't explain it, but he can't deny it either.

Vince has been dowsing now for about five years, ever since Sal Morelli found that underground spring in the rough country up behind his house in ten minutes flat during that long dry spell. Vince was right there watching when the bit of willow Sal was holding plunged towards the ground. And then when the truck with the big auger on the tray backed up and they drilled down, well, you could have knocked Vince down with a feather when they hit water. They couldn't have gone much deeper than twenty foot before they were pumping out hundreds of gallons of the stuff every hour.

Afterwards, Sal placed the forked willow branch in Vince's hands and said, 'Put your elbows against your ribs. Now, hold the two prongs of the Y in your hands. Palms facing up. That's it. Yes, yes, your thumbs away from your body. The stem of the Y must be horizontal.' Sal made a gesture with his hand. 'Flat. Now walk, walk. Not too fast.'

And Vince felt the length of willow dip, the pull on the tip of the new wood strong enough to send it straining earthwards, and the spring of water surging beneath.

'You have the gift,' Sal told him later. 'Perhaps to divine other things, too. Me, I can only find water, but my grandmother, back in Malta, she would divine for anything—a lost button, animals that had strayed, missing children.'

Sal showed him how to select a forked willow switch—not too thin, but not too thick either. It had to be green, with sap still in it.

'Does it have to be willow?' Vince asked.

Sal shrugged. 'Willow, it likes the water; it's drawn to it. For other things . . .' He shrugged again. 'My grandmother, she would use my grandfather's fob watch, you know, on a chain? She would think on the thing she wanted to find and the watch would swing in the direction that it lay. A couple of lengths of copper will work for some.'

Vince dowses for his own interest. It's a hobby. He's never set himself up as a professional diviner like some blokes do, advising farmers where to sink bores and that sort of caper. But ever since John took over the running of the farm, Vince walks out most days with his dowsing rods. Following Sal's instructions, he made a pair for himself out of copper wire. They already have a bore on their place that gives them all the water they want, so he has precious little need to look for more. Each wire is bent into an L shape so that the longer legs are about fifteen inches long. Vince made handles for the rods by drilling a hole down the length of two pieces of dowel and threading the shorter legs of the rods through them. The ends of the rods are stopped with pieces of cork to prevent the dowel slipping off. He's pleased with them—with their weight, how the butt of each rod fits into the heel of his hand and the feel of the longer leg resting flat over his index finger.

Sometimes he trims back a branch of willow, easing the thin green bark off the length of springy wood like peeling an apple, but he prefers the rods. Generally, Vince isn't looking for anything in particular. He just likes the sensation of the earth's energy humming in his hand, the pull of a lump of metal. He once found an old crowbar that had lain forgotten, grass and weeds grown up around it so that it had remained hidden for years. Like attracting like. Jean is after him to find the cameo brooch that belonged to her mother's sister. She's sure it's in the house somewhere, but he's walked every room and hasn't felt a thing, even when he's put the photograph of Jean wearing it in his pocket.

He's only once tried to find a living thing. About six weeks before Janet went missing, Meg, their daughter-in-law, brought down Sandra, their granddaughter, to spend the morning with him and Jean. Meg was going into town—shopping, banking, whatnot. The little girl, just four years old and not yet at school, was teary, clinging to her mother, unlike her usual self. She normally liked to spend time with him and Jean in the snug.

'What's up, chicken?' He picked her up, rubbing the bristles of his chin against her cheek.

Sandra squirmed in his arms, refused to play their usual games.

'It's that puppy the Rollestons gave us a couple of days ago,' Meg said. 'It's wandered off.'

They'd chained the little dog up in the kennel the night before, but it had slipped its collar. They'd been looking for it for the last hour.

Sandra continued to whinge after her mother left, refusing to be bribed into cheerfulness with cake or the offer of playing with Gran's collection of salt and pepper shakers.

'Come on, chicken,' Vince said, taking her by the hand. He led her out to the shed where he kept his dowsing rods.

'Let's see if Pop can't find that puppy.' He showed her how to hold the rods and she followed him up the short track to the big house, where John and his family lived, and around the back to the pup's kennel.

'Don't drag them in the dirt, chicken.' He took the rods from her. 'Now, what's your doggy's name?'

Her lips trembled.

'Enough of that. You help Pop find your pup. What's his name?'

'Patch,' said Sandra, still sulky, as she watched Vince hold the tips of the rods over the kennel.

'Ah, that's right,' said Vince. He hadn't been up to the big house to see the new pup, but he remembered now that John had said the little dog was a fluffy black mongrel with lopsided ears that they'd named for the splash of white on its nose.

Vince closed his eyes and tried to conjure up an image of the pup, but his mind only obliged with generic canine forms. He felt Sandra's weight against his boots. She'd plopped herself down on the ground beside him and was singing a whispery refrain of invented words.

He opened his eyes to see that she was playing with a cluster of bones the pup had chewed. 'Give me one of those, would you, chicken?'

Putting one of the bones in his pocket, he closed his eyes again, and it was like the pup literally leapt into his head, he could see it so clearly. Then, with the lightest twitch on the index finger of his right hand, he felt it come again, and took a step towards the almost imperceptible pull, but the rods fell inert almost immediately. Vince refocused. Tried to visualise Patch again as John had described him. Just the slightest pressure, very faint, but unmistakable. He took another few steps. Stopped. Felt it again, the copper wire drawing ever so subtly on the inward curl of his fingers. Then nothing. Again, Vince stopped, resummoned up the image of the little black dog.

The rods quivered very slightly, setting Vince on a path towards the abandoned chook run. The rods were suddenly heavy in his hands, their tips crossed and dragging. Then he heard it. A whimper. He followed the sound, and when he pulled aside a sheet of corrugated iron that had fallen against the fence surrounding the run, he saw a fluffy black rump and the pup's head and shoulders wedged in the chicken wire.

He was about to call to his granddaughter, but the way the little dog was lying, limp and very still, made him choke her name down. He looked over his shoulder and saw that Sandra was still playing in the dirt. Dropping the rods, he crouched down and put his hand on the puppy's flank and was rewarded by another whimper and a feeble thump of its tail.

Vince became aware of a stench. Looking through the chicken-wire fence, he saw that the decaying body of a cat had been tossed into the chook run. John had mentioned there'd been a couple of stray toms hanging about the place and he'd managed to shoot one of them. The pup, trying to reach the reeking corpse, must have worried its head and shoulders through a hole in the chicken wire and become stuck. When it'd tried to pull its head out, the strands of wire had folded back, hooking into the pup's fur. When it continued to struggle, the sharper ends burrowed into the flesh of its neck. Blood clotted its fur. Carefully, Vince freed the pup, easing the points of metal out of its soft flesh. He picked it up, cradling it against his chest, and felt a rush of relief when it licked his chin. He gathered up his dowsing rods with his free hand and walked back to his granddaughter.

'Hey, chicken, look who Pop found.'

⁓

If truth be told, Vince does know why he hasn't taken his dowsing rods down from their hooks in the shed. Twenty-four hours after their daughter Cathy went swimming and didn't come home, a woman called Rosemary Hewitt had rung them. Just found their number in the White Pages, he supposed. The story of Cathy going missing off the rocks had been on the news all over Australia. Jean had picked up the phone before it completed its first ring, desperate that it be good news. Rosemary Hewitt told Jean that she was a clairvoyant and that she was prepared to come to Quala and cast for Cathy's where-abouts. The only thing was, Rosemary lived in Katoomba in the Blue Mountains; she would need money to fly to Kaliope and to cover her accommodation expenses, she said. If Jean would send a cheque, she'd be on the next plane.

When Jean turned towards him, waiting beside her, trembling, and told him in a cluster of stumbling sentences what Rosemary Hewitt was offering and asking for, rage spewed out of him. He tore the phone out of Jean's hand and poured vile language and abuse into the handset before slamming it back into the cradle. That's why Vince hesitates. He didn't know then what he knows now, that there are people who are attuned to things that others aren't, and there are mysteries in the world that can't be explained. But he knows, too, that most people are hostile towards and contemptuous of things they don't understand, as he had been. If he knew how to contact her, he would ring and apologise to Rosemary Hewitt.

Vince remembers what Sal told him about his grandmother's divining ability. *She could find anything, a lost button, animals that strayed, missing children.* How can he not try?

In the small room next to the kitchen that he and Jean use as an office, he searches through the newspapers they keep stacked in a pile. He finds the one he wants from a month or so earlier and tucks it under his arm. Before he leaves, he places the tip of his finger on the glass covering the framed photo of Cathy on his desk.

'Hello, little Cat,' he murmurs.

Vince and Jean had known that Cathy had a boyfriend. Had met him, in fact. Eric. A nice boy, but a bit wild. Like Cat, actually. She'd been a bit too wild, but so full of life. And cheek. He smiles, rueful. 'You gave us some trouble, Cat.'

At the burn of tears, he rubs his face roughly and shakes his head. Cathy had drowned at Danger Point when she was the same age as Janet McClymont, just sixteen. At least, drowning had seemed the most likely explanation, but she'd been so badly cut up by the rocks and then the mangroves that it was impossible to really tell what the cause of her death had been.

No one saw her jump off the rocks that last time, though Cathy and Eric and a few of their school friends had all been doing it earlier. But it had been getting late in the afternoon and a few of the young folk were getting ready to leave. There was talk of a party. Eric had gone to his car to get something or other.

In the clearing where they'd parked their cars, a couple of other vehicles had turned up. The Point was a popular spot with weekend fishermen, and some blokes were getting ready to throw in a line. People were coming and going. When Eric got back to the rocks where they'd all been swimming and mucking about, no one was there. He called out and looked around and had just about convinced himself that Cathy must have left with the others when he saw her clothes and shoes where she'd left them.

Eric jumped into the water there and then to look for her, but the swell was picking up and he got into all sorts of strife. Just like Cathy did, Vince supposes. It was a good thing for him that those fishermen found him and called an ambulance. He could have bled to death, his legs were so badly gashed. They were too late to save Cathy, though. She'd disappeared well and truly by then. It was another two days before they found her.

Vince and Jean went to see her at the hospital. She was so shockingly limp and pale. And lying so cold and still. Vince tried to chafe her hands to warm her up, while Jean stood on the far side of the room with John, who held his mother as she wept.

John was beset by guilt. Cathy had asked him if he wanted to go swimming with them that day, but John, always steady, said no. There was work to do on the farm.

It turned out Cat had been pregnant when she died. The doctor at the hospital told them. Vince wishes sometimes that the doctor had kept it to herself. Not because knowing that Cathy had been pregnant when she died makes him love his daughter less, it's just that he imagines she would have been worried, fretting about telling them. She was almost four months gone when she died. She must have known.

Cathy has been dead almost ten years, but Vince can still recall the way she would run into the kitchen, having raced up the track after the school bus dropped her off on the highway. She would fling her port on the lino and throw herself into a chair beside him at the kitchen table. 'Pour us a cuppa, would you, Dad? I'm gasping.'

Her exaggerated show of thirst never failed to raise a laugh from him.

'You spoil that girl,' Jean would tell him. 'She's running rings around us.'

And it was true. But she was his Cat.

⌒

After washing up the lunch dishes, Vince takes the keys to the ute off the dresser. He looks around the corner of the bedroom door. Jean is lying down, listening to the radio.

'You alright, love?'

'Just a bit of a headache. I've taken a Bex. Where are you off to?'

'Heading up to see Sal. Won't be long.'

Over a thimbleful of grappa, Vince steers the conversation back to Sal's nanna. It isn't difficult. The old Maltese loves nothing better than to talk about the village he came from.

'Oh yes. I remember once, a village nearby, a young boy, two or three years old maybe, wandered off late one afternoon. It was December, just before Christmas, not terribly cold, but wet. Much wetter than normal. Everyone from all around out looking for him from dusk to dawn. Nothing. Fallen off a cliff onto the rocks below. The sea taken the body away. Had to be. Still, they came to see my nanna. They bring a toy belonging to the child with them, a little wooden horse. He played with it all the time. And a photo, taken at his christening.

'I was just a boy myself, but I remember when Nanna held Nannu's watch over the photo, it spun like crazy. "This boy isn't dead," she said. She knew the boy's village a little and when they described the house—the roof like this, the colour of the walls like that—she told them which direction and how far he had gone. They found him, curled up with a bitch and her newborn pups in a neighbour's barn.

'Another time, an idiot girl, almost a woman. She had wandered off while the rest of the family were picking olives. They had no photo, but my nanna knew the family well. She asked for them to bring the girl's headscarf. She held it to her eyes, thinking very hard of the girl. Then she held the watch over the scarf. The watch was still, no movement. "Your daughter is dead," she told the mother. It was true. They found her, drowned in the well.'

Vince probes Sal about how his grandmother had divined the direction and distance to the child found alive.

Sal raises his shoulders, spreads his hands. 'It is the diviner who decides. Ask for the information in the way you will recognise—how the rods move. The power is in the diviner, not in the rods or the watch.'

Sal looks at him through narrowed eyes, taps the newspaper Vince has placed on the table. 'Be careful, Vince. Don't expect to be thanked for what you want to do.'

Vince performs a version of Sal's shrug.

'My nanna would say any gift is also a burden. Finding a lost ring, no one will complain, but other things . . .' Sal swirls the liquid around in the small glass in his hand. 'You should know this better than most, my friend.'

Vince tips the last of the grappa onto his tongue. 'Thanks, old mate.'

He can feel Sal's eyes on his back as he walks towards his ute.

~

'How much of that rotgut of Sal's did you drink?' Jean has put the kettle on at the sound of his feet on the steps.

'I'm alright. Two fingers, no more.'

'You look a bit dozy. Why don't you lie down for a bit?'

'Can't a man have a bloody drink without being accused of being a pisshead?'

Jean cups his face with her hand. 'Steady on, love.'

'Sorry, darl.' He pats her fingers.

'Cup of tea?'

'Maybe later.' He tosses the keys to the ute on the dresser inside the front door and heads out to the shed.

FOURTEEN

JUST OFF THE highway, next to the cane field where Janet McClymont's things were found, is the stump of a big old swamp box that Vince cut down about fifteen years ago. He pulls the ute in beside it, avoiding the ditch in front of it that drains a culvert running beneath the tarmac. He climbs out of the ute, taking the newspaper he found in the office, which he lays on the flat, wide surface of the stump. The remnant of the tree remains a thing of heft.

From the front page, Janet McClymont looks up at him, her hair about her shoulders, her fringe held off her face by a hair slide in the shape of a butterfly. She's a plain little thing, Vince thinks, not like his Cathy, but a sweet face, nonetheless. Wide open. He'd noticed at the McClymonts' party that she had the bluest eyes. Like his Cathy, she was loved enormously. Barbara and Ted looked after her, anyone could see that. More than looked after her—nurtured, delighted in and protected her. Not one bad thing had ever happened to Janet. Not until that day she was taken.

Despite being petite, Janet seemed an independent girl. She was quick to give her opinion on a variety of subjects at a barbecue at the Tranters', contributing to the adults' conversation.

Barbara encouraged that. 'The world is changing, Vince,' she said. 'For women particularly, in work, in politics, in art. Just you wait. We'll be calling the shots soon. You men are going to have to get used to it. Move aside, make room for us.'

Jokingly, she elbowed him in the ribs to get at the plate of chops Cam had just put down on the table.

'Not in bloody harem pants and headbands, you won't,' Vince said, giving as good as he got.

They tussled with tongs over a sausage, laughing. It seems like bloody years ago.

It had been bad to lose Cathy, worse than anything Vince could have imagined. But at least he and Jean were spared the uncertainty of not knowing whether she was dead or alive. Their grief was given limits, in a way, contained within Cathy's body, which they were able to embrace and spend time with. They held her hands, torn up as they were, and stroked her dear face, even scratched and scraped as it was, the lips blue, all colour leached from her skin.

It was a reconciliation, of sorts, with Cathy's passing. But if she'd just vanished, he doesn't know how he would have contained his grief. He would have lost himself in it. And while their pain was terrible, he pities the McClymonts more than he ever pitied himself or Jean in the wake of Cathy's death. Vince doesn't dwell on the likely torments inflicted on Janet. He saw some shocking acts of lust and violence in the war, a few of them committed by men he'd considered mates. How the McClymonts must be suffering, imagining all the things that might have befallen their daughter. Their anguish must be crushing.

Perhaps he could help them. Sal had told him that he had the gift.

When Vince first holds his divining rods over Janet's photo, he doesn't know what to expect. If her body is lying somewhere close by, perhaps the rods will guide him in the direction of where it rests.

But it isn't like that. It is astonishing. He feels a jolt so strong, like an electric shock through the rods, that he involuntarily lets them drop from his hands.

Perhaps Janet isn't dead after all.

He picks up the rods again, holds them over her photograph. The rods swing to the south and a vision, like an aerial photograph, springs into his head. A cluster of tall buildings, and a wide brown river looped around it. Extending out from the skyscrapers, tens of thousands of houses sprawl out towards low hills in the west and to the coast. Brisbane.

～

When Vince tells Jean what he believes—that the rods have shown him that Janet is alive and in Brisbane—she doesn't look overjoyed but dismayed.

'I'm going to have to tell the police,' he says.

Jean pales. 'Oh, Vince. Please. Don't.' She puts her hand on his arm and he can feel her trembling.

He covers her hand with his. 'Remember when we flew down to see your sister, Merle, when she was in hospital?' he asks her. 'When we thought she was going to die?' Vince looked out the window of the plane as it swung around to begin its descent. What the rods have shown him is the same view.

'Vince. Listen.' Jean takes both his hands in hers, her mouth stiff with misgiving. 'Janet's things were strewn all over the ground. Something unspeakable happened to that dear girl. She didn't just run away to Brisbane.'

'They haven't found a body,' he reminds her.

'Please, Vince, don't say anything to Barbara and Ted,' Jean begs. And when Vince looks like he is about to argue, she says, 'You know what it was like when they couldn't find Cathy right away and Chester Connolly told us a friend of his had seen her at the Commercial Hotel in Kaliope. You remember what that did to us. How mad it sent us. And then that woman with her clairvoyant silliness on the phone.'

Vince nods, pats Jean on the arm and walks off in the direction of the office without saying anything further. Jean follows, knowing he is fobbing her off, first pleading with him and then demanding angrily that he listen to her. Finally, she rings John and asks him to come down from the big house to talk some sense into his father.

Vince pretends to listen to his son, doesn't contradict John when he says people will think he is a stupid old man. Vince knows that he won't be able to live with himself if he doesn't say something about what the rods have shown him.

The next morning, without telling Jean what he is up to, Vince backs the ute out of the shed. On the seat beside him are his divining rods and the newspaper with Janet's photo in it. He drives into Kaliope, parks, and sits in his vehicle outside the police station for twenty minutes until Bill Wren comes out and asks him what's going on.

'I'd better come in and talk to one of those detectives from down south,' Vince says, then follows Bill into the station.

Vince didn't go to the meeting at the Memorial Hall in Quala, though John has told him about the hoo-ha when their tenant Eamonn Sullivan managed in his gormless way to get himself into strife. Not that he thinks for a minute that Eamonn would have been doing anything untoward with Connie and Cam's girl, their Essie.

John spoke to Eamonn about it when he got home from the meeting later that night. The lad was embarrassed; he could see what it looked like from the outside.

John has mentioned the lady copper up from Brisbane, but still, Vince is surprised when Bill leaves him with the policewoman.

'The detective . . . ?' Vince isn't sure why he'd be more comfortable talking to a man, but there it is.

'Detective Sergeant Patterson is attending to something in Brisbane,' she says. 'It's not clear when he'll be back. Perhaps I can help you?'

Senior Constable Carmel Maitland is a mannish-looking woman to Vince's eye. Bugger-all makeup and in one of those pantsuits that hide her female shape. She looks strong too, with broad shoulders and sinewy forearms.

Vince judges that there's no use beating about the bush with her and launches into the monologue he's been rehearsing on the drive and in the carpark—about what he's discovered and how. He's come prepared to demonstrate. The newspaper with the photo of Janet is in his pocket, his dowsing rods under one arm.

He wasn't sure what to expect from this lady copper, but the fury in her face and the filthy words she comes out with set him back on his heels.

'I've witnessed this before, Mr Creadie. Someone suffers the worst of tragedies, and rather than compassion and kindness, shysters and fucking scum—excuse the language—crawl out of the woodwork to deepen their misery. I understand that your families are friendly, Mr Creadie, and I can't imagine why you would want to torture the McClymonts in this way. I would advise you in the strongest possible terms to refrain from saying anything of what you've told me to the McClymonts. And if I hear that you have . . .' Carmel Maitland takes a deep breath, 'I will personally see to it that you regret it.'

Vince has never been spoken to like this by a woman before, has never been so humiliated. The conversation has occurred behind closed doors, but from the looks Bill Wren and the young copper give him as he leaves the station, Vince has no doubt they heard everything. Maitland's bollocking of him will be all around the district by sunset for sure. Jean will be embarrassed by him. His own bloody wife. The worst of it is the insinuation that he would knowingly attempt to deepen the McClymonts' pain in any way.

Vince hates bad language. It cheapens the one who uses it more than the person it is directed against, in his opinion. Even so, he can't help himself. *That bloody bitch*, he thinks.

When he gets home, he takes the rods and Janet's picture out of the ute. There, in the shed, he holds the rods over her image. The pulse of energy is less intense this time, but still a strong sign that she is alive. Back in the house, he cuts the girl's photo out of the newspaper, folds it and tucks it into his wallet. Whenever he brings his finger to it, he sees the sweeping brown loops of the Brisbane River.

~

Bill Wren leans on the doorframe. He doesn't look directly at Carmel sitting at the desk that Patterson had been using, but rather seems occupied with scraping a tattered piece of sticky tape off the door's glass panel.

'What?' Carmel crosses her arms, waits for it. Bill Wren doesn't say much, but when he does, she's found, it's usually worth listening to.

'You should go easy on Vince Creadie.'

'That *was* me going easy, if you hadn't noticed.'

Bill continues to scratch at the tape with his thumbnail.

'C'mon, Bill. Divining rods? Janet McClymont alive and well and residing in Brisbane? Give me a break.'

Bill has succeeded in removing the last of the tape and its sticky residue from the glass. He rolls it between his thumb and forefinger. 'About ten years ago, Vince and his wife Jean lost their daughter Cathy. Same age as Janet McClymont.'

Carmel leans her elbows on the desk, bites the right index finger of her clasped hands. 'Now you tell me. What happened to her?'

Bill recounts the story: the teenagers swimming and jumping off the rocks at Danger Point, people coming and going at the end of the day, confusion about who was where. 'The boyfriend, Eric Shields, was left by himself, looking for her in the water.'

'She drowned?'

'Seems that way.'

Carmel rests her chin on her hands. 'I'm hearing a tone, Bill. *Seems that way?*'

'Her body wasn't found for several days. And when it was, it was up in the mangroves, further up the coast, miles from where the kids were swimming. Look, the swell had got up and the tides were pretty high, but it was unusual. And her body had been knocked around a fair bit.'

'You'd expect that, though, wouldn't you? Rocks, mangrove roots, a couple of days in the water?'

'Sure. But it was her hands.'

'Defensive wounds?'

Bill shrugs: possibly.

'But she definitely drowned? They found water in her lungs?'

'Yep.' He flicks the ball of sticky tape into the bin at his feet.

'Come on, Bill, this is like pulling teeth. What else?'

'Her bikini bottoms.'

Carmel closes her eyes. 'Don't tell me.'

'They were missing.'

She opens them. 'Tell me everything.'

'There's not a whole lot more to tell,' Bill says.

'What about the boyfriend? Where's he these days? Could he have raped her and then drowned her to keep her quiet?'

'Eric and his family moved to Cairns soon afterwards,' Bill says. 'He's still there as far as I'm aware.'

As to Carmel's other question, Bill tells her that apart from the missing bikini bottoms, which could have come off due to the time the body was in rough water and being scraped against rocks and mangrove roots, there was nothing to indicate she'd been interfered with. 'If Eric did harm her, he almost got himself killed in the process.'

Bill pauses in his account, places his fists on his hips, looks at the floor. 'There was evidence that Eric and Cathy had known each other in the biblical sense for some time previous,' he says finally.

Carmel guffaws before she can help herself. 'Is that what you call it around here? Knowing someone in the biblical sense?'

Bill reddens. 'It was ten years ago. Cathy was only just sixteen. Jean and Vince didn't know she was pregnant until the doctors told them after the autopsy. It didn't get out either. People were more discreet then. Now, anything goes.'

'I'm sorry. I didn't mean to be disrespectful,' Carmel says, then waits for Bill to give an indication that she is forgiven. 'What about the others who were there?'

'There were two other girls besides Cathy Creadie,' Bill says. 'Both have married and left the district. Of the three other schoolmates of Eric's, one died in a car accident the following year, another now works in the mines in Mount Isa, and the third studied engineering in Brisbane when he finished school. He still lives there.'

'And that's the lot?'

'Things got a bit more complicated later in the day. Several vehicles turned up, a few blokes looking to do some fishing off the rocks.' Bill fills in some names.

'So, Chester Connolly was there?'

'At some point.'

'And Jimmy and Frank Froome?'

'The three of them used to hare around on the weekends together, leaving their wives alone with the tots.' He looks at her over his glasses. 'You'd know about blokes like that. Reckon they work hard all week bringing in the money so they're entitled to a bit of fun on the weekend, which in their case meant going on the piss and chasing after girls they should have stayed well away from. Even if they weren't married.'

Carmel returns his gaze. 'Do you mean underage girls?'

Bill has found another errant piece of sticky tape to attack. 'I do.'

'So, they were involved in this "confusion" at the end of the day?'

'Yep. People were organising lifts home, blokes debating whether to stay and throw in a line or try somewhere else, eskies were opened, beers came out. In the end, the blokes who turned up late with their fishing lines didn't stay long. It was looking a bit rough and they decided to try somewhere else.'

'What was the official finding into Cathy's death?'

'That she drowned after jumping into the ocean off the rocks at Danger Point and that there were no suspicious circumstances. The coroner praised Eric for his bravery.'

Carmel knows that in the wake of Janet's disappearance, Chester Connolly and the Froome brothers were interviewed along with every other man in and around Quala and beyond. All three were able to account for themselves that evening, but she goes over their stories again with Bill anyway.

'Back to the night Janet went missing . . .' she says. 'The Froomes were able to show they were with their families, and Chester's wife, Gloria, also confirmed he was home with her, and there were no reports of vehicles matching the family Valiant or his farm ute anywhere near that bit of the highway.'

Bill nods.

'Do you think Gloria Connolly or the Froome wives would lie to protect their men?' Carmel asks.

'It wasn't only Diane and Mavis who vouched for Jimmy and Frank. There were other women there.'

'What about Gloria?'

'She does go to bed early and sleeps heavy, Gloria does,' Bill says.

Carmel waits.

'She's got the same doctor as my missus. He's very quick to hand out tranquillisers to ladies who "lack interest"—I think they say on the ads on TV.'

'Are you saying there might be a connection between Cathy Creadie's death and Janet McClymont's disappearance?'

'I'm saying, don't be too harsh on Vince.'

Carmel thinks back to the meeting at the Quala Memorial Hall and the grinning face of Kenny Connolly. 'Where was Chester's son Kenny the night Janet went missing?'

'Out west of Bowen working on a construction job,' Bill says. 'He'd been out there the whole week.'

'He didn't come home for the weekend?'

'Apparently not. There was a B and S ball on in Bowen that weekend. Kenny and most of the other young blokes he works with stayed out there for that.'

'B and S?'

'Bachelors and spinsters.'

Carmel considers asking what exactly constitutes a B and S ball, but thinks better of it. 'Never mind.' Then as Bill turns to go: 'We're sure Kenny was in Bowen all weekend, that he went to this B and S ball?'

'As sure as we can be.'

'What do you mean by that?'

'Have you ever been to a B and S ball?'

Carmel hopes her expression conveys the utter unlikelihood of such an event.

Bill acknowledges the redundancy of the question with a tilt of his head. 'Well, hundreds of people come from hundreds of miles away to attend, the booze is free-flowing and the drinking goes on all night. There are plenty of sore heads in the morning and people sleeping it off in swags, in the backs of utes or rolled up in tarps under a tree somewhere.'

'And your point, Bill?'

'My point is that even though Kenny said he was there at a certain time, and his mates said he was there, most of them would have been well and truly shit-faced and absolutely unreliable as to what time Kenny turned up or how long he was there.'

'How far is Bowen from Quala?'

'About a two-hour drive if you're caning it, which young Connolly is in the habit of doing.'

Carmel is aware that her pulse rate has increased and that she has risen from her chair.

Bill raises a cautioning hand. 'Before you get too excited, Kenny didn't have his motorbike with him. There was a problem with the throttle cable and he'd left it with a mechanic in Kaliope to sort out. He got a lift down to Bowen with his boss. Chester picked up the bike for him when it was fixed.'

'He could have borrowed a vehicle. Made it to Quala and back to the ball in the timeframe of Janet's disappearance.'

'Look, young Connolly's a chip off the old block, and not in a good way, but there's nothing to connect him to that young girl going missing. I shouldn't have brought it up,' Bill says, before turning to leave a second time.

'Wait—did you tell Patterson about Cathy Creadie?' Carmel asks.

'He wasn't that interested. Reckoned it was too long ago to be relevant.'

'And what do you reckon?'

'I reckon I'm getting too old for all this.' Bill taps the doorframe, signing off on the conversation.

～

Ern is not entirely surprised that the uproar regarding Eamonn Sullivan hasn't gone away. He'd hoped to arrest any further fallout from the whole *Little Red Schoolbook* palaver. But when Bev Zammit and her posse turned up in his office, any chance of dealing with the matter on the quiet evaporated. If not for the upset around poor little Janet McClymont's disappearance, it probably wouldn't have caused such a kerfuffle.

Ern doesn't want to sack Eamonn. It's hard to attract half-decent teachers to Kaliope West, and personally he doesn't give a tinker's cuss about *The Little Red Schoolbook*. A lot of fuss and nonsense about a pretty flimsy piece of propaganda. The greater the furore around it, the more attention it gets. Banning the thing was an overreach, in his opinion. Politicians should have ignored it. Their carrying on had merely succeeded in promoting and legitimising it in the eyes of young shit-stirrers. And now these parents want an example to be made of scrawny Eamonn Sullivan.

He understands that everyone is raw and on edge with anxiety over Janet's disappearance. If it was up to him, he'd corral all the girls in his care, coltish and lumpish both, to keep them safe.

Ern Shaw is not one of those men who make a habit of putting an arm around a nubile girl and giving her a squeeze. He does not secretly lust after his female students. He views their gangly, ripening bodies with protective and fatherly concern. He regards even the most deliberately provocative or heedless of the girls in his charge as children to nurture. But now—and this fills him with murderous fury towards the bastard who took Janet McClymont, a girl under *his* care—he can't look at his female students without seeing their bodies as poorly defended opportunities for defilement.

Previously, he was immune to their lithe softness seething in their uniforms; their rosy lips, pert breasts and plump buttocks. Unmoved by their experiments in flaunting their allure. Now he is contaminated, and it fills him with a raging grief. They are all besmirched; the girls—by their bodies that swell and soften for all to see, and the men who cannot help but desire them, whose minds are filled with images of rutting, whose impulses won't be denied until blood and broken flesh lie beneath them.

Ern adjusts the knot of his tie so that it lies against the knob of his Adam's apple. He straightens his socks, easing the elastic garters that sit a little too snugly beneath his knees, rubs the red marks left on his skin. He disgusts himself.

~

Ern catches up with Eamonn in the carpark as he's about to climb into his Hillman Hunter. The younger man always looks bedraggled: the back of his shirt damp with sweat, his long red hair a tangled mess, his tie slightly askew. Though he's not a bad teacher, he'd do well to cultivate some gravitas if he wants to put a stop to the more rambunctious of his Grade 12 students giving him shit. He should also stick to the bloody curriculum and keep his political opinions to himself if he wants to progress his career in the Education Department.

'It's not good news, I'm afraid,' says Ern, placing a large hand on the corner of the open door of Eamonn's car. 'I had hoped we could keep this business of your Danish friends' propaganda between us. You didn't tell me that Martin Zammit was there when you gave Joe Cassar the banned book.'

Eamonn tosses his hippy-looking satchel onto the passenger seat. Ern wants to tell him to get himself a decent bloody
briefcase, but resolves to leave that discussion for another time.
When Eamonn swings back around, the younger man's face
is glum. The droop of his moustache mirrors the downturn
of his mouth.

'Martin had left by the time I gave the book to Joe,' Eamonn
explains. 'They're friends, so I guess Joe probably told him
about it.'

'Ah well, it scarcely matters now,' Ern says, folding his arms
across his chest. 'A special meeting has been called by the P&C
Association to discuss the incident. If you want my advice,
don't concern yourself so much with mounting a defence as
preparing to plead for forgiveness. That's if you want to keep
your job.' Ern allows himself a flare of irritation. 'For heaven's
sake, Eamonn, it isn't two months since Janet McClymont went
missing. Parents and everyone else from Cairns to Brisbane are
on the lookout for perverts. What were you thinking?'

Eamonn stares at the ground, his head thrust forward, brings
his shoulders to his ears.

Ern's outburst has restored his usual ursine equability. 'Be
prepared to grovel, young fellow.'

He claps Eamonn on the shoulder, sending him stumbling
into his open car door, before wheeling back towards his office.
Two Grade 9 boys run past him. Ern grabs both of their shirt
collars, hauling them to a standstill before propelling them
towards a cluster of bins. 'Put that excess energy to good use
and pick up that rubbish I can see against the fence.'

Jean is up at the big house with Meg and Sandra when there's a knock at the front door of the snug. Vince isn't that keen on seeing anyone. No doubt the story has got around about him going to the cop shop. He's still smarting from the way that policewoman spoke to him. He even got a call from the local rag wanting him to come in and demonstrate his 'powers'. Vince caught the insolence in the young reporter's tone and shut the conversation down straight away. He isn't going to expose himself to any further humiliation.

He wonders who told the press. Not Bill Wren, surely. The policewoman? He wouldn't put it past her. Although there was that other young constable there too. Vince doesn't know his name, but the boy gave him a bit of a smirk when the policewoman showed him out.

Whoever is at the front door knocks again. When Vince pokes his head out of the kitchen door, Eamonn Sullivan is standing there. They're a pair, him and Eamonn. Both have caught a spray from that lady copper.

Eamonn gives him a wave from behind the flyscreen door. 'Just the rent, Mr Creadie.' He holds out a handful of notes.

'I suppose it's all over Kaliope.' Vince opens the door, takes the proffered cash, folds it and slips it into the breast pocket of his shirt. 'About the silly old bugger and his dowsing rods.'

The young man shrugs, pushes his hands into the pockets of his dress shorts. 'If you thought you knew something that was relevant, I reckon you probably had to tell the police. It's what they keep saying, isn't it? Any bit of information, no matter how small, could be the thing that helps them find out what happened to her.'

Vince meets his eyes for the first time. 'Yeah. Well, thanks, young fella. How did you hear about it?'

Eamonn demurs, but when Vince presses him he relates in more detail than Vince really wants to know how Allan the PE teacher asked Eamonn, 'What the bloody hell was old Creadie thinking?' And how when Eamonn failed to answer, Allan said that in his humble opinion, dowsing, divining, whatever you wanted to call it, was bullshit. Never mind that if Janet McClymont was alive, if she'd just nicked off, why had she left her wallet and her handbag lying on the ground? It didn't make sense, according to Allan. 'And she never took any of her clothes, neither. You should tell him to pull his bloody head in.'

'Allan's neighbour's a police constable,' Eamonn says. 'He was at the station when you were there talking to that policewoman.'

'Well, that's all very informative.' Vince wishes wholeheartedly that he'd never asked. 'Sounds like we'd both better keep our heads down.'

FIFTEEN

'HELLOOO!' ESSIE'S MOTHER calls through the Creadies' open front door. She has a cake tin under her arm with a bandaid stuck to its lid. *Creadie* is written on it in blue biro ink.

At old Mrs Creadie's answering greeting, Essie and Helen follow their mother into the snug's kitchen.

'I found this among my baking things.' Connie places the cake tin on the sideboard. 'I must have picked it up by mistake when they took down the canteen tent after the search was called off.'

At her mention of the search, even without saying Janet's name, something cold slips into the room. The four of them are caught fast, like insects in a flytrap. Then Mrs Creadie stirs herself and takes the kettle off the stove to fill it with water. She makes a playful grab for Helen, who is clinging to her mother's leg. Perhaps Essie could go and find Vince. 'He's outside somewhere, probably in the shed. Tell him to come inside for a cup of tea and a biscuit.'

Mrs Creadie waves away Connie's protests that she was just meaning to drop the tin off. 'Sit down, sit down. I've got some gingerbread that I know this one likes,' she says, gently pulling on Helen's pigtail.

Essie dutifully heads out of the kitchen, but before she reaches the verandah, she hears her mother ask, 'So, how is he?'

Essie pauses, waits to hear Mrs Creadie's response.

'Still a bit down in the mouth,' she says softly and then, more loudly, 'Now, Helen, fruit cup or lime cordial?'

In the snug's backyard, Essie stops to stroke a little dog with a white splash on its nose that is tied up under the clothesline. She scratches his soft ears, and when her fingers slip down to knuckle his neck, they find several areas of hard, raised skin beneath his fur, like scars. When she straightens up, she looks towards the machinery shed on the track between the snug and the big house. She can't see Mr Creadie. Essie tosses up whether to simply yell out his name as loud as she can. Then, imagining how her mother will scold her for rudeness, she decides to meander up the track.

The machinery shed, enclosed on three sides, is huge and dim. The air inside smells of grease and dust, and apart from the harvester, the tractor, the Creadies' ute and the tools on the shadow board above the long workbench, it appears empty. It is not until she is well inside that she sees Mr Creadie sitting in the driver's seat of the ute parked on the far side of the harvester. The door of the ute is open and the radio is on, tuned to the local station, but all Mr Creadie's attention is focused on something in his lap. When Essie sidles closer, she sees that it is a creased page from the newspaper. But there is also something else lying on top of the clipping, a photo of a girl.

Essie knows that the Creadies had a daughter who died when Essie was just a baby, and that the daughter's name was Cathy. No one talks about it much, but after Janet went missing, Essie heard her mother say to her father that it must have brought it all back for the Creadies.

Essie can't remember Cathy Creadie, but she supposes that she must have known her when she was little, as much as a baby can know another person. Perhaps Cathy even held Essie in her arms.

If, as everyone thinks, except old Mr Creadie, Janet is dead too, then Essie knows two dead people.

What would it be like to die and for the world to continue in her absence? Essie wonders. Now and then, when she's lying in bed before she falls asleep, she tries to imagine it. She pictures her body as a lump of meat and bones that she no longer has any use for, and her soul floating above it. Sometimes it feels peaceful, but when she thinks of her parents and Helen living in their house without her, it makes her feel like crying.

She's not sure why the thought makes her feel so sad and whether her sorrow is for herself for not being able to be with them, or for her family having to live with her absence—a huge gaping hole torn into their lives. Such a feeling of desolation comes over her that she quickly makes herself think of something else—like the time she and Helen flew to Brisbane with their mother. She took them into the city centre at night and they saw the fountain in King George Square. The lights shining through the cascading water looked magical, like something out of a fairytale.

Perhaps being dead feels the same as before you were born, like nothing. Essie can't remember being a baby, let alone what it was like before she existed in the world. Her first memory is of sitting beneath the kitchen table. She remembers her parents' legs and feet, the rumble of their voices and her father's hand appearing from above to tickle her. Stronger than the memory of what she could see and hear was the sense of wellbeing and safety flowing over her body like warm water.

On the rare occasions that her mother talks about dying, she talks about heaven. That when you die, you will be with God and the people who you loved who died before you did, and that there will be no more pain. It sounds a bit boring.

Is Cathy Creadie in heaven? wonders Essie. Is Janet with her? They are about the same age, if people don't get older in heaven. Would they become friends? Her mother says everyone in heaven is perfectly happy, but how can Janet or Cathy Creadie be happy if they know how sad their parents are?

Old Mr Creadie isn't crying but he looks like he might. Then he senses her presence and turns towards her.

'How long have you been standing there?' he asks, the soft, sad look replaced by his usual face, although crankier.

Essie points at the photo. 'Who's that?' She wonders if Mr Creadie will tell the truth or whether he will put her off the way adults often do, ignoring the question or trying to make her feel ashamed for asking it.

Air whistles through Mr Creadie's lips. 'That's my daughter, Cathy.'

'The one that drowned?'

Mr Creadie tucks the photo into the top pocket of his shirt. 'Yes, but you're not to worry,' he says. 'It's true that sometimes young people die, but I'm sure nothing bad will happen to you.'

It's the sort of stupid thing adults say all the time. No one could be sure of something like that. Essie scuffs at the shed's concrete floor with the toe of her sandshoe. Look what happened to Janet. She was young, and not one person was able to stop it.

Essie has edged her way around Mr Creadie's ute and is standing in front of the shadow board covered in tools hanging from hooks. She knows the names of most of them—pipe wrench, needle-nose pliers, mallet, chisel, hacksaw—but there are a pair of bent lengths of copper wire with wooden handles that aren't like anything on the tool board at home. She reaches out a hand to pluck them off their hooks. 'What are these for?'

'Be careful with those.' Mr Creadie stands and puts the newspaper clipping on the bonnet of the ute.

'Are they fragile?' Essie chooses the word 'fragile' carefully; it is one she has learnt only recently. It is a word a grown-up might use.

'No, but they're not toys.' Mr Creadie takes the wires from her, but rather than placing them back on the shadow board, he holds them in his hands, feeling their weight, his head cocked to the side as if he is listening for something the rods are trying to tell him.

'What are they for?'

Mr Creadie explains that there are pathways of power and energy that crisscross the earth. Some people have the power to use these dowsing rods—or even a Y-shaped stick—to find things like water, metal or lost objects.

When Essie raises her eyes to Mr Creadie's face, she knows that he is thinking the same thing as her. 'And people?' she asks.

Essie overheard her mother and father talking in the kitchen about Mr Creadie going to see the police and telling them that he thought he knew where Janet was. Her parents stopped talking about it when Essie asked if she and Helen could eat their ice cream while they were watching *The Waltons*, but Essie had heard her father say that Mr Creadie's son was worried that people would think Vince had finally gone around the twist.

Mr Creadie is looking at Essie the same way Tambo looks at her when she pretends to throw a stick but really still has it in her hand, as if he knows she is hiding something from him. 'Maybe,' he says eventually.

Essie picks up the newspaper clipping. Janet looks out at her from the photograph. She is sitting on the armrest of a chair, her body side-on, her face turned towards the camera, a butterfly hair slide holding back her fringe. She is smiling at whoever is taking the photo, although Essie doesn't think that she looks as friendly or as pretty as she did in real life.

'Could you use the rods to find someone who's dead?' Essie asks, still looking at Janet's photo.

'Maybe Janet's not dead,' Mr Creadie says. He takes the clipping from Essie's hand. 'It's possible she's still alive.'

'But why would she stay away for so long?' Essie asks. 'Why wouldn't she come home?'

Mr Creadie's eyes seem to be looking at something above her head and far away. 'You're a bit too young to know about these things,' he says, finally. 'But sometimes girls Janet's age have secrets from their parents. Things they think might hurt them if they ever found out about them.'

He doesn't say what those things might be, and Essie doesn't ask him what he means. But Mr Creadie is wrong. She isn't too young to understand about having secrets. Even before Raelene came to Quala, she understood that. Adults like to think that children are stupid with nothing to hide.

'Can you show me how to use them?' Essie says, nodding towards the dowsing rods.

They go around to the side of the shed, out of sight of the snug.

'Hold the wooden handles in your fists,' Mr Creadie says. 'That's right, but sideways. Your thumbs on top. Not too tight. Now let the longer bits rest on the side of your pointer fingers. Yes. You've got it. Now think of something you'd like to find.'

Besides Janet, Essie can't think of a single thing. It's like her mind has gone blank. 'Like what?'

Mr Creadie doesn't mention Janet either. 'I don't know. Money? Jean dropped her purse out here somewhere the other week. Maybe a couple of coins fell out.'

The lengths of copper wire feel like toys to Essie, something a little kid has made, like pretending wooden sticks are guns. 'But how do I do it?'

'Think of the thing that you want to find and let the rods guide you,' Mr Creadie says. 'Picture a coin in your mind. Or just picture the word.'

Essie holds the rods straight and steady like Mr Creadie told her to, closes her eyes. Tries to imagine a fifty-cent piece—the one with Captain Cook on the tails side and the Queen on the other. She remembers the word Mr Day taught them meaning twelve-sided. *Dodecagonal*. But the rods are lifeless, drooping. Dead things. She opens her eyes, lets the rods fall to her sides. 'Nothing's happening.'

'Try again. Take a couple of deep breaths first. Think about how you would spend that money.'

Essie shuts her eyes. Imagines going to Jensens' shop with Raelene and handing a fifty-cent coin over the counter. The number of caramel butters and chocolate bullets they would buy. Then, rather than seeing something, she feels something. A tug. No, not as definite as a tug. A touch. A tease. Not like the cold, hard edge of a coin, but more like the brush of her mother's eyelashes on her cheek. A butterfly kiss. A butterfly hairclip. The image flutters into her mind like a moth.

Essie opens her eyes. Finds she has taken several steps in the direction of the Creadies' old house. Where the red-headed teacher lives.

'No money that way. Never mind,' says old Mr Creadie, putting his hand on her shoulder. He takes the dowsing rods from her hands, then reaches into his trouser pocket and takes out a twenty-cent coin, stares at it as if surprised. 'Will you look at that. I never even knew that was there. Here.' He hands the coin to her.

SIXTEEN

WHEN ESSIE AND Mr Creadie go into the kitchen from the shed, her mother and old Mrs Creadie are at the table, a brown teapot between them. Yellow pottery cups decorated with orange flowers and filled with tea are in their hands. Helen, crumbs around her mouth and on the bread-and-butter plate beside her empty glass, is reaching for a piece of cake.

'You took your time,' says Jean, pouring tea into a third cup and giving it to Mr Creadie. She then pushes a glass of bright green cordial towards the place at the table beside Helen. Essie slips onto the chair next to her sister.

Mr Creadie drops his weight onto another at the head of the table. 'Anything other than ginger cake?'

Mrs Creadie raises her eyes towards the ceiling, pushes herself to her feet and shambles over to the kitchen bench.

She brings back the cake tin Essie's mother has returned filled with chocolate slice.

Mr Creadie holds it to his chest, prises off the lid, makes a show of breathing in the smell. 'No wonder Cam married you.'

'I was asking Jean about your tenants in the old house,' Essie's mother says as Mr Creadie has a sip of tea.

'Did you put sugar in this?' Mr Creadie asks his wife, his chin dropped towards his chest, his lips pursed in disappointment. Why do adults sometimes act like little kids, Essie wonders, and how come other adults let them get away with it?

Mrs Creadie flutters her hands at Essie. 'Oh, for heaven's sake. Pass the silly old man the sugar bowl, would you, please, dear?'

'One's the Parslow boy, isn't he?' Her mother takes the sugar bowl from Essie and places it in front of Mr Creadie.

'Yes, that's him. Works for the council, a clerk or some-thing.' Mr Creadie puts three teaspoons of sugar in his tea and stirs it thoroughly. He taps the spoon on the rim of his cup and takes a sip, then puckers his lips. 'He's Del and Ron Parslow's youngest. The older boy's running the farm now and they moved into town.'

Mrs Creadie clucks at him. 'Not the older boy, the middle one, Ned. The older boy's at university, studying to be an accountant.'

The old people click their tongues at each other and bicker about dates and circumstances, finally agree, yes, yes, Peter has been living in the old house since before Christmas.

'The other young fellow is a teacher at Kaliope West High,' Mrs Creadie says. 'Eamonn Sullivan. Up from Brisbane. You've probably seen him running in the mornings. Can't miss him, great long streak of a thing with flaming red hair.' She claps her hands together, looks at Essie's mother and then at Essie. 'Oh. Of course. I understand you met, and not under the best of circumstances.' Mrs Creadie looks at her husband and back at Essie's mother. 'Now, Connie, I know what it must have looked like, but Vince and I can't imagine there was anything awry in it.'

There is a moment of silence around the table. Mr Creadie takes a loud slurp of tea. Essie watches her mother break a small corner off the piece of cake on her plate and put it in her mouth. She chews it carefully and swallows, then asks, 'Hasn't he also got himself into hot water with that banned book?'

Essie sees the glance that Mrs Creadie gives her husband. The warning contained within it. 'That's him.'

'You're not concerned, then? About him living so close to you, to Sandra, to the primary school?' Her mother doesn't say Essie's name or Helen's, but Essie knows that the Creadies hear them anyway.

Mrs Creadie relays another plea for caution, indicating Essie and Helen, who has left the table and gone over to the side-board and is rearranging Mrs Creadie's collection of novelty salt and pepper shakers.

'People are too keen to pass judgement, in my opinion,' Mr Creadie says, draining his cup.

Helen comes back to the table and extends a hand towards the remaining slice of cake.

'No more, little Miss Piggy,' says her mother, picking up the plate and placing it out of Helen's reach.

Mrs Creadie clears her throat, suggests that Essie take Helen out to see Sandra's pup. Since he got himself stuck in the chicken wire, she explains, Meg often leaves him tied up at the snug when no one's home at the big house. Their mother ignores Essie's surly protests and Helen's whingeing that she wants to stay with her mother.

'Scoot.'

Mrs Creadie finds some meat scraps for the little dog, puts them in a plastic bowl and gives it to Helen. 'Don't let him off the chain, mind.'

Essie follows Helen out of the kitchen but lingers just out of sight. Inside, there is quiet around the table.

'Janet was in one of his classes, you know,' Mrs Creadie says.

'He was questioned by the police, as was the Parslow boy, as was our John.' Mr Creadie's voice is louder than it needs to be. 'He was seen in Kaliope around the time Janet left home.'

Essie hears the harsh scrape of a chair being pushed forcefully back from the table.

'That should be enough for anyone, I'd think. Besides, no one even knows for sure that she's dead. They haven't found a corpse yet.'

Essie hears Mr Creadie's tread coming towards the door. She runs, reaching Helen and the pup before he starts down the stairs.

~

Jean picks at the cake crumbs on the tablecloth, gathers them in small piles, dabs at them with a damp finger, says, 'It's almost ten years since we lost Cathy.'

'Yes. I know.' Connie touches the older woman's hand. 'I'm so sorry, Jean. I can only imagine what the last couple of months have done to you and Vince. And John. How hard it must be. Bringing it all back.'

They sit at the table in silence, then Jean asks, 'Another cuppa?'

While Jean puts the kettle on, Connie tells her that Cam will begin harvesting within the next few days. He's rung the mill and they'll be expecting their first cut. She knows the Creadies, like her and Cam, are behind with everything, but the strip of cleared ground between their big field and the old house on the Creadies' place is overgrown. Could Jean ask John to drive the slasher over it?

'I've told him myself already, but when it comes to the farm he only listens to Vince. I'll remind them both again. I keep telling them it's a disaster waiting to happen. What with the rain, it's a jungle over there.'

The Creadies' own cane fields have encroached further and further on the land around the old house. The fence has collapsed in several places around the yard and the cane has sent up suckers so that now it is in danger of taking over the whole garden, such as it is. Not to mention the grass and weeds that have grown like billyo with all the rain. Jean had a good go at John about it before Peter and Eamonn moved in.

'I said to him, if we're taking their money, the least we can do is make sure the yard is neat and tidy. All it would take is for one floater to settle on those weatherboards.'

Jean has worked herself up. What's more, there are regulations. If the council sends someone round, there'll be a fine. Connie will remember that a few years ago, a fire escaped from cane land up round Townsville and an elderly couple were badly burnt trying to put it out. After that there was a crackdown on anyone who didn't clear a big enough firebreak around their fields.

'If one scrap of smouldering ash lodges in an old birds' nest under the eaves—*whoosh*.' Jean gestures upwards with both arms. 'A conflagration.'

When she's back at the table with the teapot, Jean, with a glance to check that Vince hasn't decided to return to the kitchen, says, 'That policewoman from Brisbane, she came here to talk to me about Eamonn and Peter. About Eamonn mainly. She rang and made an appointment.' Jean lifts her cup. 'She's a clever miss.'

Her assessment of Carmel Maitland is not meant as a compliment, and Connie pauses with her own cup halfway to her mouth. She cocks her head at Jean's last remark.

'She got me talking,' Jean explains. 'I didn't realise until later that she'd wangled me into telling her to come at a time when Vince wouldn't be here. She wanted to talk to me on my own. Not that she got anything incriminating out of me,' she finishes with satisfaction.

As Connie drives home, they pass the old house, nestling like a bird in a bower of towering cane stalks.

Back at their house, Connie sends Essie out to the shed to tell Cam that tea will be ready at six. As Essie scampers down the stairs, Connie sees Barbara pull up in the McClymonts' Volvo and she sends Helen into the girls' bedroom to play.

At the top of the stairs leading to the verandah, Barbara pauses, leaning on the bannister. Connie comes out to meet her.

She holds her arms out to her friend, but Barbara refuses the offered embrace with the smallest flick of her fingers. She is breathing heavily as if it has taken all her strength to make it this far. Connie is shocked at how her friend has deteriorated: her unwashed clothes hang off her, her face is pale and deflated, the skin lustreless. Beneath her hair, hanging in knotted clumps, her eyes are sunken and bloodshot. And there is an odour of stale sweat beneath the smell of cigarette smoke, as if Barbara hasn't bathed for days.

Connie draws Barbara into the kitchen. 'Sit down. I'll make tea.'

Barbara remains standing. 'No, no tea.' She ignores the glass of water Connie places on the table in front of her, looks at her accusingly. 'You promised me, Connie.'

'Barbara . . .'

'I've seen the preparations Cam is making. He's about to start harvesting, even though you promised me you wouldn't burn your cane until Janet had been found.'

'It's been so much longer than we thought it would be, Barbara. We've waited as long as we could.'

'Ask Cam to hold off. Just a few more days, a week at most. Please, Connie. I don't want my little girl to burn. How would you feel if it was Essie or Helen?'

'I'm sorry, but surely it's better to find Janet, even if . . .'

A sound erupts, almost like a seal barking, hoarse and hiccupping. It is Barbara sobbing, her chest heaving so violently that Connie fears she will injure herself. Before she can try, a second time, to enfold her friend in her arms, a movement on the edge of her vision catches her attention. Essie is on the verandah just outside the kitchen. Connie quickly closes the door in her daughter's face. She doesn't want her to witness this naked adult grief. But when Connie turns back towards Barbara, her friend runs towards the door and flings it open, stumbling past Essie, who is still hovering just outside. Connie follows her but stops at the top of the stairs. Essie comes to stand beside her, and together they watch Barbara stagger to her car, half collapsing against the bonnet when she reaches it, eventually dragging the door open and slumping in the seat. She drives down the track to the main road at walking pace. Essie leans against Connie and for a long moment hides her face in her mother's side.

In the kitchen the clatter of cutlery in the sink syncopates beneath 'When You Wish Upon a Star'. *The Wonderful World of Disney* is on the television in the lounge room and Essie and Helen, in their pyjamas, are allowed to watch it before bed.

Connie thinks how tired Cam looks as he takes a handful of dinner knives, wipes each one carefully before placing them in the cutlery drawer. He's been up since before dawn trying to get the harvester to start. Although he washed his face and hands before tea, grease is still smudged beneath his right eye where he's rubbed it with his fingers. The grime has settled into the crow's feet fanning out from the edge of the socket. It makes him look older than he is.

After the washing-up and when the girls are in bed, Connie will coax Cam to sit at the kitchen table so that she can knead the tension from his muscles, bunched and rigid beneath his shirt.

Connie would like to talk of other things, but Barbara's visit this afternoon, and the horror of Janet's absence still stalking everyone, makes that impossible. Besides the crush, it is the only topic of conversation.

'Bev Zammit told me that someone found a pair of girl's underpants beneath the bridge in town,' she tells Cam.

'Christ,' says Cam. 'There's half a dozen cars parked under that bridge most nights of the week. I'd be surprised if they couldn't find a pair of girl's underpants there any time, day or night. Are the police going to show them to Ted and Barbara? After all this time, there can't be much point.'

'I suppose they have to follow everything up. They can't ignore possible evidence. Even if it's only an outside chance they belong to Janet, I guess they have to show them to Barbara and Ted.'

'They should leave them alone. Janet is dead and everyone knows what likely happened to her before she died. What good is there in knowing any more?'

'I'd want to know as much as I could,' Connie says. 'If it was Essie or Helen. I'd want to know everything.'

The tea towel hangs limply from Cam's hands. 'Would you? Really?'

'Nothing could be worse than what I could imagine.'

'I don't know about that, Connie. I wouldn't bet on it. Maybe what happened to Janet is worse than what any of us could imagine.'

A space opens up between them, just for the amount of time it takes for a bubble of detergent to slide down the plate that Connie has placed in the dish rack. Within it is a scenario where it was one of their daughters who was snatched. Violated. Murdered.

Cam takes the plate, wipes it dry, picks up another. As always, they will coordinate with the Creadies on burning and harvesting their cane. He tells Connie that when John came over to discuss arrangements they touched on the undertakings they'd given to Barbara when Janet first disappeared.

Cam says, 'But things have changed since then. We never imagined it would go on for this long. If Janet's body turns up in the paddocks near where she disappeared, then at least they'll know for sure. They can have a funeral for her. It would be best for them and for all of us.' He takes a saucepan from Connie's hand. 'Barbara's still thrashing her way through ours and the Creadies' fields even though it'd be far easier to find Janet if she'd just let us get on with harvesting weeks ago. Ted is still going into the Kaliope cop shop every morning asking for updates. He's walking around like his daughter's still alive and any day now she'll walk into the house, embarrassed about all the fuss she's caused. It will be better for him to know so he can face reality.'

'Cam.' Connie looks into his face.

'Sorry.' Cam clenches his jaw. 'I know how that sounds. If it was Essie or Helen, I would have probably driven into a tree by now.'

'Don't say that.' Connie stares into the sudsy water, wishes for a future when this time is long in the past, just a bad, sad memory. 'Have you spoken to Ted recently?'

Cam, shamefaced, performs a small movement of his chin in the negative. 'I can't even look at him.'

'You're his friend,' Connie says, gentle.

'Am I? I only used to see him when he was here with Barbara. Or at the pub very occasionally.' He stows the saucepan in the cupboard beneath the bench. 'I wouldn't know what to say to him.'

Connie pulls off her rubber gloves, lays a hand on Cam's wrist. 'Barbara was here this afternoon. She's seen the preparations we're making.'

Cam hangs the tea towel over the rack on the pantry door and leans against the kitchen bench. 'What did you say to her?'

Connie rinses out the dishcloth under the tap and wrings it out. 'I said that we couldn't hold off harvesting any longer and I told her . . .' Her voice thins, becoming hoarse and reedy. 'I told her that I was sorry.'

Cam holds out his arms, and Connie walks into them.

From the lounge room, Helen's giggle floats into the kitchen over the sound of the television. The cane would have been high above Janet's head, Connie thinks, the tasselled heads lit bright and golden by the setting sun.

Later, when Cam goes back out to the shed to have another tinker with the harvester and the girls are in bed, Connie stands at their bedroom door breathing in their smell. Earlier, in the kitchen with Cam, at the moment when they contemplated the possibility of what happened to Janet happening to Essie and Helen, she found herself wishing that her daughters had never been born.

~

That night, after her mother turns out their bedroom light, Essie thinks back to what Mr Creadie said that afternoon. She supposes it's possible that old Mr Creadie is right in believing that Janet is alive. Maybe she did slip away on purpose that night when she was meant to be babysitting her and Helen. Janet could have waved down the Greyhound coach on the highway as it headed towards Brisbane and been miles away before anyone came out to look for her. Essie can even imagine it, a silhouette of a girl stepping out of the darkness, one arm held aloft, and the coach, like a great animal, coming to a halt by the side of the road with a sharp hiss of its brakes. Its engine purring while the hydraulic door swings open and a slight figure climbs the steps and disappears inside. With a jerk, its headlights illuminating the road ahead, the coach pulling out and resuming its journey, taking Janet with it.

Or perhaps Janet simply hid in the cane in those first hours after she disappeared. It would have been easy enough to keep ahead of the adults trying to find her in the thick growth, if she didn't want to be found. In the early hours of the following morning, hungry and tired, maybe Janet dashed onto the road to hitchhike to Brisbane, dropping her bag in her hurry.

But why would Janet want to go to Brisbane or to hide from her parents? Essie knows that Janet missed her old friends. She told Essie that sometimes she cried because she missed them so much. But now Janet had a boyfriend with long eyelashes. Joe is an Islander; at least, his mother is an Islander. Not that Janet cared about this. Others do, Essie knows. 'People can be so prejudiced,' Janet once told Essie when she was babysitting. Essie's not exactly sure what prejudiced means, but she knows that it has to do with the way some people's voices change when they speak about Islanders and Aboriginal people, when they call them Kanakas or darkies or coons.

Essie wouldn't hide in the cane, especially not at night. There is the thing that looms up in her dreams, the thing that the littler children in Quala talk about. They swap stories about a monster and play games where they scare themselves silly. Essie doesn't believe in monsters, not really, not in the daylight. But there is something that lingers in the claustrophobic cane, something bad.

As Essie drifts into sleep, the muscles of her hands and fingers twitch. The memory of the dowsing rods, their weight, the way they trembled like live things, skitters into her dreams. Images whirl, create their own weather, billowing and subsiding, changing shape and form like clouds in a blustery sky.

She is in the cane, not too far, the edge of the field is just there. She will reach it in only a few steps. But with each stride she takes, another drill of cane rises up between her and open ground. She fights to escape, to push aside the thick stalks, but her hands are clumsy, and when she looks down, they are curled around the dowel handles of old Mr Creadie's dowsing rods. The rods hamper her, but she cannot let them go. Panic drives her limbs. And the cane grows ever more quickly, ever more thickly. Something is moving within it. The stalks batter and shake against each other. It is coming closer. The dowsing rods get caught up in the cane, pulling her down onto the earth.

She looks up into the face of the schoolteacher. His red hair aflame.

SEVENTEEN

ESSIE SEES THEM from the verandah. Raelene is with Danny, Gavan and Tim. They are all on their bicycles, milling in a group near the turn-off to the track leading up to Essie's family's house. The boys are taking turns to fang down the bitumen and into the corner just at the turn-off. When they hit the bend in the road, they jam on the brakes, skidding into the rough gravel lying in drifts on either side. As she watches, Gavan takes off on his bike, pedalling like a maniac. He leans into the curve, graceful, reckless, but he is travelling too fast and the bike begins to wobble. He struggles to arrest its lateral dive, but the momentum is too great and he slams into the bitumen, bouncing across the road until both he and the bike lie motionless in the gravel.

From her vantage point, Essie sees the other three are stockstill, watching, then Danny drops his bike and sprints towards Gavan. Before Danny reaches him, Gavan leaps to his feet, hooting and pointing. The entire right side of his body is dusted with dirt and small stones. He turns and waggles his bum, then dances away, cackling, as Danny attempts to slam into him with his hip and shoulder. Gavan picks up his bike and pushes it back onto the road. The front wheel, askew, knocks against the forks that cradle it. Gavan, Essie sees now, is limping and blood trickles down his leg. Danny helps him hoist up the bike so that it is standing vertically on its back wheel while Gavan holds the handlebars at the level of his chest. In this way, they manoeuvre the bike back to where the others are waiting.

There is a brief discussion and the four of them move as a group in the direction of town, Gavan still holding his bike like a dance partner and the others pedalling slowly ahead of him. As they draw further away, Gavan calls out and they stop and wait for him, turning to watch his progress. They are perhaps a hundred and fifty yards away, no more, and Essie waves at them from the verandah. Essie sees Raelene see her, but Danny is the only one who waves back.

⌒

'Don't smear it. I want it smooth.'

The following day, Raelene brings a bottle of nail polish to school. Her aunty in Brisbane has posted it up to her. She holds out her left hand, her fingers spread like a starfish, while Essie, squatting in front of the bench under the mango tree and biting her lip with the effort of keeping her hands steady, brushes the viscous lemon-yellow liquid on each of Raelene's nails. For this task, and others like it, acts of preening and adornment, Essie remains useful to Raelene. Tim, Danny and Gavan, despite how much they want Raelene to like them, how eagerly they vie for her attention and try to make her laugh, will not do this.

Raelene's aunty Colleen isn't married and she doesn't have children, Raelene tells Essie. 'She's a career lady.'

Raelene has stayed with Colleen in Brisbane a few times. Her aunty sometimes puts makeup on her so that Raelene looks older and takes her out to the pub, just as if they were friends and the same age. 'She's really pretty and has lots of boyfriends.'

Is Colleen her dad's sister, or her dead mum's? Essie asks.

Raelene darts a quick squint at Essie. 'My mum's. She was in the car the night my mum was killed. She tried to hold her head on her neck until the ambulance got there. But it was no use.'

Essie nods gravely. What a liar Raelene is. Her mother isn't dead. Just gone. Essie heard Mrs Zammit tell Essie's mum that Gordon Mason made no bones about the fact that he was glad to be rid of his ex-wife. She'd taken up with a mate of his in the west some years ago. 'He told my Tony that Camooweal and his missus deserved each other,' Mrs Zammit said.

Raelene snatches her fingers away. 'You've smudged that one. No more than three strokes from the base of the nail to the tip. That's what it says in *Dolly* magazine.'

'Sorry,' Essie says, the nail polish brush poised in mid-air. 'I'll be more careful.'

Raelene relents. Extends her hand again.

Lately, Raelene has been drawing away from Essie, spending more time with Tim and Danny and Gavan. Gavan, especially, seems to have become her favourite. Raelene prefers his company walking home from school and it is Gavan she chooses when Mr Day gives the class work to do in pairs.

Essie is working to charm Raelene back. Liar or not, there are still things Raelene can teach her, shadowy, adult things that retain the pull of a magnet. So, to re-establish their connection built on secrets and confidences, Essie is prepared to cajole and flatter her. She applies the final lick of polish to the little finger on Raelene's left hand and raises it with her own for Raelene's approval. While Raelene considers her handiwork, Essie introduces a topic sufficiently murky to entice her into speculation. 'If Janet is lying dead in the cane, what do you reckon she looks like now?'

Raelene, satisfied with the smooth sheen of enamel, brings her left hand to her lips and blows on her fingertips to dry the polish, sweeping them from side to side in the stream of her breath, producing a chuffing sound like a miniature train. She regally offers her right hand and Essie dips the tiny brush into the little bottle, extracts a droplet of polish and applies it in three careful strokes to Raelene's thumbnail.

'She'd look absolutely disgusting.' Raelene is confident in her judgement. 'Animals will have eaten bits of her. Ants, beetles, worms. Bigger stuff, maybe, too. A wild pig might have found her. She'd be a real mess.'

'But what if she's somewhere animals can't get to her?'

'Like where?'

'Like someone's house. What if she isn't even dead? Maybe someone is keeping her locked up.'

Raelene pulls her hand away from Essie's grasp. Inspects her nails, fakes a yawn, but Essie has seen her eyes, hard and bright. 'Like who? And anyway, she's gotta be dead by now.'

Essie eases the brush with its globule of sticky yellow goop through the bottle's narrow opening and screws the lid tight. She stands, puts the bottle of polish on the bench beside Raelene and brushes the dirt off her shins. Holding the skirt of her school uniform above her knees, she examines her skinny legs, the downy hair that Raelene has suggested she shave off.

'Like someone who lives not far from the McClymonts' place. Like someone who's a pervert.'

Raelene can't believe that Essie hadn't told her that the red-headed teacher lives so close to Essie's place and to where Janet McClymont went missing. Raelene has seen him in the pub once or twice; she knew that he lives somewhere close by but didn't realise that he rents the old house on the Creadies' place. Why hadn't Essie said?

Essie shrugs, hiding her pleasure at discovering the limits of Raelene's vaunted all-knowingness. Then she tells Raelene about Mr Creadie's dowsing rods. How she held them in her hands and how the image of Janet's butterfly hair slide appeared in her mind, how the rods pulled her in the direction of the red-headed teacher's cottage.

From her unparalleled access to the town gossip from her perch at the bar, Raelene has heard about old Mr Creadie going to the police and claiming that the dowsing rods had shown him that Janet was alive and in Brisbane. Chester Connolly came into the pub holding a couple of pieces of wood out in front of him and imitating old Creadie's shuffling walk. 'Bloody amazing.

I told these two sticks I was gasping for a beer and they brought me here!' he said. There was a lot of joking and laughter until John Creadie came in for a drink. Someone asked him if he thought old Vince could help him find his lost virginity. John left without finishing his beer.

Raelene grips Essie's shoulders in both hands, rewards her with her full, wide-eyed attention. 'We should sneak into the teacher's house. Maybe there's an attic and he's keeping her prisoner. Or she could be tied up in a wardrobe.'

Essie is rapt as Raelene starts prancing around her, flapping her hands like a courting bird. They decide they will ride their bikes to the Creadies' place on Saturday. The Kable boys are playing for Kaliope West High School's footy team against Candleford in the afternoon. Darren has told Raelene the red-headed teacher is taking them there in his car.

Essie joins Raelene's dance. 'We'll rescue her. They'll give us a medal.'

Raelene slings an arm around her neck, drags her close. 'I'll meet you at one o'clock on Saturday at the end of your driveway. Bring your bike.'

'What if the other man is there?'

'What other man?'

Essie tells Raelene about Peter Parslow, who lives with the teacher. But Raelene has it all worked out. Essie will hide and Raelene will knock on the door. If Peter is there, Raelene will keep him talking.

Raelene puts one yellow-tipped hand on her hip, flicks her hair with the other. 'I'm irresistible.'

Essie, she says, will creep around to the back door and search the house.

'So, you'll meet me on Saturday afternoon?' asks Raelene, holding Essie's shoulders and staring into her face. Her eyes beneath her thick black brows are narrowed. 'Promise?'

Essie thought Raelene understood that this was a game. 'But my mum and dad won't let me.'

'Duh, Fred. Don't tell them.'

'But what if they're perverts?'

'Your parents are perverts?'

Essie hates it when Raelene makes jokes like that. 'No. The teacher and the other man.'

Raelene drops her hands, rests them on her hips. Her bright, eager gaze has slid into a low-lidded stare, dull and mocking.

'I'm not allowed,' Essie says.

Raelene studies her fingernails. Rubs at an errant streak of yellow on the skin of her thumb.

'Because of strangers. Because of Janet.'

Raelene picks up the bottle of nail polish from the bench. 'You know, I'd almost forgotten that you're just a baby.'

EIGHTEEN

THE RUMOUR IS that Raelene is going with Kenny Connolly. The prospect of it is so shocking, so dislocating, Essie is not sure if she believes it. But everyone at school is talking about it.

Kenny is seventeen. He has a job and a motorbike and his way of swaggering about as if everything he sees is his for the taking. Sometimes he's away for weeks at a time working on a big construction job. Even though he's underage, when he's at home he is one of the boys who sometimes drinks with his father at the pub in Quala. Raelene has told Essie before about Chester Connolly telling someone at the front bar, 'He works as hard as a man. He should be allowed to drink like one.'

Essie is torn. Officially, Raelene is still her best friend, even though Raelene now prefers to sit under the mango tree with Tim and Danny and Gavan at big lunch. This has been noted by Sharon and Susan. They have seen Essie climbing the stairs to the classroom after eating her lunchtime sandwich. Mr Day always eats his lunch at the house with Mrs Day and the baby. There is no one to tell Essie that she should be playing outside. She draws on the blackboard and works her way through the reading comprehension cards stored in boxes beside Mr Day's desk, even the ones that she isn't up to yet. She watches the clock on the wall and when the big hand is on the ten, she uses the duster to rub off her drawings of girls lying on the ground as if dead, and creatures, hulking but indistinct, half hidden in stools of cane.

Susan and Sharon corner Essie by the drinking trough to ask her if the rumour about Raelene and Kenny Connolly is true. 'It might be,' Essie says.

She tells them the secrets that Raelene confided to her on the first day they met: that she is almost fourteen, that she already has her period. Susan and Sharon accept these disclosures as evidence of fealty. Would Essie like to turn the skipping rope?

~

Connie watches the children file out of the classroom in two neat lines and onto the verandah. Raelene surges ahead of Essie, clipping her shoulder with her school port. She doesn't even turn her head when Essie says that she'll see her tomorrow. Connie suffers a pang on behalf of her daughter, who wears her hurt and humiliation so nakedly on her face.

Gavan Connolly, Tim Froome and Danny Pine run past Essie as she squats at the racks on the verandah putting her homework book, her pencils and reader in her port. The boys follow Raelene past the children exchanging final confidences and reminders of games they will take up again tomorrow, and thunder after her down the stairs. On the asphalt the boys argle-bargle, shoving and tripping each other in a race to be the first to reach their bikes propped against the fence. In a murmuration of limbs, bicycle wheels, and hair tossed out of eyes, they swoop after Raelene as she saunters out of the school gates and down the middle of the road. Squawking and wheeling like cockatoos, the three boys swerve and circle about her, a procession of irreverent acolytes.

Because they're male and nearly thirteen, Gavan, Tim and Danny riding their bikes home without supervision attracts no comment from the parents waiting at the school gates. The risk of their drawing the attention of the person responsible for whatever has befallen Janet is assessed as negligible. They are boys, rambunctious and untidy, soon to inherit their dues and their status as men. Their fate is not to be the ones preyed upon. They will not be fondled and dandled against their will.

On the other hand, Raelene, despite her fierce black eyebrows, her knowing smiles and skilful manipulation of the Quala youth, carries the vulnerability of her femaleness even though she may not yet grasp this fact. Or perhaps she merely feigns ignorance of the danger that the flaunting of her too-early flourishing might attract. But the parents gathered at the school gates know it, and do not pretend they don't. Connie sees them look disapprovingly at Raelene walking home more or less alone. Without the supervision of an adult, at least. The pub is only a short distance from the school, perhaps a quarter of a mile, but even so. The parents catch each other's eyes as she swaggers past, hips swinging in a way that is disconcerting in a girl still in primary school. They shake their heads, clicking their tongues in concern. 'It's too bad.'

Early on, in the first week or so after Raelene started attending Quala Primary, one or other of the parents would call after her, asking if she would like a lift home. No longer. They know she will refuse the offer and with a nonchalance that contains less deference than is generally expected in Quala when a child speaks to an adult. Today, at least, she is accompanied by her squad of schoolboy protectors. Tim and Gavan and Danny fan out like a cortege behind her as she progresses down the road. The parents exchange glances, silently reassuring each other that she will reach home without incident. They murmur about how unfortunate it is that Raelene doesn't have a mother to guide her through these delicate years of becoming a woman.

Essie has another year before she will be ready for high school. Connie would like to send her to the same Catholic boarding school that she attended in Brisbane. Its high red-brick walls would confine her daughter like Rapunzel, safe and inviolate. It's a battle Connie is yet to win. Cam is insistent that he doesn't want the girls sent away to school, and in the wake of Janet's disappearance Connie hasn't broached the subject again, but she hasn't given up on her plan.

⁓

The dress that Mrs Zammit is making for Essie's mother is ready for a fitting and they call in on their way home from school. Mrs Zammit gives Helen and Essie a glass of fruit cup cordial each and two Arnott's Scotch Finger biscuits. When their mother comes out of the Zammits' bedroom wearing the almost completed emerald-green frock, she looks so glamorous, even with the dress unhemmed and trailing threads, that Helen runs to her, a mash of crumbled biscuit and sweet cordial in her mouth.

Connie sidesteps her. 'Don't touch me. Not with your sticky fingers.'

Mrs Zammit gets their mother to stand on a kitchen chair while she secures the hem, her mouth full of pins. Essie, imagining the sharp metal catching in her throat, cannot swallow until Mrs Zammit is assured that the skirt will skim just below Connie's ankles and the remaining pins are returned to their tin. She sits on her heels and gestures for Essie's mother to complete a turn. Gives a satisfied nod. 'You can hop down now.'

When her mum has extricated herself from the pinned garment and put her house dress back on, Mrs Zammit walks them out to their station wagon. She tells Connie she can come by next week to pick up the finished dress.

'I'll have it done by Tuesday. Don't forget the buckle for the belt. It will only take a couple of minutes to sew it on.'

Bev leans on the gate and the two women discuss payment and how Cam and John are finally about to begin harvesting their cane.

'I feel for that poor woman,' Bev says. 'I really do, but she can't expect you to hold off forever.'

Connie says that Cam has spoken with the sugar mill. He'll probably burn the first of their paddocks the day after tomorrow.

Essie and Helen squabble over who will ride in the front seat. Helen manages to open the car door first, but Essie grabs her around the waist and flings her away from the car. Before

Helen's wail can result in a reprimand from their mother, the roar of a motorbike causes them all to swivel around and look up towards the intersection at the top of the street near the pub. As the motorbike turns out from the pub carpark onto the bitumen, it accelerates, leaps forward, and Essie feels the rising pitch of the motor reverberate in the bones of her forehead.

Mrs Zammit holds her hand up to her brow to shade her eyes against the glare of the late afternoon sun.

'Who's that riding pillion behind young Connolly?'

The girl curled around Kenny's back is Raelene. Her arms are around his waist, her helmeted head leaning against his shoulder blades. Her blue school uniform is hitched up around her thighs, and her feet, in rubber thongs, rest on the foot pegs.

'Well, well, well,' Mrs Zammit says. 'Will you look who it is.'

Essie searches her mother's face. Finds sorrow there.

'That poor little girl,' her mother says.

NINETEEN

JOE HAS HEARD the rumours that Fantapants is going to get the sack. He feels rotten about it and pretty bloody pissed off with Martin.

'Sorry, mate,' Martin said when Joe confronted him. 'But you know what my mum's like.'

Joe didn't even bother to ask Martin why the fuck he'd told his mother about *The Little Red Schoolbook* in the first place.

It got all around the school, of course, and everyone from Brice Kable to a bunch of little smart-arses in Grade 8 asked him to tell them what was in the book. Joe told all of them to fuck off.

'Oh, Joseph,' his mother had said when she found out about the book and the resulting uproar. 'Never mind, it will blow over.'

He so wishes Janet was safe and still going around with him. He misses her. Badly. His sister Angela opened a tub of Neapolitan ice cream at the table a few nights ago and when she spooned a scoop of the strawberry flavour into his bowl, the smell brought back the night he and Janet had first kissed so strongly that he could feel the weight of it in his stomach. Weird how a memory could manifest in your guts.

It isn't only Janet's physical self he misses. He'd valued the way she wasn't afraid to talk about serious things, about ideas and what made for a good and interesting life. He would have liked to talk with her about the issues discussed in *The Little Red Schoolbook*—about young people like them taking control of their lives, not just accepting everything adults told them but developing their own sense of what was important. And, if he was honest, he would have loved to do some of the other stuff with her that the book talked about. He'd had no idea what a clitoris even was before he read about it in *The Little Red Schoolbook*.

If only he'd been able to get away to see her the night she disappeared. What a fucking mess.

Joe is almost at the bike shed, which is in one corner of the staff carpark, when he sees Mr Sullivan climbing into his Hillman Hunter. Mr Sullivan still teaches him English and economics but Joe hasn't talked to him outside of class since Fantapants gave him the book.

On an impulse, Joe drops his school port beside his bike and jogs towards the Hillman as Mr Sullivan starts it up. He raises an arm, calls out the teacher's name. When he stops beside the car, Sullivan turns off the engine.

Mr Sullivan's wary, disappointed face makes him feel terrible. He scuffs the toe of his shoe against the asphalt and can't bring himself to meet Fantapants' eyes. He even feels bad for thinking the nickname.

'What is it?' asks Sullivan, drawn in on himself as if expecting a blow. Since it got out about Sullivan giving Joe a copy of the banned book, there's been more talk about the teacher and Janet, about whether he might have had something to do with her disappearance after all. Sullivan's obviously a commie and a corrupter of morals, so the talk goes; what's to say he's not a pervert and a molester? Though Joe has no idea what happened to Janet, can't bear to think about what might have been done to her, he knows Mr Sullivan didn't have anything to do with it.

Joe takes a gulp of air. 'I don't want you to think that I dobbed you in to Mr Shaw. I didn't deliberately put you in the shit. The book fell out of my port and my dad just picked it up. After I let slip that you'd given it to me I asked my old man not to say anything to Mr Shaw, but he wouldn't listen. And then Martin told his mother, like a fucking idiot.' He puts both hands on his hips, stares at the ground. 'I really hope you don't get the sack.'

Mr Sullivan gazes out the front windscreen of his car, then says, 'Don't worry about it. Maybe it was the kick up the arse I needed. Sorry about the strife it got you into. Hopefully you had the chance to read some of the book before your dad confiscated it.'

'Some of it was really interesting. I mean, I'm not about to get into drugs or anything, but lots of the stuff it said made sense,' says Joe, then grins suddenly. 'And my dad only found one of the books.'

'Anyway . . .' They both speak at once, laugh awkwardly.

Mr Sullivan recovers first. 'Thanks for saying, you know, what you said.' He restarts the car's engine, but before he puts the car into gear he says, 'Joe, you should do pretty well in the exams at the end of the year. If you work hard enough you could qualify for a university scholarship. Talk to Mr Shaw about it, okay?'

'Will do. See ya later, Mr Sullivan. Good luck with the P&C tonight.'

'Thanks. And Joe? I'm really sorry about what happened to Janet.'

~

Through the window of his office, Ern sees Eamonn Sullivan pull into the school carpark for tonight's special P&C meeting to consider his 'case'. Even before Eamonn turns off the engine, Ern can see he hasn't heeded his advice to get a haircut. Eamonn had nodded as if he agreed with Ern that it would be a good idea to smarten himself up. But here he is, not even a trim of his long red hair, let alone a short back and sides.

Ern watches as Eamonn climbs out of his car. Christ on a bike. What's he wearing? Rather than the dress shirt and trousers Ern recommended, Eamonn's decked out in a cheesecloth tunic and flared jeans.

Before this episode with *The Little Red Schoolbook*, Ern wouldn't have pegged Eamonn as a natural rebel, but perhaps he was mistaken. He's overheard Eamonn's boasts in the staffroom about being active in the Vietnam Moratorium movement when he was a student in Brisbane and of dodging police batons on Wickham Terrace during the anti-Springbok tour demonstration. It didn't surprise Ern that Eamonn had been caught up in a bit of ratbaggery when he was at teachers' college. It's what youngsters do, although Ern suspects Eamonn has talked up his involvement a bit. A lot, in fact. He was bloody lucky he didn't get arrested during the Spring Hill melee outside the Tower Mill Hotel. He would have kissed away any hope of a career with the Education Department if he'd been charged. Well, he may very well achieve the same outcome with his latest escapade.

Not that any of the committee members have read more than the list of contents and a couple of pages of *The Little Red Schoolbook*. Ern offered them the copy that George Cassar had given him, but none felt the need to acquaint themselves with its contents in any detail. Ern has read through the thing, of course. He's not that bothered by it. The language is a bit coarse, especially for school-age girls. As for the boys, well, Ern's been a teacher for almost thirty years. Smut and profanity are par for the course as far as young men are concerned.

Ern climbs the stairs to the staffroom where the P&C will meet. No one else has arrived yet and he waits for Eamonn to join him. Ern, within the confines of the school boundaries, is, he is happy to admit, a tyrant. But not, he hopes, a petty one. He has a grudging respect for those of his students who buck against the yoke of authority—even his authority, such as it is. And he's prepared to give those rebels who throw their schoolbooks on the ground with a 'fuck you' and stride out of the school gates a second chance. He's willing to extend that same magnanimity to Eamonn. He suspects that when push comes to shove, Eamonn, despite his poorly chosen attire, will follow the script Ern has recommended—prostrate himself and beg for forgiveness.

But when Eamonn does finally drag his sorry arse up the stairs and dumps his ridiculous satchel on his desk in the staffroom, Ern catches a whiff of marijuana on the little shit. He swallows down his exasperation. He will do what he can to save Sullivan from himself.

~

An hour later Eamonn is still sitting in his Hillman Hunter when Ern turns off the lights in the staffroom and makes his way down the stairs. He lumbers across the assembly area to the staff carpark and, after wiping off the ash from that evening's cane fires, lowers his large hindquarters onto the front wing of Eamonn's car. He scratches his jaw. 'So, not a communist plot to undermine the morals of our young folk at all, but rather representing the highest principles of enlightened liberalism?'

Eamonn picks at the stitching of the steering wheel's leather sleeve. 'Too hifalutin?'

'Maybe a touch. Although I did admire your attempt to defend "fuck" and "cunt" as simply frank, forthright Anglo-Saxon words.'

Eamonn laughs, a short, sharp squawk. 'I don't think Mrs Zammit appreciated it much.'

Ern agrees this is a fair assessment. 'You couldn't put on a bloody tie and collared shirt, Eamonn? Do you want to get the sack?'

Eamonn shrugs. 'Maybe.'

'Well, I'll do what I can, but I think it's going to be taken out of my hands. The executive has already written to the Board of Education about you. So perhaps a shirt and tie wouldn't've made a blind bit of difference.' Ern shifts his rear end, causing the bonnet of the Hillman to perform a shallow dipping bow. 'I'll argue that any punishment should be limited to a formal reprimand and being placed on probation, but it'll be the Board that'll make the final decision.'

Eamonn sighs gratefully. 'Thanks, Mr Shaw.'

'And I think we'll manage to keep the police out of it. They've got enough to deal with at the moment, what with . . .' Ern pauses. 'Everything.'

Eamonn nods.

'As long as no more copies of *The Little Red Schoolbook* turn up in our vulnerable young people's hands.'

'What will happen to Joe Cassar?' asks Eamonn.

'Apart from the kick in the pants he got from his father, he won't be punished. He's a bright lad. I've got high hopes for him. As I do for you, Eamonn, but in the current climate I don't know that they will be realised in Kaliope.'

Ern stands up and stretches. 'I'll see you in the morning. Drive carefully.'

'Do you think it was someone local?' Eamonn says.

His question doesn't require further elaboration. Who is responsible for Janet McClymont's disappearance is a subject that bubbles beneath almost every conversation these days. Ern crosses his arms, rises onto his toes and then lowers himself back down onto his heels. 'I do know there are men in this town who see a young girl like that and think only about their own desires. So, yes, to answer your question, I think it could well have been someone local.'

Ern slaps the roof of the Hillman and walks over to his blue Kingswood, gets in, turns over the engine and guides it past the Hillman. He doesn't look at Eamonn as he leaves, but raises a hand, a kind of benediction.

As Ern drives towards home along Kaliope's main drag, a knot of figures stumble out of the Commercial Hotel. He slows to let the group cross the street. In the gleam of his headlights the gnarl of bodies resolves into three men and a young woman. He frowns. The young woman is actually little more than a girl, from what he can see, and she's clasped so tightly against the side of one of the men that she is walking lopsidedly, her outside foot barely touching the ground. He can't see her face, but in the angle of her head and her faltering steps he reads uncertainty. Not fright exactly, but wariness. The man with the girl crushed against his side draws ahead, and Ern sees the other two following behind them exchange a glance. Their faces are in shadow, but the animal calculatedness of it, the sense that a decision has been made from which the girl is excluded, fills him with dread. He watches them disappear into the darkness of a side street. At an impatient blast of a car horn behind him, he puts the Kingswood into gear and drives on. In the rear-view mirror, he sees the group walking down a lane that he knows leads to a sports oval.

Ern is still debating with himself if he should take any action when he notices the lights on at the Kaliope Police Station. On an impulse he pulls into the carpark. The front door is locked, but when he presses the night bell, Carmel Maitland appears and lets him in.

'Mr Shaw. How can I help you?'

Now that he is out of the car and standing in the brightly lit station, Ern is unsure whether what he saw was sinister or not. 'I might be overreacting . . .' he says.

~

Moments after Ern Shaw has explained what he suspects he may have seen—a girl, possibly inebriated, being coerced into a sexual encounter she has not consented to—and the location of the sports oval, Carmel is in the Q car and driving. When she glances into her rear-view mirror, Ern Shaw is standing by his Kingswood, his big body slumped forlornly.

Carmel finds the sports oval in minutes and pulls up next to the small spectator stand, leaving her headlights on high beam. Before she exits the car, she grabs a torch from the glove box. The headlights provide the only illumination of the oval's wide expanse. She flicks on her torch, directing its beam at the dark corners at either end. The long stretch of well-maintained grass is flat and empty.

Beneath its corrugated-iron roof, the grandstand—if you can call it that—is in pitch blackness. The banks of tiered seating reveal nothing. Carmel places a foot on the first step of the ascending aisle that divides the seating into two sections. The weathered wood creaks, and from the top row comes a gasp of masculine laughter and the sound of bodies scuttling across seats.

'Who's there?' Carmel calls.

Initially there is only silence in reply and then another snigger. Something bounces down the steps and a longneck of XXXX beer, leaking liquid, comes to a halt by her foot. When Carmel shines her torch up to the top row, the beam finds four faces: a girl and three young men.

One of the men is Kenny Connolly. He grins into the light she is training on his face. 'Good evening, officer.'

Carmel ignores him, swings the torch so the beam now illuminates the face of the girl sitting on Kenny's lap, her legs draped over the thighs of the man next to him. Smeared lipstick and smudged mascara. She looks like she's been drinking, her limbs loose and heavy, but she is alert.

Carmel advances another couple of steps. 'Are you alright, miss? Do you need any assistance? I'm a police officer.'

'She's fine; aren't you, Lesley?' the young man nursing the girl's legs answers.

Carmel recognises him as Kenny's tradie mate from the meeting at the Quala hall. 'Miss?' she says again. 'Lesley, is it? Are you safe? Would you like me to give you a lift home or to a friend's place?'

The girl settles herself further into Kenny's lap. 'Nuh. It's all good. Thanks, but.'

The third man, silent until now, hands Lesley an open longneck. 'We're just having a little party, officer. Would you like to join us?'

Lesley takes a swig and hands the bottle to Kenny.

'Yeah, officer,' Kenny says. 'Join us if you'd like.' He drinks deeply from the bottle.

Carmel ignores him. 'How old are you, Lesley?'

'Eighteen,' the girl says, airily defiant.

Carmel is still uneasy, but she can't just drag the girl away. Methodically, she shines the torch onto each of the men's faces, committing the two she is not familiar with to memory, before saying, 'I'll be at Kaliope Police Station tomorrow, Lesley, if there's anything you'd like to report.'

Jeers and catcalls follow her back to the car. Carmel doesn't care what Bill reckons; she'll definitely be looking hard into Kenny Connolly's alibi on the day Janet disappeared. And that of his mates.

TWENTY

WHEN CAM COMES to bed, he tells Connie that everything is in readiness for burning the bottom half of the big cane field below the house tomorrow.

Connie puts the book she is reading face down on the blanket, keeps a finger on the page to mark her place. Cam says he's lined up the same blokes he's paid to help with the harvest the last couple of years. They'll turn up for work the day after tomorrow, when the mill will be expecting their first cut.

'So John will help with the burn tomorrow night?' Connie asks.

Cam and the Creadies will work together as they usually do to burn the cane on both their farms, he tells her, at least over the first few days. When the cane-cutting crew turn up, there'll be more bodies to help.

Exhausted, Cam kisses Connie goodnight and turns out the light on his side of the bed. Connie reopens her book. It's not one of the volumes Barbara lent her in her now-forgotten quest to raise Connie's consciousness, but a collection of gentle tales of the life of a vet in the Yorkshire countryside, with its benign drizzle and high cold moors.

At another time, the stories in these pages would transport Connie far away from the heat and humidity, the close still air, the midday light so bright it hurts her eyes. Tonight, though, as at the beginning of harvesting every year, she is aware of Cam's anxious excitement. Knowing he has months of hard labour in front of him, his head will be full of lists and concerns, tasks to be completed, contingencies to be prepared for. He will toss and turn beside her in the bed, taking longer than usual to settle into sleep, and then wake up during the night. Despite the preoccupation with Janet's disappearance and Ted and Barbara's raw grief and naked anguish, as well as the strain from the hypervigilance they are all exercising in watching and worrying about the children, and the distrust and anxiety that hang over them all, Connie knows that Cam cannot help but look forward to the thrill and spectacle of burning the cane.

When Connie first met Cam at the wedding of her school friend and his cousin in Brisbane almost fifteen years ago, one of the first things he told her was how much he loved cane fires. He declared that if he didn't have to fly home to Quala the next day to prepare for the crush, he would take her out that evening.

His delight, the pure pleasure he took in this ritual of fire and smoke, was one of the things that drew her to him.

That and his tanned forearms, their well-defined muscles moving beneath his golden skin when he pulled out her chair for her. He'd taken off his suit jacket and rolled up the cuffs of his sleeves. When he rested his arms on the table before they brought around the meals—beef stroganoff for him and apricot chicken for her—she deliberately brushed his wrist with her hand when she reached for her wine glass, just to feel his skin against hers. At that first brief touch, she felt him shudder.

That night he told her that when he was a little kid he and his younger brother and two sisters would stand on the verandah with his mother to watch the burning cane fields. The clouds of ash would rise thousands of feet into the air and fall to earth miles away. In town, people complained about 'Kaliope snow'. They'd be fishing cinders out of their backyard swimming pools for months. But for Cam and his brother and sisters, as for most cane farmers' kids, the burning of the cane was one of the best times of the year.

On the farms, while the children played in the eddies of ash, women would fuss about the black marks on their washing and the dust drifting into the houses. Despite the wet towels stopping up the gaps between doors and floors, the ash would find its way in. The men would return to the house in sooty clothes leaving black marks on everything they brushed up against. And the smell of burning cane remained in the air for months. There was nothing like it.

Cam told her that when he was ten years old he was finally deemed mature enough to help with the burning as a runner, sprinting through the dusk between his father and grandfather on either side of a cane field to relay information about what was happening on the opposite side. If a line of flame escaped the field, flickering along a grassy verge, or a floater flew up and came down on the other side of the firebreak, he'd chase it down and beat it out with a wet hessian sack. After decades of this ritual, there are still few things Cam loves more than watching two fires on either side of a cane field race towards each other, the smoke spiralling skywards against a pink and orange sunset, the crackling of flames filling his ears, the heat of the fire on his face.

Connie knows that the tasks of preparing for the burn add texture to Cam's expectant pleasure. Checking and rechecking the driptorches, filling them with fuel, ensuring the wicks are still serviceable and replacing those that aren't. Every season, Essie and Helen hover around him as he tests them, watching the fuel falling in combusting droplets as if it's some mythical draught meant for the gods.

The girls fill the old bathtub near the machinery shed with water. They drag out the hessian sacks stored in the shed and cram them into the tub, climbing in to stomp the sacks down under the level of the water until they are saturated. Of course, it always becomes a game, the girls splashing each other so they're soon dripping wet, the dogs barking in excitement. Connie thinks the girls' squeals have become as much a part of Cam's joy at this time of year as the flames. The sodden sacks are too heavy for Essie and Helen to lift by themselves, but he lets them think they are helping when they insist on lifting a corner of wet jute and stumble after him as he heaves the sacks onto the back of the ute. He stows the jerry cans of spare fuel for the torches beside the sacks and checks he has a full box of matches in his pocket and a couple more in the ute's glove box.

This year, though, just when Cam starts to lose himself in the happy labour of tasks and planning, Connie can see the whole sorry business of Janet's disappearance flood back, marring his simple enjoyment. Not that Cam complains. His frustration is nothing compared to Ted and Barbara's loss; nevertheless, it casts a pall over what had always been a time of anticipation and purpose.

Normally, in the weeks leading up to the crush, Cam would have mown the strips around the edges of the fields, sprayed herbicide and cleared any debris that had built up and might allow the fire to leap the breaks between the paddocks. It is not all fun and games. Machinery has been destroyed and sheds lost, people injured and homes threatened, when a cane fire has got away either due to bad luck, bad preparation or carelessness.

Although there's been drier weather over the past several weeks, the earlier rain has promoted the luxuriant growth of grass and weeds. And with so many days lost in the search for Janet, this year Cam has been playing catch-up on his preparations. He and John Creadie have held off beginning their harvest for so long, but they can't wait any longer. Cam will light the first fire on their farm tomorrow.

TWENTY-ONE

CONNIE STRIDES FROM the house towards the shed where Cam is preparing the driptorches for the first burn that evening. She's wearing one of his work shirts, along with a pair of shorts and boots she puts on for gardening. Even to her own eyes, when she looked in the mirror before she left the bedroom, with her hair tied back in pigtails like her daughters, she looked pleasingly pert. She smiled at herself.

Cam screws down the brass cap on the last of the torches, straightens up when he sees her approach. When she reaches him, she leans against the side of the ute, crosses one booted foot over the other. A broad grin transforms the lines on his face. 'Well, look who it is. The woman with the famous pins. Chester Connolly, eat your heart out.'

Connie laughs. 'So, boss. What do you need me to do?' She pushes her hat back off her forehead, enjoying the delight on her husband's face.

Before Cam has time to answer, Helen is calling from the house that Mrs Creadie is on the phone.

'I hope she's not ringing to say she can't look after the girls,' Connie says as she jogs back to take the call.

She returns minutes later. 'Vince has had a fall. Tripped over something in the shed, hit his head on a sharp corner of the harvester. Jean found him at the back door. He'd crawled there from the shed after knocking himself out. She said she'll have to throw away his shirt, it's so stained and bloody.'

The phone call was hurried but Jean said that Vince was conscious and telling everybody he was fine. Their daughter-in-law Meg is in Brisbane to help out her sister who recently had a baby, so Jean is looking after Sandra while John runs Vince in to the hospital. 'Jean says we can still drop the girls over to the snug and John will be along to help with the burn as soon as he can,' Connie adds.

Cam tosses his work gloves on the ground in frustration. 'Shit. I hope Vince is alright. But it's bloody inconvenient. For safety we really need three of us for the burn,' he says. 'Maybe we should get Essie to help. She's old enough to chase down any floaters.'

Connie is shaking her head before he's finished his sentence. 'No, Cam. The thought of her running around in the dark where I can't see her? No.'

'I was helping with the burn at her age.'

'I don't care. He could still be out there. John will be here before long.'

Looking over towards the old house where Parslow and Sullivan live, Cam suggests they ask the two of them if they can help, but Connie refuses. She's prepared to accept that Sullivan had nothing to do with Janet's disappearance, but that filth he was peddling—no, she won't have anything to do with him. He's a troublemaker. A socialist. And it would seem odd if they only asked Parslow.

'We can manage with just the two of us until John gets here,' she says.

The girls are already waiting by the station wagon and Connie fishes for the car keys in the pocket of her shorts. 'I'll be back from the Creadies' in ten minutes.'

When Connie returns, Cam hands her a pair of fireproof gloves and gives her a refresher on how to use the driptorch, showing her how to loosen the brass cap of the cylinder and then remove the thumb screw from the tube that feeds the wick.

'See how the brass plate attached to the wick fits into the opening of the cylinder? And then the cap. Screw it back down over the plate to secure it.'

Connie suffers his instructions with bad grace, makes a grab to wrestle the torch out of his hands. 'Yes, I've done it before.'

But Cam is nothing if not thorough. He reminds her to open the air vent that will allow the fuel to run down the tube feeding the wick. He lets a small amount of fuel leak out of the tube and onto the gravel near where the ute is parked, sets a lit match to it. A low runnel of fire flares from the small puddle of fuel, springing up like an excited animal. 'Now you can dip the wick into the flame to light it.'

With a low *whump*, the end of the torch catches alight.

'When you want to extinguish the torch, just snuff it out.' Cam smothers the flame with his gloved hand and then kicks dirt over the fuel still burning on the ground. He goes over which section of the big paddock they will light tonight, telling her he knocked down a firebreak between it and the rest of the paddock earlier in the day. He's chucked a couple of wet hessian sacks in the tray of the ute Connie will be driving; he'll be on the tractor with the trailer.

He stresses the importance of both of them knowing where the other is at any given time.

'Don't speak to me like I'm an idiot, Cameron,' snaps Connie.

'Without a third person running between us,' Cam repeats, 'we'll have to take more care than usual.'

'Yes. I understand.'

'Keep a lookout for snakes. I've seen a few around the place. And don't get ahead of me. You concentrate on the back-burn. I'll keep an eye out for floaters until John gets here. I'll chase down any that look like they might start up a fire in the rest of the field. And watch for wind changes.'

~

Cam leaves the tractor in the north-west corner of the section of the paddock they are going to burn and Connie drives him down to the firebreak he's pushed through the cane with the big blade he attached to the front of the tractor. She waits with the engine running while he lifts one of the driptorches from the tray. He reaches through the cabin's passenger window and takes a box of matches from the dashboard.

'Start at the south-east corner and walk in the direction of the house. When John turns up, I'll send him round to your side to give you a hand. When I'm back at the tractor, I'll drive round and mop up any bits of stray ember or floater fires that start. Shit.' Cam smacks the roof of the cabin.

'What?'

'Do you know how to refuel the driptorch?'

'Oh, for goodness' sake, Cameron, do you think I'm a complete bloody fool?'

'Not at all.' He pauses. 'Constance.'

He grins at her and she makes a half-hearted attempt to slap his arm through the open window. 'Off you go.'

Cam steps back from the ute and Connie puts it in gear, gunning the accelerator and riding the clutch so that the wheels spin in the dirt before tearing off down the track. In the rear-view mirror, there is still enough light for her to see him laughing.

The sun has almost slipped behind the hills. There is precious little twilight this far north, something it took Connie years to get used to after growing up nine hundred miles south. There, the glow in the sky after sunset lit the granite hills with a soft rosy light. Here, a curtain falls, going from late afternoon to night in the space of seconds. In the minutes since she dropped Cam off, it is already noticeably darker.

She parks the ute in the middle of the break in the fields that marks the boundary between their farm and the Creadies'.

The grass outside the ute reaches over her knees. She saw John Creadie towing the slasher with his tractor earlier in the day, but he must have had to take Vince to the hospital before he had a chance to cut back the grass along this strip. Why he didn't mow along here first, who knows? Too late to worry about it now.

Connie vaults onto the tray of the ute. When she sees smoke rising from the opposite side of the field, she leaps down, finds a relatively clear piece of ground and lights the driptorch without incident. She stamps out the ignition fire, grinding the singed grass into the dirt.

As Connie begins working her way up the drill, setting the cane alight at ground level, the heat from the blaze lit by Cam on the other side is already thickening the air. The flames catch the cane's panicles, burning bright. Before long, the two fronts are surging satisfyingly towards each other across the field. The gathering darkness and the radiant aliveness of the flames; Connie's satisfaction in her competence in the performance of her task; the thought of Cam, calm and steady on the other side of the cane field, and of the girls safe in the Creadies' snug: all these things coalesce into a quiet happiness. In this moment, Connie can imagine a time in the future when once again she will be able to feel that everything will be alright.

⌒

Old Mrs Creadie gave the three girls fish fingers and mashed potato for their early tea and let them eat with their plates on their laps on the couch in the lounge room to watch *The Waltons*. She promised that she will drive them down to watch the fire later, but first she has to ring the hospital. Just wait, like good little things.

Now *The Waltons* is over and the television is off. Sandra and Helen are on the couch with a pile of Little Golden Books beside them and Helen is reading *The Poky Little Puppy* aloud, her finger skimming below each word as she utters it. 'Five little puppies dug a hole under the fence and went for a walk in the wide, wide . . .' Helen stops, her index finger planted on the page.

'Keep going,' says Sandra, her plump cheek pressed against Helen's arm.

Helen screws up her face, peers intently at the next word, but the letters and the noises she makes won't come together.

Having taken their plates into the kitchen like Mrs Creadie asked her to, Essie now prowls about the room, bored and irritable. She stops in front of the drinks cabinet in the corner, unhooks the catch on the cabinet door and glides her fingers over the bottles of luridly coloured liquor inside, silently mouthing their exotic-sounding names: *Tia Maria*, *Crème de Menthe*, *Advocaat*.

'Essie, how do you say this word?' asks Helen.

Essie leans over the armrest of the couch and flicks her finger against the book's cardboard cover. 'This is for babies. Aren't you in Grade 2? You must be stupid if you can't read it.'

She contemplates plucking the book out of Helen's hand and tossing it across the room. Decides against it when Sandra, with her dour, sulky gaze, kicks one of her fat little legs in Essie's direction.

Helen assumes a superior tone. 'Only stupid people call other people stupid.'

This time Essie doesn't hesitate. She throws the book over the back of the couch, where it hits the wall and lands on the floor.

Sandra scowls at Essie with dislike as Helen marches towards the office beside the kitchen where Mrs Creadie is on the phone to the hospital.

'Tattletale,' says Essie.

From the lounge room Essie hears the normally patient Mrs Creadie telling Helen to go away, she's waiting to talk to someone at the hospital. Essie smirks at Helen when she reappears, and gives her the forks. Helen blinks in shock at this obscenity, her mouth falling open.

Through the door opening onto the verandah, Essie sees the first tongues of fire racing each other along opposite edges of the big cane field nearest her house, and heads out to the verandah.

'Mrs Creadie said for us to stay in here until she gets off the phone,' says Helen.

But Essie is already standing at the verandah rail watching the smoke rising from her family's fields. 'Yes, yes, I can wait,' she hears Mrs Creadie say, her voice high-pitched and quavering.

Essie can just make out the flickering silhouettes of her mother and father against the leaping orange light. Their figures merge into the darkness, moving in and out of the glare of the advancing line of fire. The flames sprinting ahead are low and close to the ground. Behind them, the blaze springs skywards, climbing the cane stalks and licking at the leaves. The fire is already flinging up ash and embers and snatching at the tass-elled tops of the cane.

Essie can't forget holding Mr Creadie's dowsing rods when the image of Janet's butterfly-shaped hair slide slipped into her head like a frog into water. How the rods swung towards the old house. How they pulled her towards it, drawing her to the place where the red-headed teacher lives.

She's heard the teacher is an actual pervert. He gave some high school students dirty books with pictures of people without their clothes doing sex things. That's what Danny Pine says. When Essie thinks about the night at the hall, she can still feel the weight of the teacher's hand on her shoulder when he found her and Raelene behind the curtain. She remembers the policewoman from Sydney looking at him as if he was a cane toad that she would like to squash. And her mother's face, pinched with disgust and suspicion, as she watched him driving away from the hall. A thought occurs to Essie: perhaps it was his green car that stopped on the road that night or early the next morning when Janet stepped out of the cane field.

What might Essie find in the teacher's house if she sneaks up the tall staircase and onto the verandah so that she can look through a window? A butterfly-shaped hair slide? Janet herself?

Vivid in Essie's mind is Raelene pointing at her and laughing, telling Gavan and Tim and Danny that Essie is a goody-goody, a scaredy cat. *Just the type a pervert would want to do it to and then chop her up and leave her in a cane field for the rats to eat.* Essie's face and ears flare hot and damp. She thinks of Raelene, her poisonous yellow fingertips. *I forgot that you're just a baby.*

Essie decides that on Monday she will not run over to Raelene on the asphalt where they line up to march into school, blabbing like a little kid. She will say nothing at all to her. Not even when she is sitting beside Raelene at their desks. No. She will get on with the work that Mr Day will give them, fractions, or writing, or reading comprehension. Raelene will probably tell her some story about Kenny Connolly or the Kable boys or getting drunk, thinking she will be impressed. Most of it will be lies. Essie will nod or shrug, but she won't say anything back. At little lunch she won't offer to share her Milo with Raelene when the boys bring around the crate with the bottles of milk. She will go and sit with Susan and Sharon and later join in with their skipping games. If Danny Pine's mother hasn't packed a biscuit for his morning tea in his lunch box, she will ask him if he would like her apple.

The red-headed teacher's house is just a short distance down the track. Essie can walk there, dart up the stairs, look in the window and come back before Mrs Creadie even realises she is gone. Even if she doesn't see anything to do with Janet, she will tell Raelene and the others what she has done. Or maybe she won't. The others didn't know Janet the way Essie did. Raelene didn't know her at all. It is only Essie's heart that feels cold in her chest when the others joke about what happened to Janet, what might have been done to her. None of the other kids seem to care.

Essie imagines returning Janet to her parents. Mrs McClymont loud and bright again. Mr McClymont jolly and beaming at his daughter. Their happiness. Perhaps, in the face of all their joy, even the cane would cease to whisper.

Essie glances back into the lounge room. Sandra has brought out her Barbie doll, and she and Helen are playing with it together on the lounge room's carpeted floor. Sandra looks up to see Essie poised on the top step. Essie catches her eye, scowls and shakes her head, and Sandra turns back to Helen.

'You can brush her hair if you like,' Sandra says.

~

Within minutes of leaving the snug, Essie reaches the dilapidated fence enclosing the yard of the old house. The palings have fallen inwards as the cane in the surrounding fields has advanced. The breeze has picked up and carries the heat of the flames, lifting the hair off the back of Essie's neck and pressing her T-shirt against her skin. The crackle of the cane fire is distant.

Essie lingers outside the fence, peering up at the little house perched on its stilts and wondering how close she dares to venture. Parked on the grass out the front is the teacher's green Hillman Hunter. Its boot is open and it's loaded with boxes and a large suitcase. A brown Cortina sits nearby. The lights are on in one of the front rooms and the red-headed teacher appears in the open window. It's like looking into the aquarium in the Chinese restaurant in Kaliope that she has been to with her parents. The fish don't even realise they're being watched.

The schoolteacher's long red hair is wet and he's wearing a pair of faded jeans but no shirt. The skin of his tummy and chest is incredibly white compared to the splotches of brown freckles on his face and arms. Essie ducks down behind the fence and peers through the broken palings as he moves towards the open window. He pulls on an oddly ladyish white top that is embroidered with flowers around the neck. Turning to look at himself in the mirror on the door of a wardrobe, he draws his fingers through his hair.

Essie creeps forward and can hear him singing to himself. She listens carefully and recognises the song from the Elvis Presley record her dad sometimes plays. 'You're the devil in disguise, oh yes you are.'

Another man appears at the door to the schoolteacher's room, smoking a rollie cigarette. He is shorter than the schoolteacher, with muscly shoulders and thick arms. Pete Parslow, Essie guesses, remembering the old Creadies speaking to her mother about him when they were having afternoon tea. Essie can only hear snatches of the men's conversation as they pass the rollie between them, but she works out that Peter Parslow is advising the teacher to change his mind about something, as if he is concerned that perhaps the teacher has made a stupid decision.

She inches closer and hears him say, 'I reckon you're jumping the gun. Sounds like Ern Shaw is on your side.'

The teacher shakes his head. 'I don't care. I'm over it.'

Both men bend over, vanishing below the level of the window frame. When they straighten up, they are carrying cardboard boxes. They move towards the bedroom door and the lights go off in the house. The men disappear briefly from view before reappearing at the open front door. Staying behind the fence, Essie sneaks around to the side of the house, keeping the cars in sight. The two men clatter down the long staircase and put the boxes into the boot of the Hillman.

'Is that the last of them?' Peter asks, watching the red-headed teacher rearranging the boxes in the boot.

'Yep. Anything I've left behind you can keep, burn or give away.'

'I saw you've left your copies of *The Catholic Leader* in the dunny,' Peter says, laughing. 'Sure you don't want me to run in and get them?'

'Nah. Consider them a gift. They'll provide you with moral guidance in my absence.' The teacher slams down the boot lid. 'How are you getting back from the pub?'

'Not sure, but Marie's driving out from town to meet me for a drink there, so later on . . .'

'You bloody dog,' the teacher says. 'Couldn't even wait until I'd left town.'

The next part of the conversation is hard for Essie to make out. The men are laughing and using words that she recognises as bad. Then their discussion shifts again.

'Don't be an idiot,' Peter says.

'Nah. She'll be right. I'll sleep in the car.'

'Mate. They call it "the horror stretch" for a reason. Get to Rocky and stay in a motel.'

The teacher makes noises as if he is agreeing, but it sounds to Essie as if he is just pretending to go along with his friend's advice. Car doors slam and the car's engine turns over.

Heart thumping, Essie is preparing to make a move towards the house when she hears Peter say, 'Hang on.' He gets out of the car and runs up the front steps of the house.

As he wrestles with the front door, hauling on the knob with both hands, the teacher toots the car horn.

'I don't want that bloody cat to get in and piss on my bed again,' Peter yells over his shoulder as, with a final heave, he pulls the door to. He tugs on the knob, tests that it is shut fast.

A few seconds later, the teacher drives the car down the track towards the main road.

Essie feels something deep in her belly turn to liquid with a mixture of fear and certainty. The realisation is dizzying, and sickening. Nothing can prevent her from going into the teacher's house now.

TWENTY-TWO

CONNIE IS ABOUT three-quarters of the way along the length of the drill. Ahead of her and the advancing fire, she spots the occasional rat or mouse scrambling away to escape the noise and heat. Wary of snakes, Connie steps carefully. When a large cane toad suddenly crawls out of the cane near her feet, she shrieks. Quashes an impulse to set the thing alight.

The noise of the fire has risen, brattling and crackling. By the smoke billowing above her head, Connie knows the wind is picking up. Embers, shreds of burning leaves and ash spiral upwards. In the face of the flames' intensity, Connie is struck by how precarious their control of the burn is. So far the floaters the fire is sending up are burning out before they fall back to earth. The shifting eddies of heat-generated gas sometimes swirl into her face, tightening the skin against her skull. Sweat is now pouring down her neck and chest. She wipes her forehead with the tail of Cam's shirt. When she looks back, she's relieved to see the two fronts of the fire burning steadily towards each other and no smoke rising from the adjoining section. She waits expectantly for Cam to approach on the tractor, ready to put out spot fires ignited by floaters.

There is a sudden gust of wind, followed by a sharp, searing pain and the acrid smell of singed hair. Connie slaps at her head. *Idiot*. She left her hat on the seat of the ute. Flaming scraps from the back-burn scatter onto the grassy strip between the burning cane and the Creadies' place. Several floaters spiral down towards the paddock beside the cottage where the teacher lives, thankfully flaring out before they reach the ground. Connie's relief is short-lived. Behind her, a line of fire snakes out and onto the grass. There is no sign of Cam.

Connie extinguishes the driptorch's flame and jogs back, stamps the small flare-up out easily enough, debates whether to run back to the ute and drive it up to this point. But Cam will be here soon, and if the wind is picking up she can't afford to let the fire front he's lit get too far ahead of her. He must have reached the end of the field by now and he'll have seen that the flurry of wind that blew the embers onto the firebreak is also driving the eastern flank of the fire rapidly towards her side of the field. He'll be here in a couple of minutes. Better for her to finish lighting the back-burn.

The driptorch is lying on its side where she left it. She reaches into the pockets of her shorts one after the other, searching for a box of matches to relight it. She's sure she grabbed one from the glove box before she got out of the ute. More frantically now, she pats the breast pocket of her shirt and then runs her hands through the grass surrounding the torch. Another gust of wind, a blast of heat. She is enveloped in smoke, searing her throat. Coughing, Connie staggers back, flapping at the thick fumes blanketing her face. The wind seems to be coming from several different directions at once, and suddenly the air about her clears. The fire front on the other side of the field has leapt ahead and is racing towards her. Another line of fire has crept out from the field and is inching across the firebreak.

Jesus! Where the hell is Cam?

~

Essie scurries towards the old house. She has a fleeting image of herself climbing the stairs, shoving open the front door that Peter Parslow has pulled shut and creeping down the hall. Just like in *McMillan & Wife*, her mum's favourite TV show, she will find Janet locked in a wardrobe in the teacher's bedroom, her hands and feet bound and maybe a gag tied across her mouth. She'll take a knife from the kitchen and cut the rope around Janet's ankles and wrists and gently untie the gag. She will hold out her hand and help Janet to her feet.

Even as she imagines this happy scenario, Essie knows this rescue mission is just pretend. But still, it is thrilling. At the beginning, it was meant as a drama enacted for Raelene, but she isn't even here to see it. Because she's such a fibber and a skite herself, Raelene sniffs out lies as easily as she draws the boys around her. Initially, this adventure was a rehearsal for Essie's future telling of it. In performing it, she would make it true. But now, she is not so sure that she will tell anyone what she has done. She is doing it less to impress Raelene than to prove something to herself. And she is doing it for Janet. Or in her memory.

Essie scampers up the long flight of stairs, tries to open the front door, but Peter Parslow wedged it tight as anything in its warped frame when he pulled it shut. She kicks at it but it won't shift. Bolting back down the steps, she runs around to the side of the house adjacent to the firebreak where, only a few hundred yards away, the paddock is burning. Two enormous swags of fire churn towards each other. The cane surrounding the old cottage lists towards the flames. Her father's ute is parked in between Essie and the burning field. And there, walking in the other direction, is a black silhouette against a curtain of orange flame. It's her mother, wearing workboots and a man's shirt, but still immediately recognisable.

Around the old house, the cane in the Creadies' fields whispers as if spooked by the fire in the Tranters' field opposite. For a moment, Essie considers dashing back to the safety of the snug, but her mother's proximity—Essie could run to her in less than a minute—emboldens her. What possible harm can come to her when her mother is so close?

Essie slips through the gate and into the cottage's backyard, populated by banana trees and one big old mango, then races along the concrete path to the back steps. She looks around again, but her mother's reassuring figure is receding and the complaining cane reasserts itself. Now, with the quiet, waiting emptiness of the old house before her, Essie's night-time fears of a hulking monstrous presence seem urgently plausible. The sense of something about to pluck at her clothes, hook talons into her hair and drag her into the cane sends her bolting up the stairs.

The unlocked back door opens onto an enclosed verandah. She knows it opens onto a kitchen and a short central hall that leads to a bathroom, a living room and the two bedrooms at the front of the house.

Light from the fire seeps through the open back door, staining the walls orange. When she opens her mouth to call out for Janet, the dryness in her throat catches the sound. The vacant house draws her uncertainly down the darkened hall.

Essie looks into the kitchen, then the living room and pauses at the door to the bathroom, wrinkling her nose at the acrid reek of urine.

The bedroom on the left of the hallway is where she spied the red-headed teacher through the open window. She peers into the one on her right first, risks turning on the light. There is no sign of Janet. When she flicks on the light in the other bedroom, she sees it's been vacated. The doors of the wardrobe gape open, its drawers and hanging space bare except for a torn shirt, a pair of stained Y-front underpants and three wire coat hangers dangling from the clothes rack. There's no sign of a bound and gagged Janet. The bed has been stripped of linen, and two pillows, sweat-stained and yellow, are on the floor. She looks under the bed but there is only dust and a stray sock.

Janet is not here. No one is here. A crushing sadness descends on Essie. Where is she, the kind girl who smelt of strawberry lip gloss and who loved a boy with long eyelashes? And what has happened to her?

But there is also relief. If she runs, she can be back at the snug before Helen or Sandra have noticed she is gone and blab to old Mrs Creadie.

~

A puff of wind skimming in from over the ocean snatches fragments of smouldering cane trash and sends them corkscrewing high above the burning field. A second flurry chases the glowing swarm towards the cottage. They hang above it for moments before spiralling downwards. The old house is badly weathered and surrounded on three sides by fields of cane. The heat from the fire has leached moisture from the air, and the weatherboards, buckled and cracked, cradle tiny drifts of flammable dust and detritus collected over decades in gaps and splintery niches where scraps of burning leaf might lodge. And they do lodge. The powdery kindling smokes and then, suddenly, catches alight.

~

Essie takes a last look around the teacher's bedroom. There's an open cardboard box in the corner with copies of the red books that caused all the fuss, the ones about sex and drugs. Essie opens one and scans the contents page. Many of the words are unfamiliar, but several that she does recognise carry a sense of danger. Some she has heard Raelene use, although she has never seen them written down before.

She is about to replace the book, but the lure of the words, the promise of forbidden knowledge, keeps it in her hand. Maybe she can show it to Raelene. But the book is too wide to fit into the pocket of her jeans, so she stuffs it into the back of her underpants and flicks off the light on her way out of the room. She feels her way along the hall to the front door, but when she turns the knob and pulls, it won't budge. Using both hands and her entire body weight, Essie tugs at the door. It shifts a little, but the lower left-hand corner is stuck tight in the frame.

She will have to leave the way she came in.

Jean puts down the phone. Vince is alright. Not a stroke. Just low blood pressure and dehydration. The nurse was very reassuring. Apart from a mild concussion, she told Jean, he seems pretty good. They'll keep an eye on him for another little while but depending on what the doctor says, he might even be able to come home tonight.

Relief slows Jean's heart, which has been leaping like a mad thing in her chest for hours. A few tears spill onto her cheeks before she dashes them away.

There is no sound from the children, so they've probably gone out onto the verandah to watch the cane fire, even though she told them to stay inside until she got off the phone. But when Jean steps into the lounge room, Sandra and Helen are there, sprawled on the floor playing with Sandra's Barbie doll.

'Ready for ice cream?' Jean asks. 'Where's Essie?'

Helen points to the verandah and walks Barbie over to Sandra's foot, pivoting the stiff-legged doll on her ridiculously tiny feet. 'I'm here for my appointment,' Helen says in an approximation of a grown-up lady's voice.

Jean calls out Essie's name, and when there is no answer, walks over to the door. She breathes in the familiar smell of burning cane and the particular dancing light of the flames. Glancing down the length of the verandah, she realises the girl is not leaning on the rail, nor sitting on the sofa.

'Essie?'

~

Cam clamps his gloved hand over the lit wick of the driptorch, turns the fuel valve to off and stows the torch in the footwell of the tractor cab. So far, so good. But when he swings up into the tractor seat, it's obvious that the back-burn is less advanced than he'd like, though not yet anything to worry about. Connie's done well but he'll feel more relaxed when he's with her.

He switches on the ignition and the tractor rumbles to life beneath him. Christ, he's thirsty. He swigs a couple of mouthfuls of water from his water bottle and stows it beside the driptorch. As he switches on the headlights, a sinuous silhouette sways up in front of his eyes. Before conscious thought kicks in, he has leapt out of the cab and onto the ground, scrambling away from the tractor.

Fucking hell. He is wandering in circles, his hands on his hips, chest quivering with pent-up laughter. *Fuck me.*

He was convinced the snake was on the inside of the cab, but peering up at the reptile, he sees its creamy belly is pressed up against the outside of the windscreen. Most of its body is looped around the wipers. It's a big bastard. The illumination from the tractor's headlights is too uncertain for him to be sure, but it looks like a coastal taipan. It must have been driven out of the cane by the fire, slithered underneath the tractor, up into the undercarriage and onto the bonnet.

The roar of the fire drags his attention back to the task at hand. The wind has picked up significantly. *Shit*. He needs to get to Connie. With no sign of John, she needs his help with the back-burn. There's little danger of a floater starting up a blaze in the other section of the field now, but the fire he's lit is moving fast. If it reaches the other side it could keep going on to the Creadies' old place.

Looking back at the tractor, he sees that the snake, nervous and twitchy, has flattened the section of its body behind its head in preparation to strike. Cam knows it's capable of hurling itself forwards or sideways several feet. His great-uncle, his grandfather's brother, died from the bite of a coastal taipan when he was a young man. 'The brute flew at him like an arrow. Bit him three times before we even knew it was there,' his grandfather would say when retelling the story.

Perhaps he can flick the snake off. He'll need something with a bit of length. Cam scrabbles through the toolbox on the back of the tractor but there's nothing of use. Heart racing and conscious of the advancing fire, he scans the ground for a large stick, but then he remembers chucking his crowbar in the trailer the day before to jemmy open the tailboard. Wary of letting the snake out of his sight, he eases his way further behind the tractor, keeping an eye on it as much as he can.

Before Essie can reach the back door, she is startled by a telephone ringing. The sound shatters the muteness of the empty house into shards, pinning her against the wall. She waits, heart thudding, for it to stop. In the silence that follows the final peal, she realises there's been a fundamental shift in the sound of the fire. It's much closer. She looks up at the roof and puts a hand on the wall to steady herself. Waves of heat are rolling down from the ceiling.

~

Where the hell is Cam? wonders Connie, worried. She can't see him or the tractor. Smoke that was billowing up above the burning cane is now being blown low across the top of the field, making it difficult to see. What she can make out, however, is that fire, harried by the wind, is sending out multiple tendrils of flame and flinging dozens of floaters spiralling into the air. She has wasted precious minutes looking for the box of matches and now she is in a lather of indecision. Should she relight the torch—easy enough to do, if she's careful, by dipping the wick into a patch of burning grass—and finish the back-burning, or run back to the ute, drive it up to this point, drag the wet hessian bags out of the tray and start beating out the spot fires? Another gust of wind, another cascade of floaters, another small eruption of flame bent on colonising new ground. She can't wait for Cam any longer. If the fire reaches the Creadies' field, or a floater comes down in the yard around the old house, they won't be able to stop the ensuing blaze.

Still carrying the driptorch, Connie jogs back to the ute, several hundred yards away and parked opposite the Creadies' old house. By the time she reaches it, smoke seems to be every-where and for a moment she almost convinces herself that some of it is emanating from beneath the eaves of the old house, but before she can confirm her impression—the tangle of banana and mango trees makes it difficult to see—she glances back the way she has come. Several lines of flame are moving steadily along the ground in the direction of the Creadies' fields. Tossing the torch onto the passenger seat through the open window, she chooses to be furious with Cam rather than worried for his safety. She runs round to the driver's side and guns the engine.

~

As Cam closes his fist around the crowbar, a flash of headlights appears. A vehicle is driving up the track to their house. A ute, by the look of it, although in the dark he doesn't recognise it from this distance. Surely, whoever it is will have seen the tractor, its headlights blazing. The ute is only up at the house for a couple of minutes at most, before the driver reverses it out of the drive and speeds towards him. He holds one arm up to shade his eyes from the glare of the high beam. It's the Creadies' ute. At last. John must be back from the hospital, which means Vince can't be too bad.

But as the vehicle draws closer, he sees it is Jean in the driver's seat with the white, thrilled little faces of Sandra and Helen beside her. When the vehicle jerks to a halt, the girls almost slide off the seat into the dashboard. Jean thrusts her head out of the window. 'I can't find Essie.'

Cam looks in the direction of the snug, then at the fire, then back at the tractor's windscreen. The snake has disappeared.

TWENTY-THREE

WHEN PETER PARSLOW and the flame-haired teacher, Sullivan, turn up at the Crown in the early evening, Sullivan looks like he'd rather be anywhere else. Bev Zammit has been on the warpath and stirred things up. Word's got around about him giving the banned book to his students and that. I haven't read it myself, but I've seen the letters in the Kaliope newspaper railing against it: socialism, sex, drugs—well, that's what they reckon. It's fair to say that people aren't best pleased, and there's a bit of muttering and carry-on when he walks into the pub. And the way Sullivan is shuffling his feet and looking over his shoulder, there's no doubt he knows there's a bit of unpleasantness aimed in his direction. Why he wants to turn up wearing his hippy get-up knowing he's already drawn attention to himself, who knows?

Anyway, young Parslow drags him up to the bar and announces that Sullivan's leaving Quala for good that very night. There's a bit of a hooray and whatnot, no one's taking much notice. Most people ignore them, although Gordon Mason offers him a beer on the house, seeing as it's going to be his last in the joint. A young lady turns up just as the young blokes get their drinks. Nice-looking lass. Sullivan, like a great mooncalf, can't take his eyes off her, but it's the Parslow lad she's there for, anyone can see that.

In my opinion, public bars aren't the best place for a young woman. I know things are changing, but some blokes can be a bit rough; blokes like Chester Connolly, who's propping up the bar in his usual place. He makes a bit of a song and dance when she walks in, some crack about ducks on the pond and that sort of carry-on.

Chester starts to insinuate himself like he's in the habit of doing. Asks her what her name is and if she lives around the joint. Marie, she says. She's a teacher at the high school, lives in town. Chester's leering and going on like a galoot before she turns her back on him to talk to Pete and Sullivan, making it plain that she's ignoring Chester. He gets the pip, looks real dirty. Makes another crack. Something coarse about skinny women, but she puts him in his place, telling him not to worry, she'd rather be too thin than too thick, looking right at him. He shuts up after that.

I can hear her and Parslow trying to talk Sullivan out of leaving. Marie says he should wait for the Board's decision, the Education Board I think she means. But Sullivan says no, no; he's already booked his flight to London on the Kangaroo Route. Via Singapore, he says. Then he drains his beer and starts saying his goodbyes. Parslow and the girl make a big fuss of him. She gives him a kiss, and Parslow claps him on the back, tells him to watch out for the English sheilas. Sullivan heads for the door. Looks like he's in two minds about it, but off he goes.

Jimmy Froome and his brother are drinking at a high table near the door. Jimmy's a big bugger and Frank's not that much smaller. The two of them are built like brick shithouses. Enormous heads on both of them, hands the size of hubcaps.

Sullivan's tall but skinny and the Froome boys have half a head and three stone on him at least. He's just about out the door and he turns to give Parslow and his girlfriend a final wave when Jimmy mumbles something into his beer. Sullivan's not sure whether Jimmy's talking to him or not. He looks a bit confused. Turns to Jimmy and says something like, 'Sorry, mate?'

Jimmy heaves himself upright, that little towelling hat of his squashed on his head like a wart on a toad. He stands right over Sullivan and says loud as anything, 'I said, fucking good riddance to bad rubbish.'

The whole pub goes quiet. You could've heard a pin drop. Then Frank says, 'Ya bloody pervert.'

Sullivan looks like he's about to shit himself. Doesn't know which way to look. But credit to young Parslow, he's up beside his mate quick smart. All smiles and hail-fellow-well-met sort of caper. Tells Jimmy and Frank to knock it off, but in a friendly way. They don't need to worry. Sullivan will be on the other side of the planet in a week, he says, 'corrupting the youth of Great Britain'. He's a bit of a card, Parslow. Sends Sullivan on his way with a slap on the back. Tells him to drive safe.

Sullivan scoots out the door as if he's glad to still have his head on his shoulders. Not long after that, Jimmy and Frank finish their beers and take off too. I hear the roar of their big Bedford truck driving off in the same direction as Sullivan would've gone on his way out to the highway.

~

The sound of the fire is overwhelming. Essie can hardly think straight. And then there's the heat and the smoke. She remembers a fire drill they did at school once. Mr Day told them that in a big fire, it would be hard to see and that any good air would be down low. He made them close their eyes and creep out the door on all fours.

Essie drops to her hands and knees and crawls from the hall back into the teacher's bedroom. She finds the window and climbs into the open frame. The verandah on the front of the house doesn't extend this far, and the ground is dark and far away. Because of the overgrown bushes, which are surrounded by a border of large white rocks, she realises she'll need to leap outwards rather than straight down. One hand on either side of the frame, she gathers herself, feels the heat of the encroaching fire in the smoke billowing into the room. She imagines springing into the darkness, the fall, the landing. She will try to roll as soon as she hits the ground, avoid the worst of the impact.

A car is driving up the track. It comes to an abrupt halt. A tall male figure with long hair leaps out of the car and runs towards the brown Cortina. Before he reaches it, he looks up, sees her in the window. His face in the dancing light of the burning house is white and spooky; shadows beneath his eyes turn them into deep pits. It is the red-headed teacher. He waves frantically at her. '*Wait!*' he yells and gestures wildly towards the front door, shouts that he'll open it.

But Essie knows she can't go back into that hallway choked with smoke. It is too hot, too close. She will suffocate and die. Like Janet. Her mother will turn into a ghost, her father will become brittle and thin, Helen will cry and there will be no one to protect her from the bullies or the thing in the cane. Terrified, Essie leaps, arms pinwheeling, legs pistoning.

She sees the teacher run towards her as she falls, his arms outstretched.

⁓

Vince tests the wound beneath the dressing on his left temple, lightly pressing his fingertips against it. Sucks in air. It hurts like billyo. He winds down the car window, rests his elbow on the frame and sniffs the wind.

'Cam's gone ahead with the burn without us, then?'

John, in the driver's seat, glances across at his father. The bandage wrapped around Vince's head confers a piratical air. John is about to ask, again, if Vince is sure it wouldn't have been better for him to stay overnight in hospital. Decides against it.

The whine of a fast-approaching motorcycle builds behind them, rising in pitch and decibels. The speed of its passage as it overtakes them buffets the car.

'Bloody hell. Almost took the mirror off.' Vince peers through the windscreen as the bike disappears around a bend. 'Was that young Connolly?'

Up ahead, the glow from the Tranters' cane fire is big and bright and much too close to the old house for Vince's liking. 'What the bloody hell is Cam playing at?' he asks John.

Before his son can answer, they are rounding the curve themselves and smoke envelops the car. John slows the vehicle, his foot easing off the accelerator and onto the brake. Vince winds up the window to keep the fumes out of the cabin. They are almost out of the bend when a gust of wind dilutes the smoke.

'Shit,' says John, braking. In the gravel, at the edge of the headlights, they see the motorbike that overtook them lying on its side. Shreds of plastic and metal are littered around it. A flimsy helmet lies some yards away and a twisted human form is at the base of the large swamp-gum stump.

Once they're clear of the wreckage, John swings the car off the road, ploughing its nose into a clump of guinea grass. He clambers out of the car, leaps a ditch, runs back to where the Connolly boy lies. Vince, slower to climb out of the car, already knows Kenny is dead.

The bike has skidded into the loose stones on the shoulder of the bitumen, fishtailed and then fallen before sliding along the strip of gravel. In the light from the torch Vince keeps in the glove box, dust mingles with the smoke from the Tranters' cane fire. John looks up from the mangled form of Chester Connolly's eldest son.

~

'Are you sure you're right to drive, Dad?'

They've agreed John will wait at the crash site, slow any passing traffic, so that Kenny Connolly's body suffers no further desecration. Vince will drive to the big house, just five minutes away, to call the police and an ambulance, although the only purpose of the latter will be to act as a hearse. Depending on what he finds when he gets closer to home, he'll also call Les Comerford, who's warden of the local fire brigade. He'd be surprised if Jean hasn't called him already, but perhaps the fire's not as close to the old house as it looks from here.

Vince nods, puts a hand on his son's shoulder. Such a fine boy. A man, of course, with a wife and child of his own, but still, Vince's boy, ever and always. Oh, these young ones. Why must they cause their parents such grief?

As Vince hands John the torch, they're startled when its beam flickers over a young woman's figure, bare legs grazed and bloody. She is lying just as still as Kenny, but further from the road, almost in the cane. The girl is on her back, a mat of thick grass beneath her, as if gazing at the night sky through the helmet's visor. Vince is taken back, hit by a wave of memories, tumbling and gasping for breath, to that night, almost ten years ago, chafing the pale, lifeless hand of his daughter.

'Wait, Dad.'

But Vince is already unclipping the chin strap of the girl's helmet. He eases it off her head. Her eyes are closed, her brows, black and straight. It's the girl who lives at the pub. Except for the scrapes on her legs, there's not much blood, but one arm lies in an awkward position and a lump on her collar bone swells purplish and angry.

Vince feels for her pulse, then says, 'Help me turn her on her side. Gently, gently.' He eases a finger into her mouth. Checks for blockages in her airway. 'Now. On her back.'

After Cathy died, he learnt how to do this. And though he's never before needed to put the knowledge into practice, the instructions come back to him. He places a hand under the girl's neck, lifts. With the flat of his other hand on her forehead, he tilts her head back, clamps his mouth over hers, pinches her nostrils and blows four quick breaths into her lungs. She moans. Oh, Cathy, dear little Cat.

They consider lifting her into the car, but she cries so much when they try to move her they pause. They are concerned about her back, although she is able to move her arms and legs. She holds Vince's hand tightly in hers. Shakes her head when he tries to pry his fingers away.

'You go,' Vince says to John. 'Quickly now. Call her father too.'

John jogs back to the car. Slams the gears into reverse. Has to back out of the clump of grass before he can swing the car onto the highway. Adrenaline and shock make him careless; he accelerates too hard, sends the car careering backwards into a ditch. Hears the crack of concrete against the bumper bar. Throws the car into first. A bloody awful noise as if something is caught up between the tyre and the wheel well.

'Blast.' He leaves the car in neutral, hauls on the handbrake.

When he flings open the car door, Vince calls out to him, impatient and urging. A culvert runs beneath the road, dumping its contents into the ditch he has driven into.

A sizeable bough has snagged up around the axle, along with smaller branches and twigs. The thickest part of the tree limb is wedged in the mat of debris and vegetation at the mouth of the drain. John hauls on the mess to dislodge it, but it is caught fast. Finally, with a mighty heave, John pulls the whole half-rotten thing out of the way, splattering his legs with mud and throwing himself off balance. He trips backwards, one foot catches the edge of a stone, his ankle twists beneath him and he falls. He stops himself landing flat on his back by flinging out one arm, his fingers grappling mud and something else. He peers at the thing he finds in his palm. A familiar shape. A butterfly. A hair slide in the shape of a butterfly.

'Get a move on,' Vince calls out to him. 'Stop mucking about.'

From his position on the ground, John glimpses a pale form further back in the culvert. A slender figure is resolving out of the blackness. He crouches, leans in closer, then reels back. A sickening smell, thick and almost sweet, coats the walls of his throat, the membranes in his nose. It clings and he cannot cough it out.

John walks back to where his father comforts the injured girl. Her pallid face is clenched with pain, the black brows drawn low over her eyes, the full lips drained of colour and pressed together. She is cradling her left arm and trembling violently. Vince is sitting on the ground behind her, supporting her weight. He is about to give his son what for. Sees John's face, heartsick, his handsome mouth twisted as if he's just been hit.

'Give us the torch, will you, Dad,' he says.

⁓

Connie has succeeded in extinguishing most of the flames surging across the grass with one of the wet sacks from the ute's tray. The ones that are further advanced appear to have hit a boggy area and are burning themselves out. She allows herself to relax a little, enough to be able to curse Cam's tardiness.

Ahead, she sees a floater settle on a patch of grass and she is about to run up to beat it out when a car horn blares. She looks up to see rapidly approaching headlights flash. She shades her eyes. It's the Creadies' ute. Jean is driving, Cam beside her, stricken, his face white and streaked with ash, Sandra on his knee. Helen is crammed into the space between. Fear drenches Connie's brain, leaves no room for blood. Essie isn't with them.

Connie's mind bucks like an unbroken horse beneath the saddle. Cam leaps from the cab, Sandra and Helen tumbling out with him. In a clutch of broken sentences he tells Connie what she has already understood. Helen, badgered into heaving sobs by her mother's demands that she tell her exactly—exactly— when she last saw Essie, is rendered incapable of adding anything more to what she has already told Jean and then Cam: Essie was on the verandah of the snug and then she wasn't.

Jean says she's checked their shed, rung the boys at the old house but they weren't home. All the lights were out when she drove past the big house, so she doesn't think Essie is there, and she isn't at the Tranters' either. When she found that Essie wasn't there, she went to find Cam.

Helen is dragging at Connie's shirt tails.

'For God's sake, wait.' She thrusts Helen away from her, seizes Jean by the shoulders. 'Are the police coming?'

Jean blinks rapidly, her jaw quivering. 'I haven't called them. I thought . . .'

'Connie. *Connie!*' Cam prises her hands off the older woman. 'Take Jean's ute, drive her and the girls back to our place. Call the police. Wait there. Essie will turn up. Don't think the worst. I'll drive back to the Creadies'. She can't have gone far.'

The adults are knotted together, each intent on the others' faces. None of them able to voice their worst fear—that Essie has not *gone* anywhere, rather that she has been *taken*. Connie feels as if her heart might stop. It is a wall of shock and dread, like the force she imagines would be generated in a head-on collision, catastrophic, fatal, no way back.

'*Go. Go.*' Cam herds Connie, Jean and the girls towards the Creadies' ute.

Connie swings Helen, who is beginning to snivel, onto her hip, notices that her daughter is holding a tiny plastic hairbrush tightly in her hand. She can see it as clear as day. Why is everything so bright?

'Look, Nanna.' Sandra has planted her sturdy little feet, points a plump finger. 'The old house. It burning.'

'Christ.' Cam, his face lit by the flames from the burning house, looks benumbed. There are too many scenarios and possibilities for disaster to process, but then all at once he's sprinting towards their ute, which Connie has left idling. 'Call Les Comerford as well, tell him we need the fire truck.'

Is Essie trapped by fire or in the hands of a stranger? On which nightmare to settle?

~

The schoolteacher doesn't so much catch Essie as simply get in between her and the ground as she hurtles towards him. Her weight, slight, but given considerable heft by gravity, cannons into his chest, bowling him over like a skittle. She hears a crack, like sticks snapping underfoot, as his rib cage smacks against one of the white rocks. His body spasms as if it is about to release a howl of agony, but even though his mouth is stretched wide open, no sound emerges.

Essie has barrelled off him and landed some yards away. She is unhurt, but the teacher is struggling to breathe, his mouth opening and closing like that of a stranded fish. Haltingly, he rolls onto the side that didn't connect with rock. Essie scrambles to her feet. She would like to run back to the snug, but she can't leave the teacher there without trying to help. Tentatively she moves towards him, squats, peers into his face. 'Are you going to die?'

He seems to consider the question seriously. 'I don't think so,' he manages to say. 'But I need to get to hospital.'

Essie can hardly hear him even though she's leant down so that her face is near his. He doesn't seem to understand that they are too close to the fire. Essie is worried that the overgrown garden is going to catch alight, trapping them. She will have to drag him further away from the burning house. He is still lying on his side and she scoots around so that she is crouched behind his shoulders. She takes hold of him, one hand cupped beneath each of his armpits.

'Stop. What are you doing?' Suddenly he is hyper-alert, a trapped animal, his voice a terrified squeak.

'The fire. We have to get further away.'

The teacher glances up at the old house. It is as if he has only just registered the heat radiating from the blaze, the crash of structures within the cottage collapsing as the fire takes hold.

'Alright. I'll do it myself.' He pushes himself up on one elbow, gets his knees beneath him, lowers his other hand onto the ground so that he is on all fours.

He is so terribly slow. Essie dances beside him in agitation. 'Come on. Come on.'

Each careful movement he makes comes with a shuddering moan.

Above the wind and the crackling flames, Essie hears the whine of a truck engine. 'Someone's coming.'

'Thank Christ.' His voice is a sob. 'It'll be John Creadie.' With the prospect of rescue, other adults to take charge, something in the schoolteacher unknots. He is less turned in on himself and more curious about Essie. Still on all fours, his face to the ground, he asks, 'What were you doing in my room?'

A truck, headlights blazing, pulls up only yards away from where Essie and the teacher sweat in the heat of the house fire. The doors of the cab swing open, the hinges complaining. Two men, small hats on large heads, drop to the ground. Two pairs of workboots crunch across the grass already dehydrated by the flames.

'Am I glad to see you,' the teacher says without shifting his gaze from between his hands.

'Is that right, mate?'

The teacher looks up into the faces of Jimmy Froome and his brother.

TWENTY-FOUR

ESSIE IS PARALYSED by the violence being inflicted on the teacher in the glare of the truck's headlights. It isn't until Jimmy Froome swings his foot back and lines up a kick that she crouches, darts in between his boot and the teacher's unprotected head. The steel-capped toe connects with her hip, spinning her over the teacher's prone body so that she lands on the ground beside him.

She is back up on her feet in an instant, snarling. She flings herself at Jimmy Froome, scratching at his face. His brother grabs her, pinning her arms to her sides. She twists in the big man's hands and wrenches free, screeching the swear words that Raelene has taught her. She launches herself again at Jimmy, curls a skinny leg behind his knees and shoves him in the chest with all her strength. He is taken by surprise and lands heavily on his arse. 'Jesus.'

He lumbers upright and she sees that he's tempted to take a decent swipe at her, but his brother is already scrambling up into the cab of the truck, so he contents himself with abuse. 'Fucking little bitch.'

The horn of the Bedford blares as it tears back down the track.

Essie doesn't want to look at the teacher's face. She can hardly see his features for blood, but she forces herself to approach him, kneels at his shoulder.

'Don't leave me,' he says. Or at least that's what it sounds like through his broken teeth.

'I'll be quick,' she says. 'I'll get my mum.'

~

The old house is well alight, but as yet the fire hasn't spread to the Creadies' paddock alongside, thank God. Jean is weeping and shuddering as Connie slides in behind the steering wheel. Sandra and Helen have been shocked into silence. The Creadies' ute has a column shift, and Connie, struggling to find first in the unfamiliar gearbox, swears loudly. The coarse words erupting from her mother's mouth send Helen into an outburst of sobs. Eventually, the gearstick clunks into place and Connie swings the ute around, is about to floor it when a figure dashes into the headlights.

Relief floods through Connie with such force, she fears she might pass out. She is out of the cab and Essie is in her arms. When her daughter pulls back ever so slightly from her embrace, Connie checks the impulse to pull her closer, does not try to restrain her but lets her go. Stands her on her feet.

In the Quala pub, the drinkers pause.

'Ambulance?'

'Yep, there's another one.'

'Car accident probably.'

An additional siren pierces the fug of cigarette smoke and beer fumes.

'Coppers too, by the sounds of it.'

A jangling ring. The drinkers look up expectantly. Gordon Mason answers the phone that sits on the bar. 'Yep. Yep.'

He hangs up.

'Any of you blokes with the Bush Fire Brigade?'

Before anyone can stir themselves, Les Comerford bursts into the bar wearing his fire warden's hard hat. 'C'mon, you pissheads, time to look lively. Tranters' cane fire is out of control.'

As the men rise to their feet, draining their glasses on their way to the door, Gordon Mason answers the phone on the bar when it rings a second time. Only Marie Jarvis notices how he pales beneath his sunburn and grabs onto the beer tap for support.

TWENTY-FIVE

WHEN CARMEL PULLS up in the Q car at the accident site, one ambulance is already swinging out onto the highway, heading towards Kaliope, no lights, no siren. The initial reports are accurate, then. Kenny Connolly has been killed in the collision with the tree stump.

Back where the cane field meets the grass at the edge of the highway, and in the uncertain light of the remaining ambulance's headlights and the torch that one of the two paramedics leaning over Raelene Mason is holding, Carmel sees that the girl is sitting up but leaning heavily against an elderly man. She feels a tightening in her guts. She will have to find a moment to apologise to Vince Creadie, to acknowledge the grief around his daughter's death that must have been brought back to the surface by Janet McClymont's disappearance.

The young constable from Kaliope is hovering beside the highway patrol car. He must have arrived at least half an hour ago, but he still looks like he's trying to make up his mind about what it is he should be doing.

'I'll take it from here,' Carmel says to him. 'You can head back to the station.'

Before he slaps the car door shut, she hears him groan in protest. Stuff him. She's spent her share of time sidelined while more senior—always male—officers called the shots. It's his turn to cool his heels.

The paramedic holding the torch senses Carmel's gaze and looks up. She tips her chin questioningly, tilts her head in Raelene's direction. The paramedic nods briefly, allows himself a thumbs-up.

Standing at the edge of the dim circle of light is another man. Carmel squints. The publican, Gordon Mason. Chester Connolly has no doubt already heard that the worst has happened and maybe gone to tell his wife that their oldest son is dead. Carmel can find sympathy even for Chester at a time like this.

Approaching headlights. Carmel shields her eyes. The ute slows before the driver swings the vehicle in a tight U-turn, pulling in behind the police car. John Creadie gets out and joins Carmel where she stands at the edge of the bitumen.

'A dreadful night.' Even in situations like this the banalities must be exchanged, Carmel has learnt.

John grimaces, the only indication that he has heard her.

'What's happening with the fire?' she thinks to ask. 'Are the other houses out of danger?'

'The boys from the brigade are there. The old house is gone, but the snug and the big house are okay.' John looks over at the smashed motorbike and the ambos tending to the injured girl. 'Small beer, considering.'

Carmel nods agreement before asking, 'And Eamonn Sullivan?'

John shakes his head. 'I didn't see him. Cam Tranter said he's in a pretty bad way but he should be alright. He'll live, anyway.'

Carmel senses John's reluctance to revisit his discovery, but she can't delay the inevitable any longer. 'Where is she?'

John points to a large clump of tall grass and begins to walk towards it.

'Wait.' Carmel puts a restraining hand on his arm. 'Stay on the road if you can.'

She answers the question in his glance. 'Let's try not to obliterate any more evidence. Any that's left, that is.'

They traipse a couple of dozen yards up the tarmac, Carmel's torch lighting the way ahead. John is almost shuffling, his body reluctant to approach the place where the mouth of a culvert gapes at their feet.

'She's in there.' John's voice is unnaturally flat, devoid of emotion. As if he is somehow outside himself.

'You're sure it's the body of Janet McClymont?'

'I hope there's only one girl that's been murdered around here. At least this year.'

Memories must be flooding back for John, too, Carmel supposes. A bitterness that goes back ten years to another grim night that felt like it would never end, and to another dead girl. John would have been barely out of his teens when his sister died.

'How did you find her?'

John reaches into his pocket, hands something to Carmel. She examines the simulacrum of a butterfly, a hairclip identical to the one in the photo of Janet McClymont, before placing it in the breast pocket of her jacket.

'Where was it?'

John gestures vaguely in the direction of the ditch that begins at the culvert mouth and extends away from the road towards the cane field. The light of Carmel's torch plays over a large branch matted with wads of vegetation.

'Can you be a bit more specific?'

'Further back, in the dirt.'

The probing torch beam fails to reveal much more than the churned-up mud and half-rotted vegetation that previously concealed the body of Janet McClymont.

'I don't think we'll need anything more from you tonight, Mr Creadie, but perhaps you could call into the station tomorrow? Make an official statement.'

'When will it ever fucking end?' John is white, his mouth rigid. He utters the profanity with the weight of someone who rarely swears. He doesn't wait for Carmel to reply but walks back down the road to where the ambulance's lights rotate, patchily illuminating the road and the surrounding vegetation in scraps of red. The paramedics wheel a gurney carrying Raelene Mason over the rough ground to the waiting ambulance as her father walks alongside, his hand on his daughter's ankle.

John reaches his father, still seated on the ground. He extends his arms and his father grasps his hands. John braces and hauls Vince to his feet. The older man groans, stands for a moment still holding onto his son, then, when he's stable, lets go, rubs his joints and slowly straightens his hips. John keeps a steadying arm around his father's shoulders.

Carmel steps off the road and into the ditch. She digs into a pocket of her trousers, finds a handkerchief, holds it over her mouth and nose. She squats, shines the torch into the hole under the road just long enough to confirm what John Creadie has told her.

On her way back to the police car, she stops beside Kenny Connolly's motorbike, still toppled on its side, bits of metal and plastic scattered around it. Carmel examines its twisted form. Notices that the seat has popped up from the storage compartment beneath it. In the beam of torchlight, a handful of small objects and a folded piece of paper are revealed, thrown into a heap in a corner of the shallow well—a bottle opener, a Bic cigarette lighter, an opened packet of Wrigley's Juicy Fruit chewing gum. Carmel nudges aside the paper with the end of her torch. It's an ignored speeding fine by the looks of it. Beneath it is a tube of strawberry-flavoured lip gloss.

TWENTY-SIX

ESSIE LIES LISTENING to her mother's footfalls down the hall and the murmur of her voice as she speaks on the phone. It has hardly stopped ringing since they returned to the house. Her father is still out with the Bush Fire Brigade, but her mother has told her not to worry. The fire was controlled before it was able to spread to the Creadies' cane. The men from the brigade are mopping up the last of it.

Helen, in the bed beside hers, has been asleep almost since the moment their mother turned out the light. She looks as if she has fallen asleep in the middle of a star jump, her arms flung above her head, her legs akimbo. As if she is perfectly safe.

Tomorrow, her mother has promised she will drive Essie into Kaliope to visit Raelene in hospital. Essie wonders if anyone has told Raelene that Janet has been found.

If the doctors think he is up to it, they'll also go and see Mr Sullivan, the teacher. Her mother thinks he may have saved Essie's life.

Essie's jeans and underpants lie in a crumpled heap beneath her bed where she kicked them before her mother came in to kiss her goodnight. When she hears the door of her parents' bedroom close across the hall, she edges back the sheet and blanket, swings herself off the bed and onto the floor. On her knees, and even though it hurts her hip where a dark bruise already stains her skin, she stretches out an arm, hooks a finger into the belt loop of her jeans, scoops the tangled heap of clothes to her chest and draws out the small red book she took from the teacher's house.

There is a chair in the corner of the room piled with Helen's favourite toys, her teddy bear with its worn nose and torn ear and a large doll the size of a two-year-old child that their mother won at the shooting gallery at the Kaliope Show last year. Essie places them soundlessly on the floor and carries the chair over to the wardrobe, edging it as close as she can to its open door. On the inside of the door is the list her mother stuck there: *Never talk to strangers*. The shelf above the space where they hang their school uniforms and their good dresses is a messy jumble, stuffed with coats they rarely use, spare blankets, and toys she and Helen no longer play with but cannot bear to throw away.

Clutching the book, Essie climbs onto the chair and stretches up on her toes as far as she can. One of the chair's legs is slightly shorter than the others and it wobbles beneath her. She grabs hold of the front of the shelf to steady herself and then looks over her shoulder, but Helen hasn't stirred. Essie shoves the book under the christening gown she and Helen both wore as babies, which is wrapped in brown paper and smells of mothballs. She pushes the book with her fingertips as far towards the back of the shelf as she can reach.

The wind has dropped. Back beneath the covers, Essie can still hear the cane, but now that the fire has swept through it, burning off the leaves and trash, the sound has changed. It is more hollow and less scary, no longer muttering like a live thing. She closes her eyes. Tries not to think of the schoolteacher's face, broken and covered in blood.

TWENTY-SEVEN

A HELL OF a lot was going on that night, I can tell you.

Gordon Mason headed straight to the crash site after he got John Creadie's call about his daughter being injured and Kenny Connolly getting himself killed. I told Gordon I'd look after the place until he got back—I'm too old to be fighting fires. On his way out, Gordon had a word to the Parslow lad. Pete collared Chester before he climbed on the fire truck and told him about the accident. He managed to convince him to go home to Gloria and then to the hospital. He left it to the doctors to tell Chester that his son was dead, but.

Not long afterwards, the lady copper turned up at the pub and rang Kaliope Police Station from the hotel phone. She caught Bill as he was about to leave the station to chase up Jimmy and Frank. Connie Tranter had already called him about that nastiness with the schoolteacher. Sullivan was in a bad way.

Busted cheekbone, broken nose, a couple of teeth knocked out, ugly cut over one eye. Not to mention the busted ribs from getting knocked to the ground when he caught Essie Tranter hurtling out the window of the old house on the Creadies' place.

The lady copper—Senior Constable Maitland, I should say—told Bill about finding that tube of shiny stuff that teenage girls put on their lips in the seat compartment of Kenny's motorbike. Asked him if he was sure Kenny didn't have his motorbike on the weekend Janet disappeared.

Bill told her to leave it with him; he had a hunch about something.

Anyway, after the flogging they gave that teacher, and the threat of criminal charges, Jimmy and Frank were suddenly very anxious to clear up any misunderstandings as to what they'd originally told police about the night the McClymont girl went missing. Particularly after Bill mentioned what had been found in the wreckage of Kenny's bike. They'd already said they had a little camp down by the river where it runs through the bottom of their place. They do a bit of fishing there, a bit of drinking. They'd been there that day in the late afternoon with their wives and kids and a few others. Frank's youngest was turning ten and it was a treat for him. They lit a fire and cooked a few fish they'd caught. When the women took the kids back up to the house for ice cream and cake, Jimmy and Frank stayed by the river and got stuck into the rum. They'd told the police all this, and it had checked out. One thing they didn't mention, though, was that Chester had turned up. On his son's motorbike. Just taking it for a spin, he said, after picking it up from the mechanics earlier that day. He stayed for a couple of drinks and then left, just on dusk.

The next day when all hell broke loose about the girl going missing and the searching and that, Chester asked Jimmy and Frank not to mention that he'd been at the camp. Some bullshit about Kenny getting the pip if he knew his old man had been riding his motorbike while he was pissed. The three of them have always been pretty thick, knocking about together since they were young blokes. But now that Bill was telling them Chester was looking dodgy with regards to the death of the McClymont girl on account of picking up Kenny's bike from the mechanics that weekend, well, that was a bridge too far even for the Froome boys.

As it turned out, it didn't take much to get Chester to admit to what he did. He was beside himself after seeing his boy dead, babbling his head off. He didn't mean to kill Janet, that's what he told Bill. He was just taking Kenny's bike for a spin when he came across her not long after he left Jimmy and Frank. He tried to convince her to climb on the seat behind him, said he'd drop her off at the Tranters'. When she refused, he manhandled her onto the bike and she started to scream. He said he was just trying to stop her making a racket. I suppose a jury will decide if he's telling the truth. I couldn't tell you what, if anything, the police have found out by examining her body.

It was Chester too, you see, who volunteered to search that part of the highway, which accounts for why she wasn't discovered at the time.

He's been flown down to Brisbane. He's being held at Boggo Road Gaol. Too hot for him in the Kaliope lock-up where his cellmates threatened to take things into their own hands. He'll be tried down there too. No hope of a fair trial up here with feelings against him so strong. Gloria's taken Gavan and their youngest to Rocky to stay with her mother.

When he could make himself understood again, Sullivan told Bill Wren that he'd gone back to the Creadies' old house to get the copies of *The Little Red Schoolbook* he'd mistakenly left behind. He had dozens of them, apparently, not just the one that got into the young Cassar lad's hands. Sullivan reckoned that people had battled bureaucracy and hysteria to get that bit of left-wing propaganda published in Australia and he felt an obligation to pass them on to someone who could do something with them. The turn-off to the old house was on his way out to the highway, so I suppose he thought it wouldn't add much time to his trip to go back for them. Well, they're nothing but ash now. If he'd been happy to leave them, maybe he'd have got off scot-free. And Essie Tranter might have been badly injured or worse.

The cottage was well alight when he drove up the track, he told Bill. He thought about going in to see what he could save of Pete Parslow's things but decided against it. He was about to jump into Parslow's car to drive it out of harm's way when he saw Essie Tranter. She was going to jump and he was afraid she'd do herself some serious damage.

It says something about that young man, that's what I've been telling people. It was a credit to him, putting himself in harm's way like that.

There was a bit of kerfuffle with that detective, Patterson. As soon as he heard about Chester confessing, he caught the next plane up from Brisbane. Wanted to nab some of the glory of solving the case for himself, I suppose. The local rag had already done this big interview with Senior Constable Maitland, you see, and Patterson was pretty dirty they didn't talk to him about it. He wanted them to take a photo of him with Chester as a follow-up—Patterson marching Chester towards a police car with his hands cuffed behind his back or some foolishness. Only trouble was, Chester was already on the plane to Brisbane. Apparently, the air turned blue with the language Patterson spouted when he found out.

In the days after Janet was found by John Creadie and her body lifted out of the mud in that culvert, it was like something settled in Quala. Not just in Quala, actually, but also in Kaliope, in Candleford and in all the little shacks up and down the coast. I'm not saying that things were back to normal. There was still more than enough fear, distrust and sorrow to go around, but there was also relief. Barbara and Ted will never get over their girl's murder, no one expects that, but at least they no longer have to wonder what she is suffering or if she will ever come home. They're moving back to Brisbane, I hear.

People try to make sense of things, even those things without rhyme or reason. And there's a feeling around the place that with Connie and Cam's Essie escaping from the Creadies' old house when it went up in smoke, and with that other girl, Raelene, the one from the pub, surviving the motorcycle crash that killed Kenny Connolly, a sort of balance has been struck. Cruel and unjust, no doubt, but a balance just the same. Two have died and two were spared. It's not fair, it's not right, not by a long shot, but it's something.

When Carmel Maitland brought the McClymonts to the door of the underground room at the Kaliope hospital that serves as a morgue, Bill Wren suggested that Barbara might prefer to leave the formal identification of her daughter to her husband. Better to preserve the memory of Janet as she walked out of their house that evening in her new white pedal pushers, her fringe held back by her butterfly hairclip, he told her. It'd been two months, after all, and the weather hot and damp. But Barbara wouldn't hear a word of it. Bill said it was like water flowing down a slope, the way she was drawn to her daughter's side. She was dry-eyed, Bill said, as she stroked Janet's hair, murmuring words as if she was comforting her. Bill said that he knows it sounds strange, but he felt it was a privilege to see the tenderness and the strength of Barbara in her grief.

Ted, though, after all those weeks of holding on to hope that his daughter was still alive, he was completely undone, poor bastard. He stood at the door howling.

As for the flogging Jimmy and Frank gave Eamonn Sullivan, they told Bill that they feared for Essie Tranter's safety. Finding her with the teacher like that, what were they supposed to think? What with Janet McClymont having disappeared, and with that filth he'd been peddling at the high school, it was hardly bloody surprising they overreacted. At least they'd dragged him away from the burning house, they said. Well, no, they didn't try to stop the Creadies' old place from burning down, but the fire was roaring like a train by the time they turned up.

No word yet as to whether Sullivan will press charges against them.

The whole business has made a lot of people think back to Cathy Creadie. Not just the grief and sorrow, but the circumstances, if you like, surrounding her death. People remembering that nobody saw her go into the water. Not the last time. How the Froome boys and Chester turned up there that day. Dot and me were talking about it, how that lady copper has a certain look in her eye. She's been spending a bit of time up at the Creadies' place, but neither Vince nor Jean is saying much about what they've been talking to her about.

Bill Wren has been keeping mum too. He won't be drawn on whether he's looking into Cathy Creadie's disappearance again, but the Froome boys have been into the station a couple of times, looking like they'd rather be anywhere else. And someone's lit a fire under that young constable with the loose lips. He's gone very quiet.

Opinions vary about young Kenny Connolly. Not about his death, so much. A young man's life snuffed out before it had really begun is a bloody tragedy, no argument. More about the sort of person he was and just what was going on between him and Gordon Mason's daughter, a girl still in primary school. Although, to be fair to Kenny, she was old enough to be in high school. But still a child, more or less.

Some people say that Kenny saved her life. If he'd been wearing the full-face helmet instead of her, then it might have been him who survived the crash and she'd be the one lying on the slab in the basement of the Kaliope hospital. A real gentleman for giving it to her. That's what some say.

Mind you, that's not an opinion necessarily shared by those who saw how he looked their daughters up and down as if they were pieces of meat.

No need to write that last bit down in your notebook.

TWENTY-EIGHT

ESSIE DREAMS.

She and her friends are running like dogs let off the chain, capering and yelping with the excitement of release—Essie and Raelene and Helen; Tim and Gavan and Danny; Susan and Sharon and all the other kids from Quala Primary. Their legs beneath them long and fast and strong. Some of them career around on their bicycles, freewheeling down the hills, their feet off the pedals, their heads thrown back, their faces turned up to the sky. It is normal. Just like before. Before Janet went missing.

No adult voices bray out, telling them to stop, or to come back, or to be careful. Their parents are busy, unconcerned, absent. The children are light, free of the burden of always being in sight, always within earshot. The ground blurs beneath their feet with the speed of their passage. Quala, the primary school, all the houses and farms, all the safe places disappear behind them.

In front of them lie the inlet, the beach, the mangrove swamps, their past haunts and wild playgrounds where they used to roam at will, resolving into bright, startling clarity. All their old places restored to them. Behind them lie the razed cane fields, burnt and slashed, the cane hauled off to the mills for crushing.

Slowly at first, but quicker and then more quickly still, the cane crop ratoons. Shoots push up from the buried roots that were left in the soil. The burgeoning growth keeps pace with the children's mad tumbling progress. The cane proliferates, so fast and furious it generates a low hum. At each stride the children take, another row of cane thrusts up from the ground, pushing through the disturbed earth, the ash and the trash left behind after harvesting. It quivers and quakes, reaching out to snatch at their heels, pursuing them like a great green creature. The children run and run, but the cane keeps coming.

ACKNOWLEDGEMENTS

ENORMOUS THANKS TO Grace Heifetz and Kelly Fagan, my agent and my publisher respectively. Your enthusiasm for the manuscript of *The Cane*, coming as it did during a long winter of lockdown, was a shot in the arm and a hot toddy combined.

My editors, Louise Thurtell and Angela Handley, were vital in helping to shape and improve the manuscript. Thanks, Louise, for your firm but gentle schooling in matters of plot and structure, and your unfailing belief in the worth of the novel.

Many thanks to Clara Finlay for your careful and forensic proofreading and to Luke Causby for *The Cane*'s epic cover.

The Cane has had a long genesis and I would like to thank my stalwart and long-time writing comrades Myfanwy Jones, Spiri Tsintziras, Sam Lawry, Wendy Meddings and Jane Woollard for your wisdom and support over so many years. Here's to many more years of writing and talking, my friends.

More recently, Marilyn Miller, Trish Bolton, Catherine Jackson and Christopher Rose have also provided much-appreciated writerly companionship and counsel.

In late 2019, I brought the unfinished manuscript of what was to become *The Cane* to Antoni Jach's Novel Writing Workshop Masterclass XXV. The clear-eyed feedback and insights I received from Antoni and the other participants renewed my confidence in the project and helped clarify some of the issues I was trying to resolve.

Time and space to write are godsends. Thanks to Varuna, The National Writers' House, for its support of Australian writers, and to my friends Elizabeth and Matt for the gift of solitude in your beach house.

Thanks to Lisa Jones at the Queensland Police Museum for providing answers to my questions, Neroli Roocke at Canegrowers for her assistance, and to Ray Mencken who spoke to me about cane farming in the 1970s. Any inaccuracies in the manuscript are wholly my own.

While *The Cane* is fiction, atrocities similar to those alluded to in the novel were perpetrated against the Yuwibara people of north Central Queensland in the nineteenth century.

There are also a number of unsolved incidents of abduction and murder of children and young women that occurred in Queensland in the 1970s, and the accounts of these crimes have influenced and informed *The Cane*. In particular, I'd like to acknowledge the tragic and untimely deaths of Judith and Susan Mackay, Marilyn Wallman and Catherine Graham, whose lives were stolen from them by killers yet to be brought to justice.

The Little Red Schoolbook was written by Danish school-teachers Søren Hansen and Jesper Jensen in 1969 to encourage young people to interrogate the societal norms of the day. It was translated into numerous languages, prompting alarm in many countries that it would provoke anarchy and licentiousness.

ABOUT THE AUTHOR

MARYROSE CUSKELLY IS a writer of fiction and non-fiction. She has lived in Melbourne for many years, but she was born in Queensland, where, in the early 1970s, there were several high-profile child abductions and murders. The disappearance of Mackay schoolgirl Marilyn Wallman, in particular, made a lasting impression on her. In 2016, Maryrose was awarded the New England Thunderbolt Prize for Crime Writing (non-fiction) for her essay 'Well Before Dark' about Marilyn's disappearance and the way it percolated through her own childhood and later life. *The Cane* returns to some of the themes and preoccupations of that essay.

In 2019, Maryrose's book *Wedderburn: A true tale of blood and dust* (Allen & Unwin, 2018) was longlisted for Best Debut and Best True Crime in the 2019 Davitt Awards. She is also the author of *Original Skin: Exploring the marvels of the human hide* (Scribe, 2010) and *The End of Charity: Time for social enterprise* (with Nic Frances, Allen & Unwin, 2008), which was the winner of the Iremonger Award.